THE DOUBLE LIFE OF DANNY DAY

MIKE THAYER

THE DOUBLE LIFE OF DANNY DAY

Feiwel and Friends
New York

A Feiwel and Friends Book
An imprint of Macmillan Publishing Group, LLC
120 Broadway, New York, NY 10271
mackids.com

Our books may be purchased in bulk for promotional, educational, or
business use. Please contact your local bookseller or the Macmillan Corporate
and Premium Sales Department at (800) 221-7945 ext. 5442 or by email at
MacmillanSpecialMarkets@macmillan.com.

Library of Congress Cataloging-in-Publication Data
Names: Thayer, Mike, 1984- author.
Title: The double life of Danny Day / Mike Thayer.
Description: First edition. | New York : Feiwel & Friends, 2021. | Summary:
    Danny Day, age eleven, lives every day twice, which allows him to skip
    class, play video games for hours, and try to bring down bullies at his
    new middle school.
Identifiers: LCCN 2020039220 | ISBN 9781250770998 (hardcover)
Subjects: CYAC: Middle schools—Fiction. | Schools—Fiction. | Video
    games—Fiction. | Bullying—Fiction. | Friendship—Fiction. | Humorous
    stories.
Classification: LCC PZ7.1.T44736 Dou 2021 | DDC [Fic]—dc23
LC record available at https://lccn.loc.gov/2020039220

First edition, 2021
Book design by Michael Burroughs
Feiwel and Friends logo designed by Filomena Tuosto
Printed in the United States of America by LSC Communications, Harrisonburg,
Virginia

ISBN 978-1-250-77099-8 (hardcover)
10 9 8 7 6 5 4 3 2 1

To my wife, Jill.
Oh, that I had a double day to fix the times I got it
wrong and to relive the times I got it right.

Champions Royale

JOYLESS JUNGLE

GREEDY MINES

FANGTHORN PEAK

GHASTLY
GRAVESTONES

DRYOUT DUNES

HAUNTED PINES

LONELY ISLAND

FLOATING CASTLE

LOST LABYRINTH

SEAEDGE FORT

BANDIT'S BOG

SPASM CHASM

TOWERING TREES

WISHING WELL WOODS

PEASANTVILLE

BURIED BONEYARD

OGRE'S BOULDERS

INTRODUCTION

My name is Danny Day. I've ditched school 346 times, and I still have perfect attendance. I broke my leg last week, but I don't have a cast. I never study for a test or quiz until I've seen what's on it. I've played more than four thousand hours of video games in the past three years, and yet my parents have hardly seen me play. How is this all possible, you ask? Well, the answer is pretty simple: I live every day twice.

Yeah, that's right. Since my birth, some eleven and a half years ago, I've been living every day twice. Well . . . eleven and a half *calendar* years, that is. To me it's been twice that long, so, I guess, in a way I'm actually twenty-three. That's also probably the *only* way in which I'm twenty-three, though. Going through elementary school twice doesn't exactly make you an adult.

The first time I go through a day, it's a "discard day." It's kind of like a practice run. Nothing I say or do ever sticks.

At the end of the day, I go to bed, wake up, and—*poof*—everything gets reset, everything except my memory, that is. Most of the time that's a pretty cool thing. I get to do all sorts of stuff without any lasting consequences. My standard is just faking sick and playing video games all day, but I do enjoy my fair share of pranks and stunts. Just last week I broke my record for most candy bars eaten in a day (seventeen, thank you very much), I "borrowed" my parents' car for an evening and did doughnuts in the church parking lot, and I jumped off the garage roof to test my bedsheet parachute (did I *mention* I recently broke my leg?).

The second time I go through a day is the "sticky day." That's when everything is normal, just like it is for everyone else in the world. That's when I play for keeps, and my actions and their consequences *stick*. As you could probably guess, "Sticky Day" Danny is *very* different from "Discard Day" Danny. Sticky Danny is on time to school, does his chores, doesn't draw attention, eats a fraction of the junk food, and doesn't jump off garages.

It's not all sunshine and rainbows, though. Take today and tomorrow, for example. Instead of spending two days driving behind a moving truck from Houston to Idaho, I get to spend *four* days driving behind a moving truck from Houston to Idaho. That's when the double day becomes a curse: when I'm caught in an unpleasant situation and I can't figure a way to weasel out of it. You ever had the stomach flu, where you're either sitting on or kneeling next to the toilet? Well, I have. Nothing quite like getting another crack at one of those days. Not to mention that when I was little, my parents thought I was insane. Heck, *I* thought I was insane, always bringing up conversations and events that no one seemed to remember. It took a pretty unconventional therapist in the end to help me work through it all and convince my parents I wasn't nuts. They still don't know exactly what's going on, and ever since I learned to play things cool on my sticky days, they seem happy *not* knowing. Dr. Donaldson was a good dude, and leaving him behind in Texas was no small sacrifice.

Now, if you're wondering why all of this happens, then that makes two of us. I've been reading a lot of comics lately to see how superheroes get their powers, and I've ruled out more than 150 different ways. As far as I can tell, I'm not the product of some scientific experiment gone wrong, I was never caught in a radioactive laboratory explosion, and I have never been exposed to an alien life-form. The only thing I can point to is my birthday: February 22 at 2:22 a.m. In case you were wondering that's 2/22 at 2:22 a.m. I'm not positive, but I'd be willing to bet it was also on the twenty-two-second mark. Anyway, no matter how it happens, or why it happens, just trust me. It happens.

I'm Danny Day, and I live every day twice.

CHAPTER 1

FIRST IMPRESSIONS

(Discard Monday—Sept. 6ᵗʰ)

"Snake River Middle School." I read the brown-and-white marquee as we drove up to my new school. "Home of the Spuds."

"This is gonna be great," my dad said, grabbing me by the shoulders to give me a little fatherly shake of encouragement. He had a habit of hamming it up like this whenever things got difficult. "Your first day as a Spud."

"I can now die a happy man," I muttered, watching as row after row of kids filed out of three black-and-yellow buses and funneled toward the school entrance. The school year had started a couple of weeks ago, so not only would I not know anyone, but I was going to have to play catch-up. Not that I couldn't do that superhumanly fast, it just meant I was probably going to have to spend more discard days at school for the next little while instead of staying home and playing video games. Never a good prospect.

My dad scrunched his face. "That's not like you, son. This is sixth grade. You're in middle school now. Finally moving up to the big leagues, am I right? I thought you were excited for school."

"Kinda depends on the day, Dad," I said.

"I get it," my dad said, patting me on the knee. "Change is hard. It's a new school with new kids and teachers, but just think of it as an adventure. Put on a brave face, kiddo. You never get a second chance to make a first impression."

I raised my eyebrows. "You'd be surprised."

My dad glanced down at his smartwatch, and his eyes went wide. "Speaking of which, I don't want to be late myself. I gotta jet. Remember, you're taking the bus home."

I nodded, grabbed my backpack, and exited the car. I was almost to the front door of the school when I heard my dad's voice again.

"Love you, buddy!"

A few girls in front of me snickered as I turned around and waved at my dad. I pulled out a pocket-sized notebook with the words *Discard Day Do-Overs* written across the front in black marker and made a quick note for the sticky day.

Embarrassment: Prevent Dad from shouting "Love you, buddy" in front of the whole school

If I had a dollar for every time I had to undo an embarrassing comment from my dad, I could buy my own private island and a helicopter to take me there. That said, it was *impossible* to prevent them all, even *with* a discard day to prepare. My dad's ability to generate cringe-worthy moments in public was a force of nature. You couldn't stop it; you just prepped all you could, laid low, and hoped for the best.

I pinballed my way through the press of students, running into no fewer than five bulging backpacks on my way to the front desk. I wasn't sure what these kids were toting around, but half of them looked about ready to climb Mt. Everest. The admin looked my name up on the computer and gave me a map of the school, circling my locker and classroom locations with a yellow highlighter. I studied the map before rejoining the crowd, eventually catching the right stream of students to whisk me away in the direction of my first-period class. Breaking free of the swift current of kids to visit my locker was a lost cause and would probably have to wait until lunch.

Classroom 013 came into view, and I made my exit, slipping between two towering boys, one with dark whiskers speckling his jawline. I definitely wasn't in elementary school anymore. I walked in and stood at the front of the classroom, observing the typical pre-class chaos. Kids talked, laughed, showed each other their phones, and imitated dance emotes I recognized from the video game *Warcraft of Empires*. To be honest, it wasn't really all that different from my Texas school: columns of desks in the middle of the room, floor-to-ceiling wooden cabinets at the back, a bank of windows to the right looking out over nearby farmland, and pictures of world-famous landmarks and historical events covering any remaining wall space. I turned to see a poster on the door of a cartoon horse holding hands with a smiling potato above the words *Be a stud, befriend a spud*. So I guess *that* was different.

I pulled out my notebook and surveyed the class. I'd never be this obvious about it on a sticky day, but I needed to start mapping out potential friends and spotting bullies. When you went to school for twice as long as anyone else in my grade (with the exception of maybe Bruiser Bigelow, who'd been held back like three times), you had a better feel than most kids for how school worked. First order of business would be to bucket them into stereotypes: jock, nerd, VSCO girl, and so on. These were the faces they showed the world, but I'd spent enough discard days spying on and teasing reactions out of people to know that everyone had a second face. *Everyone.* Today wasn't for second faces, however. It was the initial assessment. Plenty of discard days ahead to see who these people *really* were. I studied the students and started jotting down a few notes.

Follow-up: Middle of classroom. Boy with long brown hair wearing a Mario Bros. shirt and a Zelda symbol wristband. Playing portable game on handheld console, NOT phone. Video game purist. Gamer and proud of it. Definite potential friend.

Follow-up: Tall kid in front. Sitting on top of desk. Black hair. Expensive haircut. Dressed like an adult (no graphics or characters on shirt), brand-new shoes, laughing at own jokes while others force their laughs around him. Appears athletic. Name most likely has an "x" in it even if it doesn't need it (e.g., Knox, Maddox, Paxton) or has a quarterbacky sound like Peyton, Carson, or Colt. In position of social power. Cool kid. Jock. Potential alpha bully.

Follow-up: Pale girl with dark hair in back corner of room. Has hood on with panda ears. She has a sketch notebook open and is staring longingly out the window. 95% chance she is drawing manga characters. Will most likely keep to herself. Anime geek. Nonthreatening.

Follow-up: Pretty girl toward the back left. Styled blond hair. Sporting Kardashian-level makeup.

Currently taking selfies with one hand and has Starbucks cup in the other. Looks disinterested in those around her. Could be top of the social ladder.

Follow-up: Tan boy near the back with parted and slicked hair. Work boots, jeans, pearl-snap shirt. Quiet, but has easygoing smile. One of the only kids not looking at a phone. Farmer of some type. Will most likely know more about potatoes than his peers.

I made several more notes before the final bell rang. The students all scrambled to their desks, and I pocketed my notebook, knowing that I'd have a few more prime chances in the day to continue mapping out the social scene: lunch, time in the halls between classes, and on the bus.

"Good morning, my bright-eyed social studies students," Mrs. Marlow announced from her desk at the front of the classroom as she clapped three times. She was about my mom's age with a pleasant, round face and long, curly, black hair.

"Good morning, Mrs. Marlow," the class said, followed by three loud claps. I guess that was a thing here.

"Class, we have a new . . . Braxlynn, please put your phone away," Mrs. Marlow said craning her neck and pointing to the blond girl in the back of the room.

Braxlynn casually swiped across her phone screen as if she hadn't heard a thing.

"Braxlynn, did you hear me?" Mrs. Marlow said, her soft voice straining to sound stern.

Braxlynn rolled her eyes without looking up from her phone. "Oh my gosh, yes. You don't need to get all salty."

Mrs. Marlow waited patiently for Braxlynn to finish up and finally put her phone away. "Class, this is Daniel Day. His family just moved to Poky. Daniel, would like to tell us some more about yourself?"

"Howdy, I'm Danny," I said, clearing my throat. "I'm from just outside of Conroe, Texas, which is just outside of Houston. I like video games and Ping-Pong, and I've never seen snow."

"Oh, well, we'll be sure to scratch that last one off your list come winter, won't we, class?" Mrs. Marlow said with a white smile.

"Oh, and I can read people's minds," I added.

"You what?" Mrs. Marlow crinkled her nose.

"I know it seems weird, but I can one hundred percent read people's minds," I said, turning from Mrs. Marlow to the students. "Dead serious."

A few kids laughed, and Mrs. Marlow's face was a mixture of surprise, annoyance, and curiosity, but she looked like she was going to humor me and allow it. Any time I did one of these weird discard-day stunts, it always provoked a reaction, and provoking reactions was one of my favorite discard-day pastimes. If you want to find out how an unfamiliar machine works, you press its buttons, twist its dials, and turn its knobs. You want to quickly find out what makes a person tick, you do the exact same thing. Discard Danny was a wizard at pushing people's buttons.

A few students raised their hands, while the gamer kid with the Mario shirt just blurted, "Oh yeah, Professor X, then what am *I* thinking?"

"I will take the Professor X comment as a compliment," I said before turning to address the other three students with their hands up. "I just need you to tell me your name and then write a phrase on a piece of paper, and I'll guess what you wrote," I responded coolly.

The gamer kid smirked. "My name's Noah."

The other three students told me their names as they scribbled something down, covering it with their hands. I gestured to Noah, who rolled his eyes and wrote something as well.

"Okay, Professor X. What'd we write?" Noah said, folding his arms across his chest.

I looked to the ceiling and rubbed my chin. It didn't really matter what I said at this point as long as I got to see what they wrote so I could accurately guess it on the sticky day, but passing up an opportunity like this to insult a loudmouth like Noah would be criminal.

"Well, Amy wrote down that you smell like a rotten potato. Shar wrote down that you *look* like a rotten potato. And Carrie wrote down that you still play with Mr. Potato Head. You wrote down that your favorite video game is secretly *Tinker Bell's Magical Wardrobe*. I'm a little disappointed that yours didn't have anything to do with potatoes, but waddaya gonna do?"

Noah's face went as red as the Mario Bros. hat logo on his shirt, and the air seemed to rush out of the classroom. Poorly restrained giggling bubbled up from the silence. I took out my notebook and scribbled down which kids snickered and which looked like they wanted to punch me in the nose.

The tall athletic kid in the front row burst out in a foghorn of laughter. "This Texas kid's savage!"

"Jaxson, quiet down please," Mrs. Marlow said, her voice too gentle to actually sound threatening. "And, Danny, that was an extremely . . . odd and unkind thing to say. That's not how we behave here at Snake River Middle School."

"Yeah, there's gonna be a lot of that from time to time," I muttered.

"Please take a seat." Mrs. Marlow gestured to an empty desk at the back of the classroom.

Jaxson held out his hand for a five as I walked past. "Sick burn, man."

I reluctantly slapped hands with Jaxson as I made my way to my desk, which happened to be next to Braxlynn's. Even though Jaxson acted like my new best friend, I had impressed him by being a complete jerk to Noah. Birds of a feather flocking together and all, my initial impressions of him that I had jotted down in my notebook were probably pretty accurate.

I sat down at my desk and glanced over at Braxlynn, who already had her phone back out on her lap. I watched as she quickly snapped a photo of another student, a heavyset girl a few rows ahead, and deftly used a filter to add pig ears and a tail before getting to work on a caption. A crumpled piece of paper beaned me in the head. I looked over to see Noah brush his hair away from his face, revealing a knotted scowl. I picked up the paper and unfolded it.

> You're Texas accent makes you
> sound like a dumb cowboy

I waved to Noah before copying the sentence (including the spelling error) into my notebook. I whispered to a few people for the three students to pass me their papers so I could see what they had actually written down. When I got the notes, I recorded what was written and put my notebook away.

The day was only just getting started, and I'd already

found a couple of real winners here at Snake River. That said, I knew better than anyone that first impressions could be misleading. Sometimes the second face that people hid looked polar opposite to the one they showed. A lot of the time, though, it was hidden because it was just an even darker version. I was committed to spending the rest of the day discovering if Noah actually was a punk, Jaxson was a jerk, and Braxlynn was a snot. And if they were and I made a few enemies, then it really didn't matter, because come tomorrow morning this day would start all over, and no one would remember a thing . . . except for me, of course.

CHAPTER 2

SPUDMASTERFLEX

(Discard Monday—Sept. 6th)

I slid my cream-colored plastic lunch tray across the metal counter and loaded up with a corn dog, sliced peaches, green peas, and Tater Tots. The lunch lady handed me a small carton of chocolate milk, and I turned to scan the lunchroom. There was no better time in the entire day to see who was who than during lunch. After spending more than a decade in elementary school, I knew there were always three basic groups: kids who didn't get made fun of for what they liked (typically the sporty boys and the fashionable girls), kids who got made fun of for what they liked (those would be the nerds), and kids who didn't care about the school social scene (those are your hunters, farmers, and outdoorsy types). The middle category was the most broad and was proudly on display as I looked for an interesting place to sit.

The music nerds sat in the corner with large headphones over their ears or around their necks while they drummed on notebooks, plates, and tables. The role-playing nerds ate with their food on their laps to clear space for an elaborate card game of Magic: The Gathering. Dozens of gamer nerds huddled around a handful of tables, their heads bowed as if in prayer while their fingers blitzed over their phones. Booming laughter shot above the chatter, and I looked to see Jaxson sitting with a group of square-jawed goons over by the door. They'd be eating as quickly as possible to use the rest of lunch for basketball or football or something. Most kids, though, just sat and ate. They would either be floaters, going from group to group depending on the day, or they'd belong to one of a dozen other, less visible subcategories: art nerds, bookworms, and so on.

I wove through the maze of chairs to find Noah at the head of a long table, staring intently at his phone.

"Who's ready to lose?" Noah asked no one in particular. "SpudMasterFlex is ready to crush dreams and hear screams!"

I raised my eyebrows at the comment. I was hoping he wasn't serious, but it looked like my dad had some competition for the cringey comment king. All the seats in the area were taken except for one next to a spindly girl with a mop of scraggly black curls and an upturned nose. I vaguely recognized her from one of my classes.

"This seat free?" I asked the girl.

"Only if you're playing in the stink-squattin' Brown Bag Game." The girl scooted her jacket over to make room but didn't look up from her phone.

I put my tray down and looked at her screen, having no clue what a Brown Bag Game was. She played on an outdated phone with a crack running down the middle of the screen and was logging on to a local game of *Champions Royale*, probably against the other kids in the lunchroom. It was a pretty new game that I hadn't played a lot, but I'd spent plenty of time on similar ones. A medieval-style battle royale with knights, wizards, dragons, ogres, and magic, where your player got dropped into a giant map in a mad scramble for resources and weapons. Last player alive won.

The girl slyly passed me a brown paper bag under the table. Confused, I glanced down and saw the bag was full of dollar bills and coins. "What the heck is this for?"

"It's not *yours*, Scrooge McDoofus," the girl said, finally looking up from her phone. "Oh, hey. You're the new kid, right?"

"Yeah," I said, laughing at the girl's choice of insults. "Name's Danny. What am I supposed to do with this bag of money?"

"Name's Freddie," the girl said, extending her wiry hand. She had on a unicorn T-shirt with a stretched-out neck and sweatpants that were wearing through at the knees. "Gamertag is FreddieCougar, kinda like the dude from the scary movies with the melted face and knives on his hands. Freddy Krueger."

"Yeah, I got it." My parents would never dream of letting me watch horror movies, but I'd seen more than my fair share on discard days.

"Anyway, the Brown Bag Game is a daily tournament. Two bucks to play. Winner take all."

"Aren't we gonna get in trouble for having our phones out?" I asked, glancing around. A teacher stood on the far side of the lunchroom casually glancing down at her own phone.

"You kidding?" Freddie said, waving a dismissive hand. "We're allowed phones during any break from class. Plus, things are pretty chill here. I've been playing in the Brown Bag Game since I was in fourth grade. As long as you're not causing trouble, no one cares. So you in or out, Texas man?"

"What do I got to lose, right?"

"Uh, two bucks," Freddie said, looking at me like I was an idiot.

I shrugged and slipped a couple of dollars into the bag

before slyly passing it to a boy on my right. I pulled out my phone, clicked on the *Champions Royale* app, and searched for the local game.

"Password is hotpotato20, no caps," Freddie said.

I typed in the password and cued up my character, who was a simple peasant. I didn't have any cool skins or anything since I'd only played the game a few times, but I was relatively confident I could still do some serious damage. Many a discard day had been dedicated to honing my gamer skills. The match started, and I dropped my character onto the north edge of Dryout Dunes, a large desert of sandy hills and stone ruins. Before I could even find a weapon, a kill notification popped up on the bottom corner of my screen.

GrizzlyAdamson was axed by SpudMasterFlex

"Sit down, son!" Noah hollered, blindly grabbing a few Tater Tots and shoving them into his mouth.

Thirty seconds later another kill notification flashed on my screen.

R2DPoo was sniped by SpudMasterFlex

"A hundred and seventy-seven yards, folks!" Noah made a gun with his fingers and pointed it to the ceiling. Even though

I didn't know the game that well, I was itching to get my hands on a long-range weapon. The physics of sniping were a bit different in every game (some had bullet drop, travel time, ricochet, and wind effects, while others were just click and kill), but I could quickly adapt to just about anything. Sniping was what I did best.

I spent the next few minutes cobbling together two kills with a spear and handful of throwing knives before a dragon swooped out of the sky and blasted me with a fireball.

You were scorched by SpudMasterFlex

The words flashed across my screen in bold letters.

"Beware the reign of fire!" Noah shouted.

I put down my phone and looked over Freddie's shoulder, since the spectating feature was apparently turned off in this custom game variant and I couldn't watch any more of the game from my phone. After another few minutes, it was down to the final four players, which included Freddie. Her knight character hid in a tree, waiting to get the jump on another player, who crouched along the forest floor. There was a flash of light, and just like that Freddie was dead, her tree burned to a smoldering crisp.

You were scorched by SpudMasterFlex

"You gotta be kiddin' me," Freddie said, slapping her leg. "There's just no pig-flippin' way he could have known I was there."

"Nobody hides from SpudMasterFlex!" Noah gobbled down a few more Tater Tots and did a pathetic attempt at evil laughter.

In another thirty seconds, the game was over. Noah yelled again and shook his phone triumphantly in the air, a small crowd now gathered around him. "That's another brown bag for SpudMasterFlex! Better luck next time, suckers!" He walked over and grabbed the brown paper bag from the middle of the table, stopping when he saw me. "If it isn't Professor Tex. Wait, is *your* money in here, too?" Noah made a show of looking into the bag and back at me. "Guess you didn't see that one coming. You honestly thought you were gonna come up here from your hick town and win at *my* game on *my* home turf? Hey, what am I thinking right now?"

I stared at Noah and twisted my face in thought. "You're thinking about how many skins you're gonna buy in *Tinker Bell's Magical Wardrobe* with that fifty bucks."

A couple of people around the table snickered. "I was *thinking* about how much I love it when talentless noobs move into town. Just means there's more suckers giving me their two bucks." Noah turned to Freddie. "Pleasure doing business with you, FreddieBooger. What does that make for you, like a billion in a row? I know you haven't ever won any money, but isn't it like *free* to take a shower? I swear, you stink more in person than you do at *Champions Royale*."

Noah leaned in close to Freddie and grimaced before plugging his nose and walking away toward the exit with a small group of kids in tow.

Freddie scowled at Noah's back and stuck her tongue out. I glanced at the final stats. SpudMasterFlex had racked up *nine* kills. He was single-handedly responsible for a third of the kills in the whole game. Freddie had gotten five.

"Hey, good game," I told Freddie.

"Thanks," she sighed, and the anger fell from her face. Her lower lip quivered, and for a second I thought she'd start to cry. "That's like the best I've ever done. I hardly ever break the top five."

"Y'all play every day?"

Freddie wrapped one of her black curls around a finger. "There's a Brown Bag Game every lunch, but I can only afford to play once a week. A lot of kids play every day, though."

I dipped a pair of crispy Tater Tots into a cup of ketchup and popped them into my mouth. They were actually really good. "Noah usually wins, I'm guessing?"

Freddie pressed her thin lips together. "Yeah. Winner chooses the game and variant, and *Champions Royale* is *his* game, so unless someone dethrones him and picks something else, he's just going to keep piling on the wins and taking our money. He always plays a custom variant that takes away basically all the monsters except the dragon, which he *always* seems to get. It's so rat-scatting annoying."

"How much money do you think he's won over the years?" I asked, tossing up another Tater Tot and catching it my mouth.

"Kendra Burg has a secret online leaderboard that keeps track of the all-time money leaders. Noah's first place, and no one else is even close. He's won well over three thousand dollars since the fourth grade."

I nearly inhaled my Tater Tot and coughed until my eyes watered. "Three *thousand* dollars? You gotta be kidding me."

"I wish I was."

"Why do people even keep playing?" I asked. "You *know* it's gotta be rigged somehow."

"Yeah, well, good luck proving it." Freddie folded her arms. "I know a lot of gamers that would like to be the one to finally knock Noah off his throne." Freddie's eyes drifted to my food. "Hey, you gonna eat those peaches? My, uh . . . lunch money was in that brown bag."

"Be my guest," I said, taking a swig of milk. I took out my little notebook and listed Freddie as a potential friend before turning to my earlier notes on Noah. I crossed out *friend*, and replaced it with *bully*. Every group had its bullies. Didn't matter if it was the drama kids, the sporty jocks, or the chess club. There was always that boy or girl who had a bit of power and liked to use it to make other people's lives miserable. A bully wasn't all-powerful, though. They could only pick on kids when they felt they had the upper hand. Noah could push around other gamers, but he'd probably be powerless in front of a guy like Jaxson.

I glanced around the lunchroom. The crowd had thinned out considerably. Noah was more than likely a mid-level bully, dominating the gamer world but nothing else. There did, however, look to be quite a few gamers at this school, so his sphere of influence was still decently big, and it just so happened to be a sphere that I cared very much about.

I pulled out my notebook and wrote three more words:

Goal: Dethrone SpudMasterFlex

CHAPTER 3

FOOLISH

(Discard Monday—Sept. 6th)

I stood outside, my back against the redbrick wall of the school, and studied the scene. A large blacktop area hosted half a dozen intense basketball games while a sprawling field of well-kept grass was home to football games, live action role-playing, and everything in between. Even with all the activity, the back of the school seemed naked and alien without slides, swings, tetherball poles, and monkey bars. Most sixth graders would probably have to go through a bit of an adjustment after having daily recess and playgrounds their whole life. I'd had them for *two* lifetimes.

In elementary school I was a bit of a floater when it came to any kind of break time. I was coordinated enough to play most games, but I wasn't the best at anything. If they had a

Ping-Pong table, that would be another story. I had spent countless hours on both discard and sticky days playing my dad in Ping-Pong. Right now, however, I wasn't trying to find a place to play or even hang out. I was here to map out the social scene, and somewhere among the chaos of screaming, laughing, and gossiping students was the most powerful group in the whole sixth grade.

Whether people knew it, admitted it, or realized it, there was a group that had even more power than the sporty kids like Jaxson, because it was this group that actually *gave* Jaxson his status. You'd think his looks, his money, and his muscles made him popular, but you'd be wrong. Those things just made sure that he'd get selected by the group that *gave* popularity. This group had the magical power to grant popularity to whomever they deemed worthy. In Texas, they were a benevolent little club and mainly used their powers for good. Summer Swanson was probably both the prettiest and nicest person in all of Conroe. After meeting Braxlynn, however, I wasn't sure I'd be so lucky here in Pocatello. I was, of course, looking for the popular girls.

I made my way around the blacktop basketball courts and scanned the crowd. Spotting a popular girl in the wild was easy once you knew how to triangulate their position. Popular students were, by definition, the ones that attracted the most attention. I ignored the kids that were playing sports, dealing

Magic cards, and reading books. You needed to find the ones that were idle, find them and follow the eyes. Some would stare, a few would gawk, but most just flashed casual glances. It took me all of ten seconds to find the popular girls sitting on a bench under a large oak tree.

Braxlynn and her squad fit the stereotype almost *too* well as they exhibited an advanced case of "selfie syndrome." Symptoms included constant outstretched arm, permanent duck-face, chronic tilting of head with occasional hand in hair, and repetitive posing. Full makeup and designer clothes at the age of eleven were also common.

Of all the characters in play on the social scene, this group would be the most important. Who were they? How easily were they provoked? What set them off? What level of nastiness were they capable of? All crucial bits of information so Sticky Danny could stay out of trouble. But there was only one really good way of finding out where a line was: You had to cross it. Luckily that was kind of my motto for discard days.

I strolled straight up to the six most popular girls in my grade and cleared my throat. "Howdy, ladies."

I waited while they finished their current round of pictures and posts. They all wore the latest Ziptalk low-profile earbuds and spoke their commands to their phones to post the pictures and send messages through Snapchat, TikTok, and a few apps I'd never even heard of.

I cleared my throat louder and spoke again. "I'm new here and was going around getting to know people."

Braxlynn fluttered her dark eyelashes and looked up at me, contorting her face like she had just smelled me pass gas after eating three spicy burritos. "Oh my gosh, you can't be serious," she muttered under her breath, and returned to her phone. Even braced against all of Braxlynn's little tricks, even with the knowledge that this day would disappear from all memory, I couldn't help but flush with embarrassment. The ability of someone like Braxlynn to make me feel about two feet tall with one dismissive glance was astounding. Behold the mighty power of the popular girls when wielded for ill purposes.

"Braxlynn, be nice," the girl next to her said. She was probably Polynesian of some sort and had wavy black hair and full red lips. "The way he talks is so Gucci. Hashtag adorbie Texas talk, right? He's definitely going up on *Stud Spuds*."

"Whatever, Sefina." Braxlynn shrugged and returned to her screen.

The popular girls cooed and looked at me like I was some kind of lost puppy, all except for Braxlynn, who couldn't be bothered to look away from her phone again.

"I reckon you don't get many folk from Texas up here in these parts, do ya?" I said, pouring on my accent.

"Oh my gosh, he's like a little cowboy or something. This

is so amaze," Sefina said, coming over to my side and holding out her phone at arm's length. "Here, say something in your adorbie accent so I can share it on *Studs*."

I had no idea what she meant by "studs" and made a mental note to check it out later. She squeezed next to me to get us both in the shot, and my stomach did a somersault. Her perfume was an intoxicating mix of passion fruit and coconut. I saw her press the record button on her phone and knew she wanted me to perform like some kind of circus monkey. Who was I to disappoint a popular girl?

"Hey, everybody," I said, waving. "Just chillin' with my new girlfriend Sefina, lighting up her Insta!"

Sefina let out a scream and flinched backward, dropping her phone as if it had just bitten her. "I was *streaming* that," Sefina said in horror as she scrambled to retrieve her phone from the grass. "What is wrong with you?"

"Me? Oh geez, a whole bunch of stuff, but it *really* kinda depends on the day." I shrugged. "I get crazy-bad cases of déjà vu, so that's annoying. It can be *super* confusing sometimes, so I always make sure to keep really good notes of what goes on. Take this for example." I held up a finger to the confused group of girls while I pulled out my notebook and pretended to scan through the pages. "Something here about my dad, there's this kid Noah who's annoying, and . . . ah. Here. And I quote: 'I saw Braxlynn take a picture of a heavyset girl today and photoshop on pig ears and a snout. Despite that, she actually seems really cool . . . the pig girl, I mean. It's obvious that Braxlynn's about as pleasant as a case of explosive diarrhea on a road trip.' Close quote."

I calmly pocketed my notebook as if I'd just recited the Gettysburg Address and panned around to see the entire group level glares at me that could strip paint from a car.

"Excuse me?" Braxlynn's two words oozed with indignation.

I took a step toward her and made a show of sniffing the air. I shook my head. "You're excused, but I typically don't even apologize unless it smells."

Her jaw dropped as her sculpted eyebrows knit downward into a sharp V. I had apparently found the line I was searching for. Accusing someone like her of publicly passing gas typically had that effect.

"Is there a problem here?"

I recognized the voice from earlier in the day and turned to see Jaxson's tall frame towering over me. The henchman had arrived.

My stomach twisted. The double day made the Braxlynns of the world toothless tigers. Her main weapon was long-term reputational damage. Any harm she could inflict was gone at the stroke of midnight. The Jaxsons were different, though. They could punch me in the face. That hurt no matter what day it was.

"Yeah, this little goblin hick put his arm around Sefina and then tried to take her phone," Braxlynn spat.

"Is this true?" Jaxson took a step toward me, his adult-sized hands balled into fists.

I looked over to Sefina, who just stared at her pristinely white Vans, avoiding eye contact with anyone.

Braxlynn's face slowly scrunched into a grimace, and she burst into tears. "Yes, it's true. I was just sitting here with my girlfriends, and he came over and was like, 'You girls are stupid.' Then he snatched Sefina's phone and my phone and said he was going to post something to all my twelve thousand, four hundred and thirty-three followers." She took a deep, shuddering breath and dabbed her eyes, careful not to smudge her makeup. However good of an actor I thought I was, Braxlynn would put most Oscar winners to shame. This girl was over-the-top ridiculous.

"First off," I said, holding up both hands, "I didn't take *anyone's* phone. I'm pretty sure Braxlynn has hers surgically attached to her palm anyway, so I'm not even sure how that would be possible."

"You calling her a liar?" Jaxson said through gritted teeth.

I bobbed my head from side to side, considering. "Well, what she said was like twenty-five percent true." I paused.

"You look confused. Twenty-five percent is like a fraction. It means one out of four—"

Jaxson's fist slammed into my stomach, dropping me to my knees. The world suddenly focused down to a single point as I gulped vainly for my next breath. I had been punched before, but this was different. This was closer to the time I misjudged a jump from my roof to the trampoline and landed belly-first onto the bars.

Jaxson leaned down over my crumpled body and whispered in my ear. "How about you stop creeping on my girlfriend and mosey on back to wherever you came from, Texas turd. I can't believe I thought you were legit."

I wheezed, struggling for air that wouldn't come, until I was sure my lungs would implode. Nothing like being proven right about your judgment of someone's character . . . by being blasted in the gut.

"What's that, Texas turd?" Jaxson said, leaning even closer. "Were you gonna read my mind, too?"

I held up a hand for him to wait as air mercifully rushed back into my lungs. "I *wanted* to read your mind."

"But let me guess. You don't know how to read." Jaxson laughed and looked around for anyone to acknowledge his sick burn.

I coughed several times and shook my head as I got to my feet, straightening with some difficulty. "Nah, the pages were blank."

I knew I shouldn't have said it. I knew it was going to cost me. But even with the guarantee of physical punishment, I couldn't help myself. I rarely could on a discard day. I could see the gears wheeling inside Jaxson's brain before his eyes flared wide. I clenched my fist, ready for him this time, although the lingering pain in my stomach told me it probably wouldn't change the outcome.

Jaxson lunged but stopped short, frozen mid-charge. I flinched backward, narrowly avoiding his flailing punches and noticed someone had grabbed him from behind.

Jaxson looked back and growled. "Get off me, Zak." He turned and pried himself away with some difficulty.

"Take it easy, man," Zak said, placing a hand on Jaxson's shoulder. "Crowd's starting to gather. Just bring it down." The kid spoke softly, like someone trying to convince the Hulk to turn back into Bruce Banner. He was big, maybe even a bit taller than Jaxson but not quite as beefy. His skin was dark, but I couldn't place his ethnicity off hand. Jaxson shrugged off Zak's hand just as the end-of-lunch bell blared from the school's speakers. He turned to me and opened his mouth, but I spoke first.

"I know, I know." I waved him off. I didn't need the double day to know what he was going to say next. "This isn't over. You'll make me pay for this, blah, blah, blah."

Jaxson hesitated before turning toward the school and storming back to class. Braxlynn followed him but glanced over her shoulder to flash a predatory smile that would make a rabid wolf whimper. The other girls gathered their things and left as well, but not before Sefina gave Zak an embarrassed smile and a little wave.

I looked on in silence for a moment before Zak finally spoke. "Dude, *what* did you do?"

"Oh, you know, just trying to make friends. Thanks, by the way." I reached out my hand to Zak. "Danny Day."

"Zak Ansah." Zak's large hand engulfed mine, his grip like iron. "I got to get to class, but you going to be okay?"

"Who, me?" I pointed to myself. "Man, that's just how we say goodbye in Texas."

Zak's eyebrows shot up. "In that case, I will just see you later, then."

"See you later, Zak." I chuckled and waved to him as he joined the mob of students headed back into the school.

I reached for my notepad and took a pen from my backpack.

Follow-up: Look more into this Zak kid. Seems pretty legit. Jaxson is easily provoked and punches like Thanos with the Infinity Gauntlet. Do not anger on sticky day. BRAXLYNN, however, pulls the dummy's strings. Alpha-level bully. Avoid at ALL costs.

I mulled over this last line. This was an important one.

She knew that I'd have to be a fool before pulling anything like that again, and she was right. It *would* be a very long time before I went toe-to-toe with Braxlynn or Jaxson on a sticky day, probably forever. What she *didn't* know was that only half my life was sticky days . . . and Discard Danny took *pride* in being a fool.

CHAPTER 4

BUS RIDE

(Discard Monday—Sept. 6ᵗʰ)

The clock ticked away the final seconds of the school day as I flipped through my notebook. I lightly touched my stomach and flinched back from the pain. Jaxson must have clipped a rib or something.

There were several markers that I used to measure how far I'd taken things on a discard day: nurse's office, principal's office, suspended, grounded, hospital, and police station. Despite the chaos of my first day at school, I was somehow on track to avoid all of them, which was somewhat disappointing. If the fight with Jaxson had escalated, I probably could have checked off three or four of them. I'd never gotten all in one day before, but I always thought it would be fun to try.

The bell rang, and kids scrambled to their backpacks and

out the door. I made my way onto the bus, and although I recognized a few kids, it was mostly full of unfamiliar faces.

I passed Noah, who looked up from his phone and flashed a stupid grin when he saw me. "Hey, my wish came true," Noah said, pointing to my stomach. "I heard you're somehow worse at fighting than you are at *Champions Royale* . . . or reading minds."

Word must have gotten around. I didn't have a witty comeback, so I just shook my head and walked on by, Noah's jittering laughter pelting me from behind. It was moments like this that had me racking my brain for the entire evening to develop the perfect comeback for the sticky day. I didn't plan on being in this same situation tomorrow, however, so I just had to let that one go.

I sat on an empty bench and pulled out my notebook. I hadn't taken down so much new information in my life. Usually it was just a few quick notes about ideas for clever things to say, questions on tests, or embarrassing moments to avoid. I had to memorize as much of this as I could before I went to sleep and it all vanished. First thing tomorrow morning, I'd copy down everything I could remember in my sticky-day notebook.

"Hey, this seat taken?"

It was Zak. He wore neat, expensive clothes, held a violin case in one hand, and had a full-sized notebook in the other.

"It's all yours," I said, gesturing to the seat. "Unless you're here as one of Jaxson's assassins or something."

Zak slipped his backpack off and slid his violin under the seat. "If I was an assassin, I would have taken the seat *behind* you."

"Good point." I shrugged. "Thanks, by the way, for holding Jaxson back."

Zak waved a hand. "Don't mention it. Although it looks like he still got you good." Zak mimicked a punch to the stomach. "Dude, what *were* you doing rocking up to the Clique anyway?"

"The Clique?" I lifted an eyebrow.

"Braxlynn and her friends," Zak said. "That's what they call themselves."

"The Clique, huh?" I said. "They like the popularity mafia or something?"

Zak weighed my comment. "That's one way to put it. To be honest, a lot of them are pretty cool if you get them one-on-one. Most of them are in my neighborhood, and Sefina's actually my next-door neighbor. Braxlynn does run the show, though, if you haven't already noticed."

"I noticed," I said flatly. I flipped through my notebook and stopped on a term I had written down after the fight. "Hey, I've been meaning to ask someone. I heard Sefina say something about posting a picture to *Stud Spuds* before . . . well, before things went south."

Zak winced and let out a little sigh. "I might as well just show you." Zak took out his phone and opened up Instagram. "It's a shame no one warned you before you went headfirst into this buzz saw. You cross paths with Braxlynn, on purpose or not, and you either end up as a Stud Spud or a Dud Spud." Zak swiped to an account, which showed filtered pictures of Braxlynn, her friends, Jaxson, and others before switching to a second account.

"Oh dear," I said. The latest post showed a picture of me, mouth open and eyes bulging, complete with a photoshopped cowboy hat, fake tears, and text bubble that read *Everything's bigger in Texas . . . especially the DUDS!* The picture already had twenty comments.

"Sorry, man." Zak patted me on the shoulder.

"Wow," I said, rather impressed. "They must have taken that picture at the *exact* moment he punched me. They should be photographers for *National Geographic* or something. Can I see that?"

"Your funeral," Zak said, handing me his phone. I flipped through more pictures and noticed the picture Braxlynn had taken in the morning of the girl she made into a pig. She was put in a side-by-side picture with Shrek. A heart was placed in the middle with the question *Ship or Dip?* The comments were not kind.

"Ship or dip?" I asked.

"Do you think they'd make a good couple," Zak explained, rolling his eyes.

"Yikes," I said, shaking my head and handing back the phone. "Pocatello's a rough place, man. No one shuts these down?"

"What's someone going to do?" Zak said. "One comes down, another takes its place. Welcome to Snake River Middle School. Getting on Duds your very first day is a tough break."

"Meh." I waved my hand. "Everyone will forget by tomorrow. Trust me."

"I admire your optimism, but I'm not so sure you know how the internet works, or Jaxson for that matter. The kid can't remember how to spell his last name, but he never seems to forget a grudge. You had a heck of a first day."

"I aim to please," I said. "I gotta ask, though. If Jaxson never forgets a grudge, then why'd you risk jumping in to grab him? Oh, and how did you even *manage* to grab him? That's like wrestling a Russian circus bear . . . and not one of the nice ones. One of the old ones who turns on their trainer."

Zak laughed. "Jaxson and I have a . . . mutual respect for one another."

I stared at Zak, squinting my eyes. "You guys got in a fight before and you won, didn't you?"

Zak shrugged modestly. "It's not like you think. Jaxson's wrestling team came to my judo dojo last year as kind of a cross-training exercise. Again, we respect each other's skills."

I pressed my lips together. If this Zak kid could take on a guy like Jaxson—and apparently refuse to brag about it—then he *was* one to keep an eye on as a potentially valuable ally.

The bus took a sharp turn, and Zak's violin case slid out from under the seat into the center aisle.

"I bet that thing's a pain in the rear," I said, pointing. "I don't see anyone else having to lug one of those around. You lose a bet or something?"

Zak pushed his violin case back under the seat. "I actually take private lessons."

"Dude." I shook my head in astonishment. "What *don't* you do?"

"In discipline there is power to accomplish all things," Zak recited. "Within rules there is freedom from everything that would stand in your way."

"What, is that some ancient judo proverb or something?"

"No." Zak chuckled. "That's what my dad tells me every morning before I go to school."

"Yikes," I winced. "So your parents are pretty intense, then?"

"I guess so," Zak said. "My dad was born in Ghana, Africa, so he had like absolutely nothing until they came here when he was little. Worked super hard and ended up playing college football for Oklahoma, where he met my mom. She was a concert violinist for the Tokyo Junior Orchestra Society when she was younger. They're pretty accomplished people."

I pulled out my notebook and scribbled down some of the information. "So when do you have time to do anything?"

Zak looked confused by the question. "Like in *addition* to all of the stuff I do?"

"No. Like when you do have time to just chill?"

"So you're asking me when do I have time to do *nothing*?"

I opened my mouth to reply but stopped, considering his comment. "That's a weird way of putting it, but yes. When do you have time to just sit there and like play video games or something?"

"I'm not much of a gamer," Zak admitted.

"Well." I put my hands on the seatback in front of us and stood. "I appreciate you saving my life at lunch and all, but I believe we've reached the end of our little conversation." Zak's face froze in an odd twist of confused surprise before I laughed and sat back down. "I'm just kidding. No one's perfect, I guess."

We continued chatting as the bus weaved through town dropping off students. Turned out his dad was one of the big bosses at the computer chip factory that my dad now worked at. He may have been a bit more straitlaced than my Houston friends, but I had a good feeling about Zak. The video game thing was fixable with the right amount of effort. I jotted a few more things down in my notebook.

Goal: Introduce Zak to the marvelous world of gaming.

Strange how most of my goals revolved around video games.

"I'm home," I called as I opened the front door. I followed a narrow path between stacks of moving boxes to the kitchen, where my mom was busy unpacking the pots and pans.

"Oh, honey, how was your first day?"

"Just daa-andy." I winced reflexively as I said the word, favoring my left side. Dang that Jaxson.

"Honey?" My mom's face deepened with concern. "What's wrong? Are you okay?"

The best answer to these kinds of questions was typically whatever would get me out of trouble until tomorrow morning, when everything would reset. Could it really be considered lying if it ended up never actually happening? The lack of physical markers with this particular injury gave me near-limitless options for an explanation. "I tripped over someone's bag in class and fell into a desk. I'm fine."

"You have all the grace of your father," my mom said,

digging through a few boxes before pulling out a dishcloth that she filled with a handful of ice cubes from the freezer. "Well, put some ice on it, and be careful, please. I knew a kid once who tripped on an extension cord in the middle of class and split his head open on an overhead projector. Had slurred speech for a month."

"Really?" I said, grabbing the towel and pressing it to my side.

"No," my mom admitted, "but it *could* be true, and that's all that matters."

I chuckled. I could never tell if my mom was making a joke with stuff like this or some serious point. "I'm sure I'll be fine tomorrow, Mom. Where are the twins?"

"They've been playing upstairs since lunchtime. Thank goodness for their fascination with large empty boxes. With them distracted, I've been able to get a lot more done than I thought I would. Now you go on upstairs and get settled. I'll need your help later on with the rest of the unpacking."

I gave my mom a kiss, worked my way back through the maze of boxes, and went upstairs. I popped my head into the twins' room and immediately realized why my sisters had been so quiet all afternoon.

"Oh, that's not good." Black scribble marks covered the walls and carpet. I ducked into one of the big moving boxes and found Sarah and Alice asleep, dual-wielding uncapped permanent markers. They had apparently used each other as canvases as well. I pulled out my notebook.

Crisis: Find permanent markers . . . before the twins do.

I went to my room, tossed my backpack on the floor, and crashed onto my inflatable mattress. We didn't know how long it was going to take to set up the beds, so we'd packed the camping gear in last. Not a bad discard day. I rolled over and pulled a blank sheet of paper from my backpack and began mapping out the school's social scene as much as I could from memory. While anything I drew today—just like any notes I wrote down—would disappear overnight, I found the best way to retain a lot of information was to make it visual. I plotted out the various groups, drawing different-sized circles depending on their relative power, numbers, and influence. I then placed all the confirmed bullies and potential friends. By the end, I only needed to refer back to my notes a few times. When I had it all mapped out, I went on to memorizing my task lists, which I organized into different categories: follow-ups, embarrassments, comebacks, goals, deep thoughts, stockpiles, and crises. It was a method I'd devised with Dr. Donaldson to bring a bit of order to the double day.

Some things needed to be implemented the very next

day, like hiding the permanent markers from my sisters, while others were longer-range goals, like staying off *Dud Spuds* and winning the Brown Bag Game. Having at least one long-range goal that involved kicking butt at a video game was always a good thing. Taking on Jaxson and Braxlynn during a sticky day would require a near-impossible degree of leveling up, but there might be something I could do about this Noah kid.

"Well, I better get to it," I told myself as I got my phone out and opened up *Champions Royale*. "It's a tough job, but someone's gotta do it."

CHAPTER 5

STICKY DAY

(Sticky Monday—Sept. 6th)

"This is gonna be great," my dad said, pulling up to Snake River Middle School. "Your first day as a Spud."

"I feel pretty good about it, too," I said, matching his enthusiasm. "I'm nervous, but excited to finally start our life here in Idaho."

My dad parked the car and turned to me. "That's the spirit, buddy. I know you can be a bit shy sometimes, but try to make some new friends, okay? They're out there. You've just got to find them."

"Sure thing, Dad," I said, remembering my last line. I needed to take care of this in the car so he wouldn't yell anything in front of the other students. "Love you, Dad."

"Love you too, buddy."

I got out of the car and walked toward school. When I had a lot of notes from the discard day, the sticky day always felt a little like some kind of living performance where I had to find my mark and recite my lines. Most people got anxious because they didn't know what was going to happen on any given day, Sticky Danny was anxious because he knew *exactly* what was going to happen and had to make sure he didn't screw it up even worse.

A car honked three times, and I turned to see my dad waving through an open window. "Go, Spuds!"

A few kids snickered around me, and I copied their laughs. "Wouldn't want to be *that* guy's kid," I said to no one. Sometimes an embarrassing comment from my dad was just inescapable. I always tried to go into sticky days with backup plans for my backup plans.

I bypassed the front desk this time and went straight to my locker, deposited a few books, and made my way through the crowd to classroom 013. I waited patiently in front of the class until the final bell rang. It was a weird thing to look out at people who *should* know me (like Jaxson, Noah, Freddie, and Braxlynn) but didn't recognize me at all.

"Good morning, students," Mrs. Marlow announced from her desk, clapping three times. The class repeated their reply. "Class, we have a new . . . Braxlynn, please put away your phone."

I watched the familiar scene play out. After Braxlynn finally did what she was told, Mrs. Marlow addressed the class again. "This is Daniel Day. His family just moved to Poky. Daniel, would you like to tell us some more about yourself?"

"I'm Danny from just outside of Conroe, Texas," I said, clearing my throat, "which is just outside of Houston. I like video games and Ping-Pong, and I've never seen snow."

"Oh, well we'll be sure to scratch that last one off your list come winter, won't we, class?" Mrs. Marlow predictably replied.

"Oh, and I can read people's minds," I added. My voice shook ever so slightly as I tried to stick as close as possible to what I had said and how I had said it the day before. I typically didn't care or even need to stick this close to the discard-day script, but when I did tricks like guessing what people were thinking, it helped if I could accurately re-create the conditions from the discard day. Over the years I found the timeline to be pretty resilient, though. Unless I took the day hardcore in a different direction, it was amazing how many things seemed to proceed down the same path.

"You what?" Mrs. Marlow asked.

"I know it seems weird, but I can one hundred percent read people's minds," I said, turning from Mrs. Marlow to the students. I wiped my sweaty palms against my thighs and hoped no one noticed. "Dead serious."

The same three students raised their hands, and I could see Noah leaning forward to make his comment.

"Oh yeah, Professor X, then what am I thinking?"

"I will take that as a compliment," I mumbled, turning to the three other students. "I just need you to tell me your name, jot something down on a piece of paper, and then I'll guess what you wrote."

Noah grinned. "My name's Noah."

The other three students, Shar, Amy, and Carrie, told me their names and then wrote their sentences down.

"Okay, Professor X. What'd we write?" Noah said. It was the exact phrase from the discard day. I was one hundred percent sure they'd written down the same things. I opened my mouth to say something to Noah, but I hesitated. I wanted to put him in his place, to embarrass him in front of the class and make it stick, but I . . . couldn't. Well, Sticky Danny couldn't. It had been so easy to do the day before. To poke fun, to take risks, to be courageous, to take the bullies down a few notches. I hadn't even thought about the consequences. There was nothing anyone could do to me that wasn't tolerable for half a day, but this was the sticky day. Anything I did here was for real. It was for keeps.

My heart began thundering in my chest, and I turned my thoughts and eyes from Noah to the three other students. I rubbed my chin and squinted my eyes. "Shar wrote down,

'Fuzzy Wuzzy was a bear.' Amy wrote, 'There's no way you'll guess what I wrote.' And Carrie wrote, 'Why doesn't Pocatello have a Chick-fil-A?' Was I close?"

The class slowly turned from me to the three girls, who sat still as statues and gawked in amazement.

"There's no way," Shar, a short girl with straight brown hair, finally managed.

Amy looked from side to side and then behind her, searching for some explanation. "How'd you do that?"

Carrie remained silent, her mouth open, looking from her paper to me and back.

I shrugged. "Call it a Texas party trick."

"You never guessed what I wrote, Professor Tex."

I turned and saw Noah brandishing his little paper. He had no idea that I knew exactly what was on that paper, word for word, spelling error and all. He could never guess that I was already two steps ahead with a dozen different things to say already planned out. Doing the trick for the three girls and the rest of the class was simple. They'd think it was cool. It would earn me some easy street cred on my very first day. But Noah was different. Knowing that goading him would only cause permanent sticky-day problems, I bit my tongue. Even if I just predicted what was on his paper, that could still create problems. Kids like Noah, Jaxson, and Braxlynn didn't like being shown up or making a mistake in front of a crowd.

I knew from the discard day that Noah wasn't used to losing, and even though I wanted *desperately* to introduce him to a new way of life, I just couldn't will my sticky-day self into action. If I wanted to avoid making an enemy, I would have to let Noah win this one, and probably a lot of other ones.

I squinted again and acted like I was struggling for an answer. "I don't know for sure on this one. Something about how you're good at video games?"

"Wrong!" Noah gloated. "Although you *are* right about me being *incredible* at video games!"

"Noah," Mrs. Marlow chided. "Let's try to be more encouraging to our new student. Be a buddy, not a bully, please. Danny, that was a fantastic little trick. We're excited to have you on board. Now if you'll please take your seat . . . as long as there aren't any rabbits you're going to magically pull out of your backpack."

"No rabbits, Mrs. Marlow," I said, unzipping my backpack to show her inside. The class laughed, and I walked to the back of the room, a trail of impressed whispers in my wake. I sat down and stared at the back of Jaxson's head. I apparently hadn't been sufficiently mean-spirited to deserve a high five from the alpha bully today. All the better. Staying off his radar on sticky days was a top priority.

I didn't even dare turn my head in Braxlynn's direction. I looked out of the corner of my eye to see her with her phone out. It would have been noble to do something to help out Mrs. Shrek, or at least that's what people would be calling the girl a few rows in front of Braxlynn by the end of the day. But nobility was also a great way to tangle yourself up in other people's messes, a goal that Sticky Danny avoided like baggy jeans at a rodeo.

To my right, Noah showed his paper to a few kids and flashed a cocksure smile. I pulled out my sticky-day notebook, flipped to my daily list, checked off one box, and retraced the words on another.

☑ Perform a standard "guess trick" with Shar, Amy, and Carrie

☐ Dethrone SpudMasterFlex

I didn't know how I would ever get the guts to actually check the second box. Not on a sticky day. Not when it counted. I cursed my sticky-day self for being such a wuss. Mrs. Marlow turned to write something on the whiteboard, and I tried to put the thought from my mind. I had a lot of things to try to get right today, which meant there were a lot of things I could get wrong if I wasn't careful. I read back through my sticky-day notes for my next steps. This day was far from over.

CHAPTER 6

FRIENDS

(Sticky Monday—Sept. 6ᵗʰ)

"Could I trouble you for a double helping of them Tater Tots and peaches?" I asked, dialing up my Texas accent. The storklike lunch lady tilted her head and smiled as she piled on two scoops of the crispy, golden tots and gave me an extra bowl of peaches. I was quickly learning that a little Texas charm went a long way up in Idaho. I walked over to the gamer tables and took the closest seat to Noah I could find.

I passed the brown bag along without putting in any money and kept my phone in my pocket. I'd played nearly four hours of *Champions Royale* yesterday, but I knew as well as anyone that I'd need more than a few hours of practice to beat the infamous SpudMasterFlex. However much I hated to admit it, the dude was a legit gamer. I was itching to test my skills (especially my sniping), but my plan wasn't just to eventually defeat Noah, it was to do it in spectacular fashion— if I ever got the courage.

The game started, and Noah immediately began shouting out insults every time he eliminated a player . . . which was often. My plan to watch his gameplay and pick up on his strategy was a bust as he had one of those polarized privacy screens and pulled his phone right into his chest. For a guy who loved to show off and gloat, I found it odd he would be so secretive about his screen.

"Sit down, son!" Noah yelled, and pumped his fist.

Not getting anything from Noah—other than the growing desire to give him a throat punch—I left my lunch for a second and walked around the table, taking in the action by glancing over a few kids' shoulders. The ending changed slightly without me in the game. FreddieCougar got fifth instead of fourth and SpudMasterFlex racked up twelve kills instead of nine, but the end result was the same. If I was going to outplay Noah, I was going to need some serious help.

Noah taunted a few kids as he walked by before stopping at Freddie. I knew what was coming, how mean it was going to be, how much Freddie didn't deserve any of it. Some brave discard-day part of me took half a step forward before I caught myself, wavering like a little kid with his toes at the edge of the high dive. I wanted to help. I had the knowledge to help. But I couldn't risk it. Not on a sticky day.

"Thanks for the two-dollar donation," Noah said, shaking the brown bag in front of Freddie's face. "I hope this wasn't your laundry money, because you ree-e-k!" Noah plugged his nose and walked away just as he'd done the day before.

I went back, grabbed my lunch, and made my way over to Freddie. I told myself it was because I wanted to get more info on Noah and the Brown Bag Game, but I knew full well it was more about trying to get rid of my guilt for not sticking up for her. "Hey, which player were you?"

"Huh?" Freddie said, her face a mask of surprise. From what I had seen, not a lot of people just walked up and chatted with Freddie. "Uh, FreddieCougar."

"Like the scary dude in the movies with the melted face and knives on his fingers?"

"Yeah," she said, perking up. "No one ever gets that reference."

"Texcalibur," I said, holding my hand out.

She shook it, and her eyes widened with recognition. "Oh hey, you're that new kid who did the mind-reading trick in Mrs. Marlow's class. That was pig-stickin' crazy. How'd you do that, seriously?"

"Would you believe me if I told you that I just transferred here from Hogwarts?"

Freddie giggled. "No, I don't think I would."

"Well, then you probably wouldn't believe the *actual* answer," I said, glancing at Freddie's old, busted-up phone. "You did pretty well. Top five."

"Yeah"—Freddie gave a dejected smile—"that's like one of the best I've ever done, but it's all or nothing with the Brown Bag Game. Noah is good, but no one is *that* good. He wins *all* the time. It's so frigging annoying. Ratbag cow poop! I just don't dog-digging get it."

I chuckled at Freddie's word choices. "Ratbag cow poop?"

"Sorry." Freddie hunched her shoulders. "My older brothers cuss like crazy, but my grandma told me that ladies shouldn't do that, so I just invent my own phrases."

"Makes sense," I said. "Do you think you could teach me?"

"What, to cuss?" Freddie asked.

I laughed. "No, to play *Champions Royale*. I've got a gamertag and everything and I'm a pretty quick learner when it comes to games, but I could use someone to show me the tips and tricks before I toss my dollars in the bag. Maybe we could take down SpudMasterFlex together."

"Really?" Freddie perked up. "Like, you want to come over to my house and stuff? I mean, if it's not weird or anything that I'm a girl."

"A gamer's a gamer. Doesn't bother me." I had no idea

whether I was actually going to go over to this girl's house to play games, but after all the bullying I'd seen since showing up at school, I'd take friends where I could get them, and it seemed like Freddie would do the same.

Freddie smiled and nodded her head. "Cool. I'll message you my info. I've never really had a teammate before. This is gonna be awesome."

"Wait, there's teams?" I asked. "I thought it was every man for themselves."

Freddie shrugged. "Well, yeah, in the end there's only one winner, but it's not like you're gunning for your best friend first thing. People aren't walking around in squads or sharing guns and ammo or anything, but there's technically no rule against ganging up on someone or avoiding skirmishes with your buddies until the end. We call them 'shadow teams' since it's not *really* a team, but it sort of is."

"And you got top five without any shadow team of your own?" I asked.

"Yeah, flying solo makes it a bit tougher, especially when I'm garbage at long range. Get me in close quarters and I'll be dancing on your worm-squirming grave, but I can't ever seem to get close enough to Noah. He's either sniping me, raining dragon fire on my head, or I get double-teamed before I can close the distance."

"So is that how Noah wins all the time? His shadow team?"

Freddie slowly shook her head, black curls bobbing. "He *claims* no one helps him, but I highly doubt that's true. Hey, maybe you can read his mind!"

The comment, however absurd Freddie meant it to sound, actually gave me an idea. "Yeah, I'll see what I can do."

"Wait . . . can you read *my* mind, too?"

I pursed my lips and slid over my extra peaches and Tater Tots. "You're thinking you're hungry because you put your lunch money in that brown bag."

Freddie's eyebrows shot to the ceiling. "Whoa, Texcalibur. Maybe you *did* go to Hogwarts."

"Something like that," I said, taking out my list and checking off another box.

✦ ━ ✦ ━ ✦

The remainder of lunch was distinctly less painful on the sticky day than it had been on the discard day, but that wasn't all that uncommon. Freddie and I rotated in and out of a winner-stays game of four square while I shot occasional glances over at the Clique. Looking at Braxlynn duck-face for photo after photo and laugh as she took pics of other kids made my stomach burn like I'd just chugged a ghost chili milkshake, but I knew I wouldn't do a darn thing about it. The fear of me ending up on some "ship or dip" post on *Dud Spuds* made sure of that. Why did she have that kind of power to begin with? I wasn't aware of anyone who actually *liked* her, outside of her little gaggle of friends and Jaxson, but somehow she still ruled the school.

I also kept an eye on Zak over at the football field. He played on the opposite team from Jaxson and actually gave the bully a run for his money, which gave me an odd sense of pride. Odd, considering the kid didn't even officially know who I was yet.

The rest of the school day went by without incident. I hung back and waited for Zak to board the bus first. Without having broken up the fight between me and Jaxson, I couldn't be sure he'd choose to sit by me again. On sticky days, you sometimes had to take matters into your own hands. I boarded the bus and saw Zak sitting about halfway back. The seat next to him was empty.

"Hey, this seat taken?" I asked.

"Be my guest," Zak said, scooting over a bit more.

"Danny Day," I said, holding out my hand. "I'm new here."

Zak placed his notebook on his lap and shook my hand with a strong grip, recognition washing over his face. "Oh, you're the mind-reader kid."

"The one and only." I held my hands out. "What gave it away?"

"Not too many new kids from Texas around here pulling off magic tricks. It was the locker talk of the day." Zak had a precise diction when he spoke, like he was carefully choosing each word. He didn't sound robotic or overly formal or anything, just extremely measured, which wasn't all that surprising given his strict upbringing. He looked around, then leaned in close. "So how'd you do it?"

"There's no magic to it, man," I said, trying to downplay the moment. "Nothing you can't look up how to do on YouTube."

Zak squinted one eye with a look that he knew there was more to it than a simple YouTube video, but he let it go. "Well, it was quite the first impression regardless."

"Practice makes perfect, I guess." I shrugged.

Our conversation continued much as it had during the discard day, with talk about Zak's interest in sports, judo, and violin. I wasn't following a script exactly, but it was important to retread all the main points of a "getting to know you" type conversation like this. Even with all my notes it was impossible to keep up on everything I learned about someone during a sticky versus a discard day, and it made for some awkward moments when I asked someone about their sick grandma when they never remembered telling me that they even *had* a grandma. The more and more I talked to Zak, the more I liked the kid. I was 100 percent comfortable around him on a sticky day. That was rare for me.

"You know what I was thinking about?" I asked, looking out the window as we turned the corner into my neighborhood.

"What's that?"

"What if I had a second crack at today?"

"What do you mean?" Zak asked.

"Like what if you had this strange ability where you could repeat the day?" I clarified. "Like let's say if the first time you lived a day was a trial run. Nothing really mattered, because everything would just reset itself, and you'd have another shot at the day."

I had asked this question to a few friends over the years, since it was usually a great source for new ideas of things to try out. It didn't really matter if I brought it up on a sticky day. It wasn't like anyone suspected that I actually lived a double day. To them it was just a cool thought experiment.

"Hmmm." Zak looked up and rubbed his chin. "So I'd like remember everything I'd done during the first go-around?"

"Yeah."

"Okay." Zak nodded. "Easy answer. I'd split that first day between practicing the violin, drilling judo moves, and then doing something new like learning a language or something."

I opened my mouth to reply, then closed it. "Hold on. You'd spend the extra day *practicing*?"

"Yeah, I'd get crazy good at stuff, crazy fast."

It was my turn to squint at Zak with disbelief. "You wouldn't like spend a hundred dollars on candy, run through the school in your underwear, and throw a paint-filled water balloon at your neighbor's dog?"

Zak gave a confused laugh. "You would run through the school in your underwear?"

"You know what I mean," I said, although I *had* done it one time in fourth grade. Very freeing. "Like something spontaneous. Something you could usually never get away with."

Zak thought for a while. "Oooh, maybe I would be a superhero! You'd read the news and then figure out where all the bad stuff happened, and then you could go save people and stuff."

I leaned back and stared at Zak. Of all the kids I had ever asked this question, not a *single* one had given Zak's answer. Once I brought up the idea of doing mischievous stuff, the thought exercise always went in that direction. I had only ever heard that they would do the same things as me, but here Zak was wanting to become a concert violinist, judo ninja, and protector of old ladies' purses. Even crazier still, I didn't get the feeling that he was putting me on. He was completely serious. I had taken a peek at Zak's second face and just found one that seemed to smile more brightly.

The bus pulled to a stop, and the squeak of opening doors jolted me from my thoughts. I said goodbye to Zak and headed for my house, all the time dwelling on what he'd said.

"I'm home," I called, opening the front door. I made my way to the kitchen, expecting to see my mom unpacking the pots and pans, but heard her voice call from upstairs.

"Up here, sweetie."

I walked upstairs and saw my mom slumped in a camping chair, surrounded by an explosion of toys and empty boxes. My two crazy sisters ran around in circles and launched stuffed animals from one end of the room to the other.

"Geez, Mom, you okay?" I asked.

"I'm fine." She rubbed her eyes as she sat up. "I think the girls have a lot of bottled-up energy from being stuck in the car for two days. I didn't get much unpacking done today, unfortunately."

I shrugged. "Well, it could have been worse. They could have gotten hold of some markers or something and drawn all over the walls while you unpacked."

A stuffed animal smacked my mom in the face, and she barely reacted. "Right now, I think I'd prefer the markers."

However stressed my mom looked, I knew for a fact that she *wouldn't* have preferred the permanent markers. I had made a point of taking them out of the box and hiding them above the fridge this morning. That was the funny thing about sticky days. It was easy to prevent something from happening that I didn't want, but it was impossible to tell what other things might happen instead. Did I sometimes create an even bigger mess on a sticky day by trying to avoid something that happened on a discard day? Yes. Yes, I did. My middle name could be Unintended Consequences. All in all, though, if you added up the damage I caused versus the damage I prevented, I would have to say I was doing pretty well.

"Hey, do you know where my bike is?" I asked, slipping my backpack off my shoulder.

"It'll be in the garage somewhere. You might want to wait for your dad to come home."

"Bike ride?" Alice said, her pigtailed head popping out of a cardboard box like a prairie dog out of its hole.

"Bike wide, Danny?" Sarah echoed, unable to pronounce her *r*s. She ran at me and latched on to my leg like a four-tentacled octopus. You had to be very careful what words you said around the twins. Certain phrases like *bike ride*, *ice cream*, *candy*, and *horse* were like uttering the words to a magical spell that drove my sisters mad with desire.

"No bike ride today, twinsies," I said, trying to pry Sarah from my leg. I finally resorted to the foolproof release mechanism known as the "armpit tickle."

"Are you looking to go somewhere?" my mom asked.

"It's nothing urgent. I just had someone invite me over to their house to play video games one of these days. I can go some other time."

"Video games?" my mom said, looking confused. "Most of the systems we get you just end up gathering dust."

Did every parent know so very little about their kids, or was it just a double-day problem? "I know, Mom, but I still like to play. Plus it'll be a good way to make friends."

"So you met some nice kids at your new school, then?"

Today I did. "Oh yeah, basically everyone I talked to today was super nice. There's Freddie, the one who likes video games, and another cool kid named Zak. I met him on the bus ride home."

"Oh, that's such a relief. It's so important to find good friends and not get mixed up with the wrong crowd. I'd drop you off at your friend's house, but I really need help unpacking. We just need to get settled, and then you can have all sorts of playdates."

"*Hang out*, Mom," I corrected as I walked over to my room to drop off my backpack. "The twins have playdates. I go over to hang out."

I looked down from the second-story balcony at the labyrinth of big, unopened, cardboard moving boxes. My mom hadn't asked me to help with the boxes on the discard day. Scrub the walls of permanent marker, yes, but not unpack boxes. All real superheroes got punished in some way for trying to do the right thing. I was no exception.

I spent the next three hours pulling clothes, books, picture frames, and toys from about a million different boxes. It was pretty tedious work, and most of the time it just seemed like we were making more of a mess, but it had to be done, and it gave me time to reflect on the day. I replayed several moments again and again in my brain: seeing Braxlynn piggify that girl's picture, not using the mind-reading trick to put Noah in his place, watching him tease Freddie. I may not have shown it, but there was always something nagging me at the end of a sticky day, something I did or didn't do, but this was different. I had known they were all coming. I was the *only* person who had known they were all coming, and yet I did nothing. Zak would have. This ate at my stomach like a worm burrowing through the center of a bright red apple.

Dr. Donaldson had always pushed me to be responsible with the double day. It wasn't like he didn't expect me to have fun with it, just to not spend *every* discard day trying to eat all the items in the school vending machine. When I wanted to be flippant, I'd tell him a phrase I heard my dad say when he beat my uncle in a very uncoordinated game of one-on-one basketball: "In the land of the blind, the one-eyed man is king." Roughly speaking, no one else had the double day, so I wasn't in competition with anyone about how to *use* the double day. On top of that, I was also pretty sure no one would use it all that much differently than me anyhow.

But then there was Zak. He didn't know it, but he had me

calling into question my whole *approach* to the double day. I was reminded of Dr. Donaldson's response: I may very well be in the "land of the blind" when it came to the double day, but that didn't mean that I shouldn't do more with it. I wasn't the one-eyed man because I only had one eye. I just refused to open my other eye.

I pulled out my sticky-day notebook and sighed.

Deep thought: I hate it when Dr. Donaldson ends up probably being right.

CHAPTER 7

STOCKPILE

(Discard Tuesday—Sept. 7th)

"Let's see who did their reading yesterday," Mr. Wilding said from the whiteboard, pushing his round glasses up his pointed nose. "Who knows how to solve a fraction divided by another fraction? Take two-fifths divided by four-ninths."

It was fourth-period math, but by the number of students asleep, you'd have thought it was midnight. The only response from the class was a cough, a sneeze, and some gentle snoring.

I looked over at Zak, expecting him to pipe up. Turned out he was in both my fourth-period math class and my sixth-period honors English class, which was pretty cool. He looked back at me and mimed playing the violin. I guess the kid was human after all.

"Nobody?" Mr. Wilding asked. He seemed more offended than surprised. He spent a long while casting a sharp, hawkish scowl over the class before continuing. "It was on page one of your reading. Page *one*. This is preposterous . . . Look, I will give five bonus points on your next quiz to whoever can tell me the answer. Anyone?"

"You find the common denominator?" a girl offered from the back of the room.

"You find the common denom—" Mr. Wilding sputtered in disbelief. "No. You multiply the first number by the reciprocal of the second number!"

I took out my discard-day notebook and jotted down the answer just as Mr. Wilding angrily penned it on the board. Discard days weren't all just flippant quips and high-risk pranks. Sticky Danny's pristine and impressive reputation required a lot of upkeep, and ol' Discard Danny was tasked with most of the legwork. I already had two copies of quizzes stashed in my backpack from first and third period that I'd need to study tonight. Some discard days were about using ammo, and others were about stockpiling it. Stockpiling days were necessary but were never as much fun.

At lunchtime, I went for the ultra-healthy selection of a giant pink cookie and twenty-ounce bottle of soda from the vending machines before heading to the video gaming tables.

Freddie perked up when she saw me and gestured to the empty spot next to her. I held up a finger for her to give me a second and walked over toward Noah, who had just taken his seat at the head of one of the long tables.

"Cool shirt, man," I said, nodding to Noah. His T-shirt had two dragons on it with what looked like Chinese lettering underneath.

Noah looked down at his shirt and then at me. "You know what game it's from?" The question came off more as a challenge than the start to idle chitchat.

I had played a lot of video games in my life, but I didn't recognize the symbol. "Are those the dragons from the latest *Shimmer and Shine* show?"

"*You* would know," Noah scoffed. "Shows how legit of a gamer you are. It's from *Double Dragon*, you noob. Freaking awesome retro game. One of the all-time best."

Although Noah spoke with more confidence than Spider-Man in a rock-climbing contest, I highly doubted he knew as much as he put on. First off, he was like eleven years old. Second off, video games had been coming out for basically forty years. There were millions of them. Third off, I'd checked his online stats. He played a *lot* of *Champions Royale*. It didn't leave much time for other games. He probably got the shirt as a gift, played the game once, knew no one else would be able to call him on it, and used it to smugly show

how much he "knew" about retro games. I pulled out my notebook.

Stockpile: Learn more about the old game Double Dragon

"I'll have to check it out," I replied. "So, I hear you're like the best at *Champions Royale* in the school."

Noah spoke as someone passed him the brown bag. "I'm the best at *every* game in the school. You gonna play in the Brown Bag, or what?"

"Of course," I said, holding up my phone. "Just letting you know, I was like the best in my school, especially at sniping."

"This is my scared face." Noah tilted his head and gave me a bland stare. "Buckle up, buddy. And just to let you know, my sniping's straight fire. No one's better than me." He gave a predatory smile as he handed me the paper bag.

Noah claiming that he was better than me at *Champions Royale* was forgivable; I hadn't played nearly as much as he had, after all. A challenge to my sniping ability, however, was an offense on a personal level. No matter the game, no matter the opposition.

I eyed Noah as I pulled out a wad of cash. "It's five bucks, right?" I asked, testing to see if Noah would correct me.

"Yep," Noah said, watching me place a five-dollar bill into the bag.

"Good luck," I said, walking over to take my seat next to Freddie.

"Don't need it," Noah called out after me.

Freddie leaned over to me as if she were some spy slipping me top secret information. She wore an oversized T-shirt and the same worn-out sweatpants from the day before. "What was *that* all about?"

"Mind games, Freddie," I said, queuing up *Champions Royale*. "Mind games."

A few minutes later, the round started and my character was zooming through the sky toward the map. I dropped into a barn at the southeast corner of Peasantville and watched two other players land in nearby houses. After a quick search, I almost shouted for joy when I opened a chest behind a hay bale.

"The worm-squirming wizard's cloak," Freddie hissed in excitement as she watched my screen. "Danny, that's huge."

"I know—keep it down," I whispered back, not taking my eyes from the screen. The wizard's cloak was one of the most powerful objects in the game. It took up your magical item, armor slot, and weapon slot, but it was worth it. I equipped the cloak and began levitating a few feet off the ground. You couldn't exactly fly around with it, but the minor levitation allowed you to move over any terrain with ease. I floated out of the barn and found the two players who had landed in nearby houses. After a few blasts of lightning from my hands, I reduced the population of Peasantville to one.

Texcalibur zapped DontFeedAfter12

Texcalibur zapped BigBaller50

"Texcalibur takes the lead," I shouted, knowing that Noah would have just seen the kill notifications pop up on his phone. I felt Freddie's hand squeeze my shoulder and flitted my eyes to the side. She was more intently focused on my phone than I was.

Even though I couldn't hold any other weapon while wearing the wizard's cloak, it gave me the ability to command the dragon, which was usually how Noah ended up not just winning but *destroying* the competition. If I could get to the dragon at the top of Fangthorn Peak before SpudMasterFlex, then there was a decent chance that I could beat him right here and now. And, typically, if I could do it on a discard day, I could do it *better* on the sticky day. Toppling this kid might not be so hard after all.

I left Peasantville and third-partied another pair of players in Haunted Pines before making my way to the base of Fangthorn Peak. I wasn't super familiar with the best route up the mountain but still made good progress. From the corner of my eye I could see Noah lean forward over his phone and bite his tongue. He was nervous. This one was slipping away from him. In another thirty seconds I'd be at the dragon's lair at the top of the mountain, and this thing would be over. I just needed to get to the dragon—

My screen flashed red as a waterfall of fire rained from the sky.

You have been scorched by SpudMasterFlex

"No friggin' way!" I yelled.

"Class is in session, Professor Tex." Noah laughed and pumped his fist.

Freddie let go of my shoulder and leaned back. "Yuuuup," she said with the understanding of one who'd been in my spot far too many times before.

I clenched my jaw and shook my head in disbelief. How on earth had he gotten to the dragon before me? The rest of the game was a slaughter as Noah piled on a blistering seventeen kills. Something wasn't right. This went beyond the fact that Noah was a good player. Freddie had said earlier that it just didn't make sense how much SpudMasterFlex won. I took a few screenshots of the end-of-game stats to look over later.

"You did all right, Tex," Noah said, walking by me with the brown bag in hand, "but it looks like the competition in Texas isn't quite what it is up in Poky!"

"So are you gonna cheat every time you play, or just when I jump out ahead with four quick kills?"

"Ha, in your dreams, noob." Noah jostled the brown bag in front of my face. "Get all the quick kills you want to. You do realize the winner is the last person standing, right?"

I wanted to snatch the bag from him with one hand and punch him square in his rat face with the other. I could do it. He deserved it, and it was a discard day, but I muscled down the growing rage. I had a quiz in fifth period today, and I needed to see what was on it for the sticky day. I couldn't spend the next hour in the principal's office.

I glared at Noah. "I'm gonna beat you."

"You couldn't beat a drum," Noah said. His comebacks were worse than my dad's jokes. He turned to Freddie. "Smell ya later, Frede-*reek*-a."

Instead of replying with one of her colorful insults, Freddie wilted like a dying flower.

My lip curled as I watched Noah stroll out of the

lunchroom, a group of four of his cronies in tow. I knew two things in that moment. One, I would make him pay a hundred times over for being such a turd. And two, I would probably never have the guts to do anything on a sticky day. Such was the curse of living the double day.

CHAPTER 8
THE ROOST

(Discard Tuesday—Sept. 7ᵗʰ)

Freddie's one-story house was tucked behind a patchy, brown lawn and a row of overgrown shrubs. A rusty Ford sedan was parked under a slanted carport roof, which hung off the side of the rectangular home. I leaned my bike against one of the shrubs and walked up the chipped cement steps. I stood on the porch and gave my legs a little stretch. Freddie's house was at least five miles out, and most of it was uphill. I tried the doorbell but couldn't hear anything from inside, so I knocked three times on the screen door. Just when I was ready to get back on my bike and ride home, I heard the sliding of a chain lock, and the main door opened. I stared through the warped screen-door mesh at an old lady in a floral muumuu.

"Uh, is Freddie home?" I asked.

"Freddie"—the old lady turned back inside and cawed with the sound of a dying crow—"there's some kid here."

After a few seconds, Freddie came running to the door. "Thanks, Gammie," she said, standing on her tippy toes and giving the old lady a kiss. "Here, let's actually go outside."

I stepped back as Freddie opened the screen door and led the way around the side of the house but stopped. "Hey, is that your bike?"

"Yeah, do I need to put it somewhere else?" I asked.

"Let's bring it around back," she said, walking over and wheeling my bike toward the backyard. "If you don't lock your stuff up around here, it tends to become someone else's stuff. You get my drift?"

"All right, then," I said, eyeing the other houses in her neighborhood. "Thanks for the pro tip."

I followed Freddie into her huge backyard. It was a maze of trees, long grass, and untrimmed bushes. Nestled back between two towering trees stood a sprawling oak tree. Half a dozen or so wooden rungs were nailed into the wide trunk, leading up to a hidden tree house some ten feet in the air with an extension cord dangling down and running to the back of the house.

"Cool," I said, watching Freddie go up the ladder after she stashed my bike under an overgrown bush. She took out a key and removed a heavy padlock on a small hatch on the tree-house floor and climbed inside.

"Come on in," Freddie called out.

I made my way up the rungs, poked my head into the tree house, and gawked at the surrounding awesomeness. The walls of the small space were lined with posters of *Champions Royale*, *Minecraft*, *Portal*, and other video games. A poster-sized whiteboard hung on one wall and was covered in anime-style drawings of iconic video game heroines like Princess Zelda, Samus, Cortana, Wraith, Tracer, and others. There was a small TV mounted to the wall with no fewer than ten different retro systems set up below it and shelves with neatly organized game cases to the sides. One small beanbag chair was pushed off in the corner. "This place is incredible."

"You like it?" Freddie said, her face lighting up with an expectant smirk. "Most of the old systems were my dad's, but I've managed to scrounge a few from yard sales and stuff. Sorry, I'll have to get another chair up here somehow. I don't get a lot of visitors. My dad built the tree house. He's in the army, so I don't get to see him very much, but he's really awesome at making stuff."

"And what's your mom do?" I said, climbing into the tree house and closing the trapdoor.

"I've never actually seen my mom," Freddie said casually. "My grandma takes care of me and my three older brothers.

They're pretty big turd brains for the most part, which is why I spend so much time up here."

I gave a small laugh. "Yeah, I've got two younger sisters who I'm pretty sure are part goblin, but you can get away with a lot when you're cute. Your brothers don't come up here?"

"Nope." Freddie smiled, jangling her key. "It's my own private little space."

"It's perfect." I would definitely have to come back on the sticky day. "A place this cool has to have a name."

Freddie nodded. "I call it the Roost."

"That's awesome." Freddie was a funny girl. She was nice but had a flair for colorful expletives. Her appearance was a bit messy, but her tree house was super clean and organized. She was an interesting person, and I liked interesting people. I also got the impression that she'd been waiting a very long time to share the Roost with someone, and I was totally fine being that someone. "So is this what you'd spend your money on if you won the Brown Bag Game? Some upgrade to the Roost?"

"A new bike, actually," Freddie said without hesitation.

"Why? What's wrong with your . . ." I trailed off, putting two and two together. "It got stolen, didn't it?"

"Danny the mind reader," Freddie said, snapping her fingers and pointing to me. "Some pig-blathering snot brain stole it from my front lawn like a week after my birthday. You have any idea how long it takes me to walk to and from the frog-sliming bus stop every day?"

I tried to remember where the bus dropped Freddie off. It wasn't close. "Yikes."

"Just wait until winter." Freddie nodded knowingly. "That's mega yikes. I swear I spend half my day walking. Cuts down on my sleep, my time to do homework, the time I have to help my grandma."

"Not to mention your gaming time," I added.

Freddie gave me a strange look. "Nothing cuts down on my gaming time, Texcalibur."

I laughed. "So a new bike and anything else?"

"Well, a new phone is too expensive, but maybe I'd get some data for my current hunk of junk. Now I just bum off of hotspots and free Wi-Fi and stuff. Kind of annoying." Freddie looked at the floor, her next words coming out in a mumble. "Maybe some new clothes as well."

"New clothes? There's nothing wrong with your clothes," I lied, partly to make her feel better and partly to make *me* feel better. Here Noah was, using Freddie's lunch money to buy new skins for his *Champions Royale* characters, while she needed *actual* clothes. It made something inside me burn.

"Are you kidding?" Freddie said, pinching her shirt and pulling it out. "You see a lot of girls in our grade wearing their *brothers'* hand-me-downs? And these ain't exactly fresh hand-me-downs, either. These suckers have seen some action. I look like I'm homeless."

"Don't listen to what tools like Noah say."

Freddie gave a short laugh. "Don't worry about what people say? Yeah, well, just wait until you get shipped or dipped on *Dud Spuds* with Oscar the Grouch and people comment how Oscar would never go for Freddie because 'she's too much of a slob.'"

I winced. "Geez. That Braxlynn is ruthless." As if I needed any more reasons to make staying off Duds one of my top double-day priorities. Was I seriously going to sit here and give Freddie advice about not caring what other people thought? I'd have a nervous breakdown if someone like Braxlynn, Jaxson, or Noah made a fool of me on a sticky day.

"What makes it even worse is that Braxlynn actually used to be my friend."

"Come again?"

"Yeah, she used to live just a few houses down, believe it or not. We were actually pretty decent friends until about kindergarten, although I'm sure she either doesn't remember or at least would never admit to it. Her brother had some ATV accident, got messed up pretty good. They just keep him at home now. He like doesn't even come to school or anything. Her family sued, they got a bunch of money, and they moved."

"No kidding?"

"No kidding."

However unexpected it was to admit, I actually felt a little bad for Braxlynn, or at least for her family. There wasn't ever a good excuse for being a turd like Braxlynn, but there was always an explanation. She'd have to layer her public image on pretty thick to bury her past deep enough that no one would ever find it. Half of me wondered if the part of her that had been friends with Freddie was completely dead or whether there was anything left to resurrect. The other half of me just wanted to spend the next twenty discard days putting rotten fish guts in her backpack. Life was complicated like that sometimes.

"So what game do you want to play?" Freddie said, changing the subject back to why she'd invited me over in the first place.

"You don't want to practice up on *Champions Royale*?"

"I don't know." Freddie shrugged her small shoulders. "It's just so cow-farting frustrating. No matter how much I practice, I just can't ever get close enough to beating him. I've even looked up his online stats. He's darn good at sniping, but overall he's not *that* much better than I am, you know."

"If you want to get better at sniping, I can show you some tips and trick shots you can work on in your spare time."

"Kind of like video game homework?" Freddie said, perking up.

I shrugged. "Yeah, like video game homework. Noah's definitely got a knack for it, but we can close the gap, Freddie. I guarantee it."

"That'd be awesome, but I'm not even sure it would matter, honestly. I think I just choke when money's on the line."

"Maybe not," I mused as Freddie turned on the TV and pulled up a side-by-side view of her online stats and SpudMasterFlex's. Seeing the numbers reminded me of the screenshots I'd taken of the post-game numbers after today's Brown Bag. "I agree that something feels off, Freddie. You saw how quickly I got the wizard's cloak today."

I pulled up the screenshots and shared them to Freddie's TV.

"These from today's Brown Bag?" Freddie asked, squinting her eyes and scanning the numbers.

"Yeah, something just didn't feel right, so I saved them before they disappeared. Look at the overall kill list. I was totally in the lead. He only had one kill before he scorched me. If I had gotten that dragon instead, I could have wiped out the whole map."

"Wait a second," Freddie said, tilting her head. "That doesn't make any poop-tooting sense."

"What doesn't make any poop-tooting sense?"

"Look here." Freddie pointed to the kill map. It spelled out who killed who, where they were killed, and how. They could be scorched, crushed by a boulder, shot with an arrow, zapped by magic, or any of the hundreds of other ways to die in the game. "You zapped two people right off the bat with the wizard's-cloak lightning; then SpudMasterFlex killed someone with a holy grenade shortly after that. You got two more zaps at Haunted, a few other people got kills, and then you got scorched."

"That's a pretty good summary, yeah," I said, not seeing where Freddie was going.

"Noah couldn't have rat-sacking done that." Freddie frowned.

"Why not?"

"Because the custom settings for the Brown Bag Game only allow for *two* wizard's cloaks on the whole map." Freddie help up a pair of fingers. "Otherwise it would just be wizard's-cloak chaos, which can be fun, but it's not for the Brown Bag. The cloaks always spawn on the opposite ends of the map from one another. Aside from getting your four kills, you basically ran straight to Fangthorn Peak from the start, which means that he would have had to be booking it in order to get to the dragon before you."

"And he couldn't have done that?"

"Keep up with me here, Texcalibur," Freddie urged. "If he got a wizard's cloak at the beginning then he would have put it on right away because it lets you float, which is faster than running. But he *didn't* have it on when he got his first kill one minute and eleven seconds into the game. It says right here he got his kill with a holy grenade, not a zap."

I rubbed my chin. "Couldn't he have taken the cloak from the person he killed?"

Freddie shook her head. "The wizard's cloak is immune to the holy grenade, you know that."

"Right . . . ," I said. "Couldn't he have gotten the kill, *then* found the cloak?"

"Look at where the kill was." Freddie pointed to a grenade icon on the map on the west side of Bandit's Bog. "If you got your cloak in Peasantville, then the other cloak most likely spawned up in Lost Labyrinth. There's no way he would have had time to go up there, in the wrong direction, find the cloak, and still beat you to the dragon."

I studied the map, trying to take in everything that Freddie was explaining. She obviously had a level of understanding and familiarity with the game well beyond my own. "So what are you saying?"

Freddie clapped her hands together. "I'm saying I finally have proof. Someone *else* found that cloak."

"But how did he get it, then?" I asked.

"Someone must have given it to him." Freddie gritted her teeth. "He poop-tooting cheated. What I would have given to have been there to catch him in the act."

"Well, Freddie, it's your lucky day." I pulled out my discard-day notebook and smiled. "I know someone who just might be able to help with that."

CHAPTER 9

MIDNIGHT SNACK

(Discard Tuesday—Sept. 7ᵗʰ)

The twins took turns using their spoons to catapult broccoli across the dinner table. I had no idea why my parents even bothered giving them vegetables. They might as well have just dumped the plate on the floor at the start of dinner to save themselves the time. Better yet, they could just dump it in the garbage. That's where it went anyway.

The front door opened, and my dad burst into the house. "Sorry I'm late," he said, hanging up his jacket and quickly making his way to the table. He gave each of the girls a kiss and sat down.

"Hands," my mom said.

"Sorry." My dad rushed over to the sink to wash up. "It just smelled so good." If I had to guess, I would say my dad spent half of his life apologizing for something, which I guess was better than never apologizing for anything.

"How was work?" my mom asked.

"Busy." My dad chewed on the word and didn't seem to like the taste of it. It was strange, having him come home so late, but *everything* seemed strange since moving to Idaho. My dad returned to sit at the table. "They do things a bit differently around here, so I'm scrambling to keep up at times, but I've got a good team. Mawuli Ansah is the new department head. I think his son Zak is in your grade, Danny. I see the last of the moving boxes are gone. That's good."

"Yes," my mom sighed, "while the twins applied your shoe polish to an entire basket of laundry."

My dad's eyebrows shot up, wrinkling his forehead. "Ah. That's bad. I may have forgotten to put that away." My dad spent the *other* half of his life forgetting things . . . which was probably where all the apologizing came from.

I waggled my finger at the twins, and they responded by pelting me with broccoli. I pulled out my discard-day notebook and added a comment about shoe polish.

"So, how was school today, buddy?" my dad said, trying to change the subject.

"Pretty good. I went to Freddie's after school and played video games, so that was cool."

"Video games, huh?" my dad said, dumping two spoonfuls

of lasagna on his plate. "You hardly touch those things. Oh, before I forget again, I got something that I forgot to show you yesterday." My dad fished around his pockets until he removed a pair of tickets.

I leaned forward. "Idaho State University football tickets. Sweet."

"Sweet is right, buddy. It's not exactly the Houston Texans, but it's on the fifty-yard line, third row. Zak will be there, too, but he'll be up in the corporate box with his dad. From where *we're* at you'll be able to *smell* the blood and sweat. Work's going to be busy for a while, unfortunately, so this will be a good way to lock in a solid bros day."

"Cool beans," I said. "When is it?"

"Not until the middle of next month. The twentieth, I think it is," my dad said, inspecting the tickets. "The . . . sixteenth. Geez, I wasn't even close. Shows where my brain's at."

After dinner I helped with the dishes and then went to my room to pore over my discard-day notes. There wasn't too much in the way of embarrassing moments to avoid or things I wished I would have said, but there was a good deal of studying. Three blasted quizzes tomorrow. I didn't *have* to study for them, but the Sticky Danny in me couldn't *not* look over the material when it was sitting right there in my backpack. What I really wanted to be doing was practicing *Champions Royale*. With a bit of luck, I would get to the bottom of this "Noah and the wizard's cloak" business tomorrow and be one step closer to taking him down.

Going to bed on time really wasn't an issue on a discard day, since how I felt in the morning only ever depended on when I went to sleep on the previous sticky day. As long as I got my discard-day business done by the stroke of midnight, I was all good.

After feeling pretty confident about all the quiz material, I finished the rest of my discard-day routine by stockpiling sports scores, news, and even a bit of celebrity gossip. Sticky Danny wasn't one for drawing too much attention with ultra-bold predictions (a caution from Dr. Donaldson), but I still liked to go into the day armed with a bit of info in case it came in handy. I checked my notes and added a quick Google search on *Double Dragon*. It was nearly 10:00 p.m. before all my duties were done, which left two hours for video games. I turned off the lights, sat back on my bed, and pulled out my phone, not bothering to slip into my pajamas. I also didn't have to brush my teeth or floss, which was a plus.

I lost myself in the game. I had a couple of quick rounds with unlucky drop locations but managed to crack the top five on three different occasions before my five-minute alarm buzzed on my phone: 11:55 p.m. The discard day was almost up. I stashed my phone in my pocket and made my way downstairs to the fridge. Capping my discard days off with a midnight snack was a tradition I tried to keep as often as I could.

When I got to the kitchen, I froze. My dad sat at the table, the light from his open work laptop illuminating his sleeping body in a pale glow. His head lolled to one side as he breathed heavily in the darkness. Catching my dad like this was about as surprising as it would have been for my dad to catch me playing video games at 11:55 p.m.

"Dad, what are you doing?" I said, jostling him on the shoulder.

"Wha-what?" My dad startled awake, and I had to steady him to keep him from falling out of his chair. "Danny? What are you doing up?" My dad rubbed his eyes and squinted at the clock on the wall.

"Getting a drink." Of Dr Pepper. "Sorry to wake you, Dad. You looked super comfortable in that hard chair."

My dad winced as he rolled his neck from side to side. "Yeah, I'm going to be feeling that one for a while. Get your drink and go off to bed, buddy."

I paused a moment and glanced at his laptop screen. The page was filled with row after row of *L*s. He must have fallen asleep with his hands on the keyboard. Beyond being tired, my dad also didn't notice that I'd come downstairs to get a drink in my school clothes. "You okay, Dad?"

"I'm fine, I'm fine. Just trying to get ahead of

something." My dad reached over and closed his laptop. "Let's go to bed, son."

"Yeah, okay." I reached for my discard-day notebook to write something down, but I'd left it upstairs in my room, and before I could get it, the discard day was done.

CHAPTER 10

OATMEAL RAISIN

(Sticky Tuesday—Sept. 7ᵗʰ)

Mr. Wilding peered down his sharp ski slope of a nose. "Class, who knows how to solve a fraction divided by another fraction? Take two-fifths divided by four-ninths. Nobody?"

I waited to give the answer. No use giving something away that could earn you extra quiz points.

"It was on page one of your reading. Page *one*. This is preposterous . . . Look, I will give five bonus points on your next quiz to whoever can tell me the answer. Anyone?"

I looked at Zak and gave him a sly smirk before raising my hand. "I believe you multiply the first fraction by the reciprocal of the second."

Mr. Wilding flinched, like my answer had just given him a mild electric shock. Zak gave me an impressed nod.

"Why, yes, actually. That's correct. Very good. David, is it?" Mr. Wilding walked over to his desk to write my name down.

"Daniel, sir." I played up my Texas accent. Kids made fun of the accent, but the adults seemed to like it. I was off to a great start. I'd aced my first- and third-period tests and now nabbed the math quiz bonus points. Doing whatever I wanted on a discard day was awesome, but really pulling off a flawlessly executed sticky day had a satisfaction all its own.

After another twenty minutes, the bell rang, and a mad rush of students fled toward the lunchroom. I made my way to the door, but paused at the sound of Mr. Wilding's voice.

"A moment, please, Daniel, if I could."

I couldn't risk missing the Brown Bag Game, but Sticky Danny wasn't about to blow off a teacher. I had a few minutes.

"Yes, Mr. Wilding?" I turned and looked expectantly back at my math teacher.

"That was some very fine work today. Very impressive, especially for a new student. How do you find the curriculum here in Idaho compared to Texas?"

I could see he was looking for affirmation more than the truth, so I gave him what he wanted. "Oh, just as good if not better. Very pleased to be here."

Mr. Wilding gave a satisfactory nod. "Great to hear. We

work hard up here to present engaging material. Gotta think differently with this rising generation, you know. You're used to instant gratification. High-speed internet, computers in the palm of your hand, binge-watching TV shows."

"Uh-huh." I stood there awkwardly, waiting for him to say something else before speaking up. "Well, I need to be getting to lunch now, Mr. Wilding. Don't want to miss out on those Tater Tots."

"Already converted you, did we?" He gave a nasally, snorting laugh. "You know, most folks think the Tater Tot was invented in Oregon, but they'd be wrong. My grandfather was making those over in Inkom before the Second World War."

"I'd love to hear more about that someday," I said, inching for the door.

"Ah, yes. Another time, then. I always eat lunch in my office if you ever want to hear the whole story." Mr. Wilding pushed his glasses back up his nose.

"All righty, Mr. Wilding," I said.

"Well, okay. Run along to lunch. Again, great work today."

Odd dude, I thought as I rushed out the door and made my way to the vending machines. Even though I typically made better dietary decisions during sticky-day lunch, I still opted for the pink cookie and soda. Partly because I was now running behind and partly because I was a bit superstitious when it came to pulling off stuff like this. No need to unnecessarily upset the balance of the cosmos by getting a plate of Tater Tots instead of a giant sugar cookie.

I turned the corner to the commons area outside the lunchroom and skidded to an abrupt stop. Not ten feet in front me, Jaxson and two of his goon friends stood at the vending machines, surrounding a kid in tan slacks and a tucked-in polo shirt who came up to Jaxson's armpit. Braxlynn stood off to the side, her face in her phone.

I froze, not even daring to swallow, praying I hadn't drawn too much attention when I'd clumsily thrown on the brakes. I should have just kept making my way to the lunchroom, but it was like I was in *Jurassic Park* and I didn't want the T-Rex to see me. If I didn't make any sudden movements, they'd never even notice I was there.

"C'mon, Wallace," Jaxson said, walking right up into the littler kid's face. "You're saying you can't spot us a few bucks for lunch? Unless you're telling me you don't want to be cool with us. Unless you're telling me you're some kind of dud."

Braxlynn looked up as if Jaxson's final word was some sort of hypnotic command phrase. She swiped at her screen a few times, most likely queuing up her camera. Wallace looked around with all the nervous skittishness of a cornered mouse trying to avoid becoming cat food. "Nah, yeah, we're cool.

No worries, guys. I got you." He shakily reached into his pocket to take out his wallet.

"My man." Jaxson laughed and roughly shook Wallace by the shoulder as Braxlynn rolled her eyes and returned to her phone.

If I were Zak, this would be a different story. I'd have no problem stepping in and rescuing this poor kid. As I tried to will my body to do anything but stand there like a statue, one thing became abundantly clear: I was not Zak.

I watched as Wallace shelled out a few bucks to Jaxson and his friends. They each took their turn buying something, and it was only from some primitive survival instinct that I was able to lower my head and step past them unnoticed as they walked by. I took a couple of deep breaths before I put my money in and punched the numbers on the vending machine.

"Crisis avert— What the crud . . . no!" I banged on the glass as I saw an oatmeal raisin cookie spiral out and thunk into the retrieval bin. I was so distracted I'd punched the wrong item number. I let out a disgruntled growl as I collected my garbage cookie and reached into my pockets for more money. I pulled out two dollars but stopped just shy of inserting them into the machine. Two bucks . . . "The Brown Bag Game!"

I raced to the lunchroom, swimming past kids as I made

my way to the gamers' tables. I could already hear Noah hurling insults at the other gamers. I was too late.

"You gotta be kidding me." I slapped a hand to my forehead and emitted a pained grumble that was thankfully drowned out by the lunchroom chatter. My perfect chance to catch Noah cheating had gone up in a smoke of cowardice.

The day had started out so well: acing quizzes, getting bonus points in math. I looked down at my hand, now balled into a fist of frustration, and saw yet another victim of this debacle: the oatmeal cookie. I relaxed my grip, but the damage had been done. As if that cookie wasn't enough of an abomination already. I shook my head. Some days you thought life was handing you a soft, delicious, pink sugar cookie, and all you got left with was a lumpy, mangled oatmeal-raisin mush. I didn't know if I was more mad at myself for freezing up at the vending machines, at Mr. Wilding for delaying me, or at Jaxson, Braxlynn, and Noah for being turds. I *did* know a few things, though. I knew I was incredibly mad, I knew tomorrow wasn't a sticky day, and I knew that Snake River Middle School was about to see exactly what Discard Danny was capable of.

CHAPTER 11
EMERGENCY BOX

(Discard Wednesday—Sept. 8th)

"Danny, you're going to be late for the bus," my dad yelled upstairs. He seemed a little less pleasant than usual this morning.

"I'm coming." I reached into my backpack and pulled out an old pencil box with the words *Discard Day Emergency Box* scrawled across the lid in faded marker. I popped it open and did one final check of the contents. It was all there. I had never used every item in one day, but I didn't want to leave behind a single thing. You were just never quite sure what opportunities would present themselves.

I put the emergency box back into my backpack and sprinted for the door, giving my mom a kiss and my dad a hug, and poking my sisters in the bellies on my way out the door.

I boarded the half-filled bus and found Freddie sitting by herself close to the front. Zak was toward the back but already had a few other kids sitting next to him, so I gave him a wave and plopped down next to Freddie. The green leather seat had clashing black duct tape running across a hole on the backrest. Freddie looked surprised at my choice in bus companions but gladly scooted over to make a bit more room.

"Hey there, Texcalibur," she said, grinning. "Any wild predictions or mind-reading tricks today?"

I had gone back over to the Roost during the sticky day afternoon, but without the evidence of Noah's cheating or even the screenshots to cause suspicion, the visit was much less eventful than before. However disappointed I had been at school, I just felt too bad for Freddie to ditch out on her when she'd been counting on me coming over.

I massaged my temples and exaggerated a squint. "I think I wore out my telepathic powers for a bit. I'm just a normal kid today, I'm afraid."

Freddie shrugged. "Too bad. You're gonna be way less fun as a normal person."

I smiled. "Oh, you might be surprised. You gonna play in the Brown Bag Game today?"

"No"—Freddie cast her eyes to the floor—"I don't have the money today. If I give up milk at lunch for the next week or so I should be able to get another shot."

I reached into my pocket and pulled out a ten-dollar bill. "Keep the change," I said, handing it to her. It was a good chunk of my personal savings, but it wasn't like I was actually giving it up. Plus, sometimes a prank of good fortune was as fun to do on a discard day as a mischievous prank . . . sometimes.

Freddie's mouth fell open as she dumbly held the money up. "I can't take this."

I shook my head. "You're *not* taking it—I'm *giving* it. Seriously. Keep it."

"I don't know what to say."

For a moment, I thought Freddie was going to tear up right there in the middle of the bus. An unfortunately familiar voice broke up the moment.

"Oh no, Freddie. You have to sell the family's prized cow or something?" Noah stood in the aisle, mock concern on his face, before turning around to the rest of the students on the bus. "I'm shocked she didn't come back with magic beans. Check your wallets, everyone, looks like we have a pickpocket on the bus!"

A few kids laughed, but most of them just ignored Noah, probably used to his loud outbursts.

"Stuff it, Noah," I shot back.

Noah froze then slowly turned to stare at me. "What, are you like her *boyfriend* or something, Professor Tex? Moving pretty fast there, don't you think?"

I made to stand up, but someone spoke up from behind me. "Sit down, Noah, and leave her alone."

It was Zak from a few rows back. He didn't say it threateningly or even raise his voice. Miraculously, Noah obeyed, while muttering a few additional insults under his breath. Zak had totally just shut down Noah. I looked back and nodded my thanks. Who *was* this kid? I didn't know exactly what I was going to end up doing before this discard day was over, but I knew full well it wouldn't be something Zak would do. But maybe I was going about this all wrong. Maybe Zak's approach was worth looking into. I dwelled on the thought for about five seconds until Noah's irritating laughter ripped it from my brain. I needed to do something about this kid . . . today. I'd have other discard days to reinvent myself.

Freddie did most of the talking as I mulled over all my options for pranks. Some pranks were elaborately planned, while others were more shoot from the hip. You couldn't go wrong either way, really. Each was fun in its own right, but today was for shooting from the hip. The plan was to run through as many pranks as I could before eventually getting caught. I've had a few perfect runs before, but it was easy to get greedy when I was on a roll.

The bus pulled up to the drop-off, and I told Freddie I'd see her at lunch before hustling straight to my first-period class, not even bothering to swap books out at my locker.

Rarely was I more excited to get to school than on a prank day. You had to space these days out, though. Prank days were like eating a piece of my mom's super-rich homemade cheesecake. You eat it every now and again, it's like the best thing ever. Eat too much too often and you start to lose your taste for it. And trust me, I once tried to eat an *entire* cheesecake in a day. Amazing how throwing up a food through your nose will affect your long-term appetite for the thing.

I rushed into the classroom and was rewarded for my initiative: not a student in sight and Mrs. Marlow had her back turned as she busied herself with some elaborate drawing on the whiteboard. These were the opportunities you were looking for when shooting from the hip. I quietly unzipped my backpack and opened the emergency box, retrieving the remote-control fart machine I affectionately referred to as the "robo-toot." I looked over the empty desks and pictured where everyone sat, counting from the left and right side of the classroom just to make sure I had it correct. Even though my actions wouldn't have any lasting consequences on a discard day, it wasn't an excuse to be sloppy or hasty. I took one last glance at the door, then at Mrs. Marlow, and made my way to Jaxson's desk. I knelt down, made to tie my shoe, and suction-cupped the robo-toot on the underside of his chair.

I quickly made my way to my seat and waited for the other students to trickle into the room. I lost track of time as

I thought through my next steps. I'd put fresh batteries and stink-bomb spray into the machine last night before I went to bed. I was primed for action.

The bell rang, and the last few students scrambled to their desks, except for Jaxson, who sauntered through the door, purposefully taking his sweet time. Mrs. Marlow clapped three times and had to tell Noah twice to put away his phone before he obeyed. I think Mrs. Marlow just gave up with Braxlynn, who was currently using her phone as a mirror to apply another coat of lip gloss.

I hung on every word Mrs. Marlow said as I ran my fingers over the rubbery buttons of the robo-toot remote stashed in my pocket. I didn't know exactly what I was waiting for; I'd just know it when it came.

"One of the richest and most distinct cultural expressions we have from peoples around the world is their music," Mrs. Marlow said, pointing to a group of expertly drawn musical instruments on the board. The right moment was close. "Here in America, we have more modern expressions like rap, blues, and rock and roll. Europe is known for its contributions to classical music, of course, while ancient religious and tribal songs cover the world over. Archeologists have even found harp fragments from Mesopotamia that date back some five thousand years. I can almost *hear* what those ancient melodies must have been."

A long squeaky fart sounded from Jaxson's desk.

Mrs. Marlow's eyes flared wide. The whole classroom froze as if taking a huge breath before erupting in laughter. Jaxson's name echoed around the classroom.

"Jaxson Johnson," Mrs. Marlow said aghast. "Excuse you."

"That wasn't me." Jaxson's face turned beet red as he glanced around the room, scowling at the entire class. "It wasn't me."

Mrs. Marlow shook her head, her round, pleasant face twisting with disappointment. A discard-day amateur would have released the stink-bomb spray on the very first fart, but I was no amateur. You had to pace yourself, draw these things out, wait for the right moment. Ten minutes later, it came.

"All right, class," Mrs. Marlow said from the whiteboard. "I would like you to take the next five minutes to do some silent reading from your textbook. Look for a culture you find interesting. You need to choose one for your upcoming paper on the history of music around the world."

I usually stayed pretty cool and collected on discard-day moments like this, but the anticipation of knowing I had Jaxson precisely where I wanted him had me bouncing my leg something fierce. I spun the remote control over and over in my pocket and aimlessly took out my textbook, flipping it open at random.

I waited until everyone was reading and the classroom was

still, save the soft scraping of turning pages. A small squeak split the silence, and a few students from Jaxson's side of the classroom muffled their giggles.

"Quiet, please," Mrs. Marlow warned, looking up from a book she was reading at her desk.

This was it. In response to Mrs. Marlow's plea for silence, I went for the kill. I moved my fingers down the remote in my pocket and found the big button at the bottom. A deep, robust, bubbling fart reverberated from Jaxson's seat, followed by the foul, inescapable stench of rotten eggs. Kids both laughed and covered their noses. One kid in front of me started to gag, and two girls near Jaxson actually stood up and ran to the hallway. Mrs. Marlow looked on in horror as the thick odor spread through her class before making its way to her.

"Good heavens," she choked, standing to open a window. "Jaxson Johnson, I'm afraid you've crossed the line this time. Please excuse yourself to the restroom and continue on to the nurse's office if you need to."

"But it wasn't *me*!" Jaxson stressed.

Mrs. Marlow didn't reply. She merely pulled her blouse up over her nose and pointed to the door.

That was the issue with trying to plead your innocence as a chronically disruptive and misbehaving student. Just like with the boy who cried wolf, no one believed you when you actually needed them to. Jaxson, shoulders slumped in defeat, slowly got up, snatched the hall pass from Mrs. Marlow, and left the classroom.

To most people the eggy, gag-inducing funk that hung in the air was nauseating. To me it was the wonderfully rancid scent of victory, and I was just getting started.

Talk of Jaxson's bad gas filled the hallways during passing time, ranging from something near the truth to him pooping his pants and clearing out the entire room. The more absurd the rumor, the more my discard-day heart warmed with satisfaction.

On the way to lunch, I made a quick stop at my locker to stash my backpack, but not before retrieving a few needed items from my emergency kit.

As I worked my way through the lunch line, I made sure to ask for an extra-large serving of beans, a second bowl of peaches, and two chocolate milks. While I would typically be more than happy to share the extra food with someone like Freddie, I actually had someone different in mind today. I wasn't just going to share this food. I planned on giving it *all* to Braxlynn . . . whether she wanted it or not.

After transferring the chocolate milk from cartons to open cups, I was ready to rock and roll. I scanned the lunchroom and found Braxlynn and the Clique sitting at a table on the far side. I whistled tunelessly as I walked in their direction.

"Hey, where you going?" Freddie asked, appearing at my side just as I was passing Braxlynn. "You gonna play in the BBG?"

"Yeah, I was just gonna check—" I threw my hip out, bumped the chair beside me, and stumbled forward, tipping my entire tray of food on top of Braxlynn's head.

I let out a yelp as I convincingly tumbled to the floor but was soon drowned out by the shrill shriek that shot above the lunchroom chatter like a fire alarm. Braxlynn slowly rose to her feet, her hair, face, and body covered in a beany mixture of chocolatey peaches. She wouldn't have looked more horrified had I dumped a gallon of pig's blood on her head, which was good, because pig's blood was hard to come by . . . even for Discard Danny.

"Oh my gosh, I am *so* sorry. Did I get any on yoooou . . . oh wow," I said as I stood and faced Braxlynn. She drilled into me with a gaze that could have turned Medusa to stone.

"Are you kidding me?" Braxlynn screamed. The whole lunchroom stopped and stared, pulling out their phones. I smiled inwardly. Let's see who the dud was now. "This shirt is Adagio, you idiot. You've ruined it."

I picked a bean off Braxlynn's shoulder and ate it. "I think it's quite tasteful."

My puns were always better on sticky days, when I could think of them ahead of time, but that one wasn't half bad.

"What the crud do you think you're doing?" Jaxson announced before shoving me into a nearby table. I had no idea where he'd even come from, but he obviously kept a close eye on Braxlynn. "Keep your hands off her."

"That's weird," I said, making a show of sniffing the air before turning to Jaxson. "I didn't smell you coming."

Jaxson vibrated with rage and lunged toward me. I was ready this time and darted away to the other side of a nearby table. A growing crowd of students cheered on the game of cat and mouse as I tried desperately to keep the table between me and my attacker.

"I'm gonna freaking kill you," Jaxson yelled, pushing away chairs as he stormed after me.

I plugged my nose. "You get too much closer and I'd have to agree."

Jaxson let out a string of cuss words and made to climb over the table but was wrangled by a pair of teachers coming to my rescue.

"We're done here," a burly male teacher said, bear-hugging Jaxson. "Let's go have another one of our little chats, shall we?"

A second teacher came to check on me while a third attended to Braxlynn. The lunchroom activity soon returned to normal as Jaxson and Braxlynn were ushered away and the janitor rolled in his industrial mop bucket. I stood there, heart hammering in my chest, not believing my good fortune. I'd had no plans other than dumping food on Braxlynn. To get Jaxson hauled away as part of the deal was like reaching into the couch cushions after a quarter and finding a five-dollar bill.

"Holy toad-boogers." Freddie gawked, taking me by the arm and leading me away to the gamer tables. "That was *unreal*. You know you're a dead man, right?"

"Ah well, whatever." I shrugged it off as we sat down. "She totally had her chair sticking out."

"Wait." Freddie leaned closer. "Did you do that on purpose? Oh my gosh. You totally did that on purpose. Jaxson is *totally* gonna murder you."

"I'll be fine," I reassured her. "Brown bag's coming."

Freddie grabbed the bag and slyly put in her two dollars. "Are you not playing?"

"I'm gonna watch this time."

"Sure?" Freddie said, confused. "I'll totally pay for you . . . considering it's *your* money anyway."

"No, no," I said. "Don't worry about it."

Freddie shrugged, and after a few more minutes the Brown Bag Game was underway. It wasn't long until Noah started yelling from the end of the table.

"SpudMasterFlex cannot be stopped!" I eyed Noah as he shoved a couple of Tater Tots into his mouth. It was like a ritual. Kill, mock, tot. Kill, mock, tot. I reached in my pocket and fingered the small vial of Texas Atomic hot sauce. Maybe it was time for Noah's ritual to get a fourth step.

I left Freddie playing and casually walked over to Noah, making a show of checking out gamers' screens as I passed. Most of the time to pull off a stunt like this you needed a diversion, but every kid sitting at Noah's table had their eyeballs glued to their screens. I fished a few coins out of my pocket, walked up next to Noah, and dropped the change on the floor. Noah didn't so much as flit his eyes in my direction as I bent down to retrieve my coins. I placed a hand on the table as I stood back up, quickly reached over, and pinched out a drop of hot sauce onto one of his tots. I only needed a drop. In reality, I probably only needed about one one-hundredth of a drop, but it was better to be safe than sorry.

I retreated to my seat next to Freddie and waited for the show to start. On most days it was unfortunate that Noah got so many kills on *Champions Royale*, but today wasn't one of those days.

"How do you like *that*, BuckinBlueBronco?" Noah yelled, pointing at one of the other players. "That's what it feels like to get *shanked*!" Noah gave a weaselly chuckle as he grabbed a handful of Tater Tots and slammed them into his mouth. He chewed fast and swallowed. Some hot sauces came on slow, the heat gradually building as the sensation progressed from mild to molten. This wasn't one of those kinds of sauces.

Noah coughed twice and his eyes bulged as his face turned red as a gym dodgeball.

"Waaaaah!" Noah threw his phone into the air and reached for his milk, chugging it like oasis water in the desert. "It doesn't help. It doesn't help!"

"You have been scorched by Texcalibur," I said under my breath.

For the second time today, the lunchroom stopped and turned in the direction of a student gone mad. Noah sprinted around the room, desperately grabbing any food he could find and shoving it into his mouth like some kind of ravenous savage breaking into a banquet hall. Peanut butter sandwiches, crackers, fruit, juice boxes. The whole room was in chaos as students scrambled to protect their food from Noah's spice-driven rampage. Like any dedicated prankster, I took the opportunity to retrieve Noah's cell phone . . . and superglue it to the lunchroom table. It would seem that Noah's mouth had finally caught up to him.

After Noah was restrained and carted off to the nurse's office, the rest of lunchtime was abuzz about Noah's, Braxlynn's, and Jaxson's outbursts. It seemed like the whole school was going insane. The conversation continued in the hallways as I made my way to fifth-period science. Normally, both Noah and Braxlynn were in my class, but their seats were predictably empty. Noah'd be down and out for at least an hour. I knew because I had spent one fateful discard day personally acquainting myself with the power of Texas Atomic hot sauce. As far as Braxlynn was concerned, I had no idea what the recovery time was for getting your designer clothes dirty.

I leaned back in my chair and smiled. I had done good work today, *great* work actually. In fact, I'd made such short work of everything that I was running out of bullies. Just when I thought the fun was winding down, however, a voice came over the intercom. Danny Day was wanted in the principal's office.

CHAPTER 12

BE A BUDDY

(Discard Wednesday—Sept. 8ᵗʰ)

I hummed softly as I sat in one of the two chairs in the hallway outside Principal Picatilly's office. In the other chair was a smaller boy with messy blond hair. He sat hunched forward with his head down as if he was saying a silent prayer.

I tapped him on the arm and leaned over. "So what'd they get you for?"

"Throwing my gum in the teacher's hair," the boy mumbled without looking up.

I clicked my tongue. "Savage."

"What about you?" he asked.

"Hmmm," I said, rubbing my chin. "I'm not sure yet."

The door opened, and Principal Picatilly's head leaned into view. "Daniel Day," he intoned from beneath a large brown mustache.

"Looks like I'm up," I said as I swung out of my chair and strolled into the principal's office. For most kids, this was like the long walk to the electric chair. For Discard Danny, it was the dessert after one of my very favorite meals. Sometimes I got caught right in the act and there was no mystery or suspense, but in cases like this one, I was genuinely curious as to how they traced any bit of the chaos back to me.

"Take a seat, Daniel," Principal Picatilly ordered, gesturing to one of the large, high-backed chairs across from his desk. He was a predictably stern-looking man with a wide mustache that looked like a mini version of the janitor's push broom.

I sat down in the unnecessarily large chair and felt like I was one of the twins sitting in my dad's recliner. "What can I do ya for, Mr. Piccolo?"

"Principal *Picatilly*," the principal growled. This guy was already furious. It took my last principal *way* more goading to get to the growling stage. "And what you can do for me is start by explaining why you think you're in my office right now."

Ah, the ol' "you tell me what you did" technique. Over my life of discard-day mischief, I learned that adults usually did this when they knew you did *something* but didn't know *everything* and were hoping you'd spill the beans . . . well, I *had* spilled the beans, but those beans were on Braxlynn's head. I wouldn't be giving up any information in this office without a fight. It was time to see who I was dealing with in the principal of Snake River Middle School.

"I am in your office because you called me down and I am an obedient boy." I nodded.

Principal Picatilly pressed his lips together, bristling his mustache. "But *why* do you believe I called you down here?"

"It's hard for me to say." I paused and looked to my shoes for dramatic effect. "But I think it may be because you are lonely."

The principal clenched his fists when he spoke, and I could sense he was right on the edge of going full-on nuclear. "I know you are new here, but trust me when I say this, Daniel Day, that I do *not* suffer fools. You are *here* because of *this*."

Principal Picatilly pulled out a remote and turned on the large flat screen hung on the wall to my left. The screen showed a still image of the lunchroom. From the angle and time stamp in the corner I could only assume that it was from one of the school's surveillance cameras. He pressed play, and the video zoomed in on me walking up to Noah, dropping my coins, and then briefly reaching across his basket of Tater Tots, where the principal paused the footage.

"Care to explain?" He leaned forward menacingly. I was quickly understanding why that kid out in the hall seemed so nervous and defeated. If I had to meet this principal on a sticky day, I think I'd be wetting myself by now.

"Principal Pinocchio, you want me to explain the underground video-gambling tournament that has happened every day right under your nose for the past three years? Well, it's called the Brown Bag Game, you see, and while I know it sounds like a stupid name, it's actually quite—"

"Mr. Day!" the principal bellowed, hammering down both fists. A cup fell over, clattering pens and pencils across the desk. I almost shot out of my chair, Discard Danny or not. "You think this is a joke, do you? That student is *still* running cold water through his mouth."

"You should really use bread and milk," I added mildly. "The water just kind of sloshes it arou—"

"You will not speak!" The principal jabbed a finger toward my chest. "I don't need you to admit to it—I just need you to know that you've been caught. The janitor is also *still* trying to pry Noah's cell phone from the lunchroom table. I'm sure your parents will be *thrilled* to learn you now have to buy Noah a brand-new phone. New here or not, Mr. Day, *if* I decide not to expel you, let me make this crystal clear: We do not tolerate bullying here at Snake River Middle School, of any sort."

I burst out laughing. It wasn't even to intentionally provoke the principal; I honestly just couldn't restrain myself. "You don't? No bullying at all? Well, I can't even tell you how relieved that makes me feel."

After several more minutes of being dressed down like I was being dishonorably discharged from boot camp, the principal finally kicked me out of his office. I walked out the door, and the small blond kid looked up at me in shock, face pale and eyes wide as an owl's.

"I softened him up for ya." I leaned down and patted him on the knee. "Good luck in there, buddy."

+ — + — +

Zak sat next to me on the bus ride home. Whether he knew about my day's exploits or not, he didn't let on. The secretary had tried to call my parents to come get me, but my dad couldn't get out of work, and my mom was at a doctor's appointment with the twins. A hint of nausea brewed in the pit of my stomach. It was nothing near what I would have been feeling if this had been a sticky day, but I still didn't *enjoy* going home and seeing my parents' irate and disappointed faces. It wasn't like Discard Danny was a *complete* unfeeling monster. I'd be greeted by my parents in utter shock for having their perfect Danny act so completely out of character for the first time in his life. They wouldn't know how to handle it, how to react, whether they should ground me, sit down and talk to me, or what. They will have never been in that situation before . . . that they could remember. For me it would be only one of hundreds of other times. There was something deeply strange about that. Even I recognized it, and I'd known no different my entire life.

"So, how you liking Poky so far?" Zak finally asked.

"No shortage of excitement," I replied, staring out the window. Today had been a solid day of pranks. Rarely had I been able to cleanly pull off so many before getting caught. I took a deep breath. I should have felt proud of myself, happy that someone was able to put those punks in their place for once, but instead I felt a growing emptiness. And filling that emptiness came a flood of something I thought Discard Danny would never feel: actual guilt.

Most of the time when kids got caught misbehaving, they only felt bad because they got caught. For Discard Danny, even when I got caught, I didn't *really* get caught. You'd have to catch me on a sticky day for that. My pranks hadn't done any lasting damage to anyone. The only remaining effect from today's actions would be yet another funny memory. So why were my insides souring like I'd just eaten my grandma's warm egg salad?

"You okay?" Zak said, waving his notebook in front of my face to get my attention.

"Dude, I'm good," I said unconvincingly.

"Sure there's not something I can do, man?" Zak asked.

I exhaled loudly, my internal conflict pressurizing to a sudden breaking point. "You can act like a normal freaking human for once, stop being so friggin' perfect all the time, and give me some blasted space! Can you do *that*?"

The whole bus grew quiet, and Zak leaned back, a confused look on his face like he didn't quite know if I was joking or not.

"Fair enough." Zak stood, shouldered his backpack, grabbed his violin case, and moved to an empty seat a few rows back.

I couldn't even meet the kid's eyes. Zak didn't deserve that. He'd only ever tried to be helpful, but that was precisely the problem. His notion of the double day had ruined me. I should have been celebrating today's accomplishments, not feeling guilty for them. What use was the double day if I couldn't enjoy the discard day?

Dr. Donaldson had once described my situation as only ever living life on either end of the pendulum swing. I was either brazenly jumping off garage roofs on a discard day or cowering from bullies with my tail between my legs on a sticky day. My life may average out in the middle, but I'd never spent a single day there. He wondered what effect it would have on someone in the long run. Back when he'd made the comment, I couldn't have cared less. But now, sitting alone on a bus with my head in my hands, I thought I was beginning to understand the answer.

CHAPTER 13

PHONE CALL

(Discard Wednesday—Sept. 8ᵗʰ)

"Daniel Douglas Day, I have never been so disappointed in you in my entire life." My mom stood, arms folded, in my bedroom doorway.

"Uhhh, that's not actually true," I said from my bed, holding up a finger and remembering the discard day that I borrowed the minivan and took it off a few jumps at a nearby BMX track.

"*What* has gotten into you?" My mom shook her head, spreading her hands in disbelief. "I would like my old son back, please."

"He'll be here before you know it," I mumbled.

"Yeah, well, so will your father, after he gets back from the chiropractor. I can promise you one thing, Danny. He will not be in the mood for . . . for . . . *this*." She made an exasperated gesture in my general direction.

"Chiropractor?" I asked. "What happened to Dad?"

"He fell asleep at the kitchen table working late. Can hardly even move his neck. Your behavior at school is the last thing he needs right now."

My dad. *Dang it*. I *had* remembered to hide the shoe polish from the twins yesterday morning, but I'd completely failed to go downstairs and wake him up last night. I'd been so amped up and distracted with checking over my emergency box and prepping for the prank day that it must have slipped my mind.

"You act like you don't even care, Danny," my mom continued, apparently not done with my scolding. "What if the boy had had a reaction? What if he'd stopped breathing?"

I rolled my eyes. "I didn't slip him rat poison, Mom. It was hot sauce."

"It doesn't matter *what* it was—"

"So you'd get mad if I dumped a sugar packet on his Tater Tots?" I interjected.

"Well—I mean—it *does* matter what it was," my mom spluttered. "I just don't know why you decided to put anything at *all* on this kid's food. It just doesn't seem like something you'd do."

A lifetime of raising Sticky Danny had set my mom up to

be completely blindsided by Discard Danny. However angry she got, she always left moments like these more confused than anything, which worked in my favor. I could handle confused, but I didn't like seeing my mom upset or disappointed. It was tolerable on a discard day, but I still didn't *like* it. I'd been in this spot before, however. Any moment now she'd just throw her hands up and leave.

"Danny—" My mom's voice cracked, and she pressed her lips together hard. "I guess I thought you were okay with the move. You never complained, so I never asked. Do you think it would help if you, I don't know . . . spoke with Dr. Donaldson?"

I opened my mouth for some kind of smart-alecky comeback, but the words fizzled out in my throat. This prank wasn't nearly as bad as some I'd pulled in the past, but I couldn't remember the last time my mom had suggested I speak with Dr. Donaldson. Something was different for her, and I didn't know what it was, and that made me uneasy.

It wasn't until I was about four years old that my parents began to worry that something was wrong. I was always talking about stuff that had never happened, conversations we'd never had. They first wrote it off as an overactive imagination, but it was harder to deny when I began talking about things *before* they happened: some bit of news I'd overheard on the TV, unexpected weather, sports outcomes, things like that.

After a tour of doctors, neurologists, psychiatrists, and even a psychic, we stumbled on Dr. Donaldson. He was the first person who *really* listened to what I was trying to say, and he was unconventional enough to not dismiss it. Over the years, my parents were apparently content with the progress, and I saw him less and less. They rarely spoke about how things used to be. Even on discard days I struggled to tease much information out of them.

"Just think about it," my mom said, her voice noticeably softer, her face shifting from angry to concerned. She heaved a deep sigh and shut the door. I heard her muffled footsteps go down the stairs.

I stared at the door in silence before pulling out my phone. It wasn't that I was afraid to call Dr. Donaldson, or even that I thought it was a bad idea. In fact, if I talked to Dr. Donaldson, I was sure to get useful advice, but that advice wouldn't come without a cost. I didn't want to dial his number, because it would be admitting that my mom was right and that I *needed* an extra session with a therapist. You don't go to a doctor unless you're sick, and however much I missed my chats with Dr. Donaldson, the feeling that I was mentally well enough to *not* need them was something I didn't want to easily give up.

I tried to distract myself by pulling out my discard-day notes, but there wasn't much there, never was on a prank day. I went through the rest of my discard-day evening routine of stockpiling a few sports scores and news stories. Curious, I checked out *Dud Spuds* and *Stud Spuds*, but they were predictably without an update since lunchtime. I should have claimed it as a small victory, but nothing felt right at the moment. I even tried a few games of *Champions Royale*, but it did little to ease the nagging feeling in my gut.

"This thing's not gonna go away now, is it?" I mumbled to myself. If this feeling was only getting worse, then maybe I *wasn't* well. Maybe I *did* need help. I checked the time. It was close to 7:00 p.m. I swiped over to my contacts and scrolled down to Dr. Donaldson's number. I stared at the name. What did I have to lose anyway? It was a discard day after all. No one would know but me. I pressed the button for video chat, and after five rings Dr. Donaldson answered.

"Howdy, Danny." The image on the phone was poorly lit and mostly showed the bottom of Dr. Donaldson's hipster beard. It was like he had placed the phone on the floor or table. He stared intently somewhere off-screen as he spoke. "One moment, please."

I watched as his eyes darted from side to side, his tongue sticking out in intense concentration. I'd seen this look before, not on him, but something about it seemed familiar.

"Wait a second," I said, realization dawning. "Are you . . . playing *video games*?"

"Not very well, I'm afraid." The doctor winced and then

let out a disappointed sigh. "Darn this infernal game. That's three bad drops in a row."

"What alternate dimension did I just dial into?" I said, scratching my head.

I could see Dr. Donaldson put down a black Xbox controller before reaching for his phone. "Sorry about that. Doing a bit of research is all. Can't tell you how many kids I see about addictions to this kind of stuff. Thought I'd get a firsthand account. How can I be of service this lovely discard-day evening?"

"Very admirable of you, Doctor," I said. While I was surprised to see him playing video games, it was just the kind of unexpected coolness I'd come to expect from the man over the years. "So, I'm just calling to—wait. What makes you so sure it's a discard day?"

He stood and walked over to turn the light on before returning to his chair. "Well, Sticky Danny is typically a bit more self-conscious about calling me at home at eight p.m. Houston time."

"Oh," I said, realizing immediately that he was right. "Sorry about that."

"Bah, you know I'm always free for a chat, Danny, *especially* when I end up repeating today and getting my evening back anyway. I don't make a habit of giving my personal number to clients, but you know I make exceptions for those who regularly bend the space-time continuum. So what's up?" Dr. Donaldson settled into his chair as he always did before we got into the serious stuff.

I explained everything that had happened since coming to Pocatello: every run-in with Jaxson, Braxlynn, and Noah, my interactions with Freddie, my most recent conversation with my mom, and most important, Zak's answer to my question about how he'd use the double day. "I'm doing all the same stuff I always do. I'm still having fun on the discard days and staying disciplined and out of trouble on the sticky days, but it just feels, I don't know . . . empty."

Dr. Donaldson steepled his fingers and tapped them against his lips. "Danny, do you wish that something would come along and cause harm to your sisters?"

"Uh, no," I said, having been through Dr. Donaldson's lines of questioning enough times to know they were never what they seemed. "A whole section in my daily notes is dedicated solely to twins damage control."

Dr. Donaldson nodded. "Yes, that makes sense. You love your sisters dearly. We wouldn't wish failure, loss, heartache, or disappointment on anyone we love, but what kind of girls and women would they grow up to be if you removed *every* harmful thing from their lives? If they were never confronted with anything unpleasant? If they never had to struggle to overcome an obstacle?"

"Trust me," I said. "Trouble follows them like a shadow. I only take the edge off."

"And what about *you*? You're in a tough spot, Danny. You'd be crazy to know something bad is coming and not avoid it, but in doing so, how many of those challenges, uncomfortable situations, and hardships have you missed out on? How many opportunities for growth have you self-selected out of your life and have passed you by?"

"With all due respect"—I held up a hand—"I'm pretty sure I've lived through more broken bones, ER visits, and trips to detention than any ten kids combined."

"But what causes growth, Danny?" Dr. Donaldson replied. "Experiencing the moment of hardship or wrestling with the consequences that come after? Consequences that you often don't have to contend with."

"So I *shouldn't* avoid bad stuff on a sticky day? Gonna be kind of hard when I know that the school corn dogs cause food poisoning to just muscle one down on a sticky day and take one for the team."

"I do miss our talks." Dr. Donaldson gave a slight chuckle. "I'm not saying you should eat a rancid corn dog, but I do think a bit more balance in your life would help you work through your current funk. I'm all the way out in Texas, Danny. You could call me every day for a year, and it would still be hard for me to understand exactly what you're going through up there. I'd never be able to appreciate the nuances of your school's social scene, your specific challenges, the potato-centric culture."

"So what do you suggest? I get a doctor up here?"

"No." Dr. Donaldson shook his head and leaned closer to the screen. "I think it's time you found someone you could trust, that speaks your language. Someone to help you balance your two worlds and work through things. I think it's time to tell a friend about the double day."

I inhaled sharply. "I just don't know, Doc." However much a part of me always wanted to do it, I could simply never picture myself taking that leap of faith.

"Look." Dr. Donaldson stroked his long beard. "Maybe I've been giving you the wrong advice this whole time."

I furrowed my eyebrows. "What do you mean?"

"I've been telling you that being the one-eyed man in the land of the blind isn't enough, that to get a better perspective on the double day and on life you need to 'open your other eye,' but maybe that's *not* the best way."

"No?" I said, not sure where he was going.

"Maybe instead of opening your other eye, you need to help one of the 'blind' open *theirs* and have them tell you what *they* see." He paused. Even though I was 1,500 miles away, I knew he could read my reluctance like I was sitting in his office with my emotions written on my forehead in black ink.

"Danny, if you want change in your life, then you've got to want *to* change your life. That's as plainly as I can put it."

I twisted my mouth. I didn't know whether it was the move, or Zak, or the bullies, or all of it combined, but this emptiness inside me was different from anything I'd ever felt, and I wanted it gone. *If I want change, I have to want to change.* I repeated the phrase a few times in my head.

However much the prospect of telling someone about the double day terrified me, I knew deep down that it was the right answer, and I knew who it needed to be. It was finally time to share my secret.

CHAPTER 14

CONFESSION

(Discard Thursday—Sept. 9th)

The next discard day I boarded the bus and saw Zak sitting toward the back, Bluetooth earbuds in, bobbing his head.

Even though it wasn't a sticky day, I still had a knot in my stomach. These were uncharted waters. I had never managed to convince someone of the double day without having them first think I was crazy. If I told Zak on a sticky day and he told *anybody*, I'd have a permanent spot on the *Dud Spuds* hall of fame, if there was such a thing. This wasn't like telling Dr. Donaldson. He was *paid* to listen and not judge me. He was also required by law to not tell anyone.

I took a deep breath and sat next to Zak. I needed to be confident I could pull this off *perfectly* before I tried anything on a sticky day, which meant I'd be spending a whole bunch of discard days working out all the kinks. I wasn't expecting much from my first attempt other than getting the lay of the land.

"Hey, man, what're you listening to?" I asked Zak.

He plucked out one of his earbuds and offered it to me. "Vivaldi."

"Vi-who now?" I said putting the earbud in. A chorus of violins played some piece of classical music I'd never heard. Or maybe I had. They all sounded the same to me.

"Vivaldi. It's from his third opus. *L'estro armonico*. It's my morning jam. Afternoons are Brahms."

I motioned for his phone so he would show me all the info. I pulled out my notebook and wrote it down.

"So you like it?" Zak asked, his face a mix of hope and surprise.

I gave Zak a flat stare. "No."

"Oh." Zak's expression slumped. "So why did you write it down?"

I looked around and leaned in close, keeping my voice low. "For another one of my mind-reading tricks."

"I'm not sure I follow."

"Look, I will tell you my secret, but you gotta promise not to tell a soul. Deal?"

Zak shrugged. "Sure."

"This is going to sound kind of weird," I said, leaning in even closer, "but I need you to know that I'm completely serious when I tell you this."

"Okay, okay." Zak laughed. "I get it. I'm ready."

"I am able to do those mind-reading tricks because I actually live every day twice." I paused. If today was all about getting a baseline to see what I was dealing with, then from Zak's reaction, that baseline was one of profound confusion.

Zak cocked his head to the side, as if not hearing me correctly. "Uh . . . what?"

"I told you it was going to sound weird." I leaned back and put my hands up. "I will explain as simply as I can. I live every day of my life twice. Once where I can kind of do what I want, including learn what people are going to say, and then the day resets itself and I get another crack. That's why I know what people are going to say or write down."

Zak stared at me, blinking, his eyes presumably searching for any signs that I was joking. "So what am I going to say next?"

"It's the first time I've lived this day, so I don't actually know."

Zak pressed his lips in a flat smile. "Not your most impressive trick."

Attempt 2: (Discard Friday—Sept. 10th)

"Hey, man, what're you listening to? Wait." I held up a finger, closed my eyes, brought my other hand to my forehead. "Let me guess. Vivaldi. Third opus. *L'estro armonico.* Am I close?"

For a moment Zak looked like he had stopped breathing. He glanced over his shoulders two times each before returning to meet my eyes. "The mind reader is back at it, huh? So did you see it on my phone, or are my earbuds on too loud?"

I pursed my lips. "Zak, this may come as a shock to you, but not every eleven-year-old kid can name every piece of classical music he hears. In fact, I think it's pretty safe to say that no one, besides you, can name *any* piece of classical music. Trust me, it's more believable that I'm reading your mind."

"All right, so what else you got up your sleeve?"

"Not much for right now." I clicked my tongue. "But I can tell you *how* I do these little tricks as long as you promise not to freak out."

"Your *method* is going to freak me out?"

"No." I waved my hands back and forth as if trying to reset the conversation. "I'm just saying that my method is a bit weird, and I want to make sure you *don't* freak out."

"Well, now I'm getting worried that I *should* be freaking out."

Attempt 4: (Discard Tuesday—Sept. 14th)

"All right, so what else you got up your sleeve?" Zak asked.

"How about knowing that your full name is Zakari Kaito

Ansah. Your dad was born in Ghana, Africa, and played college football for Oklahoma. Your mom was a concert violinist for the Tokyo Junior Orchestra Society when she was younger. You're also a blue belt in judo. How's that?"

Zak's expression betrayed no emotion until he spoke. "So you cyber stalk people. That's just wrong, bro."

Attempt 7: (Discard Friday—Sept. 17ᵗʰ)

"All right, so what else you got up your sleeve?" Zak asked.

"Well"—this was now the fifth time I was trying to answer this question without torpedoing the conversation—"you make fun of me for playing too many video games, but I know for a fact that you play *Clash of Warbands* before you go to bed every night." I had snuck over to his house the discard day before at around 10:00 p.m. to see if I could get any useful info and saw him through the window.

"Wait." Zak's face went slack with panic. "Can you look that up online or something? How'd you find out? How do I delete it?"

"Whoa there, partner." I made a calming gesture with my hands. "You can just go into your game center settings on your phone and erase your activity history," I lied. I had no idea how to erase your activity history. I just needed him to calm back down so I could get some more useful information out of him to use at the next discard day. Today was looking like yet another bust, unfortunately.

Zak put his notebook on his lap and massaged his forehead with both hands. If he was this worried about his parents finding out he played a video game for a few minutes a day, I wondered how they'd react if I ever got him into some serious discard-day trouble. It was definitely a new goal.

The bus took a sharp turn, and Zak's notebook slid off his lap onto the floor, splaying open. Before Zak could pick it up, I saw an incredible sketch of some kind of ripped superhero blasting energy from his hands.

"Uh, what's that?" I asked, pointing.

"Nothing," Zak dismissed quickly.

"Like it's Captain Nothing or Mr. Nothing or the Mighty Nothing? 'Cause that actually looked like a pretty awesome superhero."

Zak let out a little sigh and opened his trusty notebook. "Don't tell anyone, please." He flipped through the pages, revealing character after character of expertly drawn superheroes.

"Dude," I said, genuinely impressed. "Again I ask: Is there anything you *can't* do? I mean, apart from being allowed to play video games."

"Drawing helps me relax," Zak offered, as if that explained everything.

"Well, you must relax a lot." I paused. "Or I guess you must need a lot of relaxing. What's that one there?" I gave a short laugh and pointed to a character with a mop for a weapon and garbage-can armor.

Zak gave a half smile. "Haven't named him yet. Was thinking of something like Smasher Trasher. Don't tell anyone, but I actually used a picture of Mr. Wilding from the school's website as a model."

"Interesting," I said, writing a few things in my own notebook.

Sticky Day: (Sticky Monday—Sept. 20th)

School was over. I waited outside the bus and chewed on my bottom lip. After nearly two weeks of discard-day trial and error I had come to the sinking realization that the most convincing things I could tell Zak couldn't be done on a discard day. No matter what information I could secretly learn about him on a discard day, none of it would be as powerful as predicting the future, and I could only do *that* on a sticky day. It was now just a matter of two things: waiting for the right day and having the guts to take the leap of faith. The bus ride home on the discard day had provided me with the opportunity I was looking for. Now for the leap.

I pulled out my sticky-day notebook and flipped between

a few pages, mumbling the lines I'd written down. I swallowed hard against a heartbeat that had somehow migrated to my throat. My legs suddenly swayed like I was standing on a boat in choppy water and not the sidewalk in front of the school. I had to steady myself on the bus to keep from toppling to the ground.

I checked my watch. It was do-or-die o'clock. I wasn't going to get a better opportunity than today. I slapped my face a few times and quickly boarded the bus, stashing my notebook back in my pocket. Zak sat three-quarters of the way toward the back. The seat next to him was predictably empty. I stopped and shared the same small talk with Freddie that I had on the discard day about stopping by the Roost later on today. I took a deep breath and continued down the aisle.

"Hey, man. How was school?" Zak said, taking out his earbuds as I walked over and sat down.

My heart fell back into my chest but was still slamming around like a feral hog in a steel trap. "Good. It was good."

Zak paused and leaned forward. "You all right? You don't look so hot."

"Yeah," I said, trying to regain my composure. This had been so easy on the discard day, but doing it now was like playing the final boss on *Mega Man* with no extra lives. A screw-up here and it was game over. I needed to get back on track. "Sorry, man. Intense day. I could sure go for some Brahms's Violin Sonata number three right now, am I right?"

Zak flinched like I'd flicked water in his face. He checked his earbuds and then patted his pants to find his phone. "How'd you—"

"Meh, don't worry about it." I waved my hand. "Just mind-reader stuff." I needed to get him curious. Going in too strong too quick didn't work.

"Uh-huh." Zak gave a skeptical raise of the eyebrows. "You get your test score back from Mr. Ziggler today?"

Mr. Ziggler was our science teacher, but we had him during different periods. "Yeah, how'd you do?"

Zak rolled his eyes. "I swear Ziggler takes pleasure in putting the most random facts ever on his tests. If we don't cover something in class and it isn't on the study guide, then it *shouldn't* be on the test. Plain and simple." I'd heard Zak's same rant on the discard day. I smiled inwardly at the sight. It was nice to know that he could get worked up over *something*. "I seriously think I'm going to complain. Writing a test no one can do well on doesn't mean you're smart. It means you're a bad teacher. At least he'll grade us on a curve. Still stupid that I've never gotten anything less than a ninety-three on any test in my entire life, and you know what I got on this one? Eighty—"

"Seven point five?" I said, finishing Zak's sentence.

Zak scrunched his eyebrows and tilted his head back. "Yeeeah, how'd you know that?"

I pulled my test out of my backpack and handed it to him. "The same way I was able to get this."

"A hundred?" Zak's eyes went wide as he glanced from my test to me and back. "Dude . . . wha . . . what? *How* did you pull that off?"

"Dude." I looked at him like the answer was obvious. "Mind-reader stuff."

"You don't just 'mind read' your way through one of Ziggler's tests, man. If this is some trick you learned off of YouTube, then please send me the link. What else you got up your sleeve?"

I brought two fingers up to my temple. "Let's see here. You stacked your books in your backpack in the following order, back to front: history, math, science, then there's a music folder, and then a library book—*The Count of Monte Cristo*, if I'm not mistaken. Oh, and there's a note from Sefina in your outermost compartment."

Zak gave me a strange look before unzipping his backpack. I could hear him mumbling the names of his books before looking back up at me with a blank stare. "Danny, I *just* pulled those books from my locker and stashed them in here like three minutes ago. How did you . . . and the note from Sefina . . . What?"

"Hey, man, you asked what else I had up my sleeve." I shrugged. This thing was building momentum. I was past the point of no return. "I was just getting warmed up, but you don't look like you're in the mood for more."

"Danny," Zak said, his face vacant of any humor. "How are you doing this?"

I sucked at my teeth and took another deep breath, ducking my head down. "I'll tell you on two conditions."

Zak tentatively ducked down as well. "Go on."

"You have to promise you'll give me a chance to explain myself and promise you won't tell *anybody*. Like not one of your other friends, or parents, or anything. Deal?" I said, holding out my hand. "On your blue belt's honor."

Zak paused, as if only now realizing how serious I was. He nodded, then shook my hand. "Blue belt's honor."

I cleared my throat. The moment of truth. "So I kind of have this thing where I . . . I live every day twice."

Zak squinted. "Come again?"

I nodded slowly. "Every day of my life, for as long as I can remember, happens once, and then it resets and happens again. The first day just kind of disappears, and I get to repeat it. We actually had this conversation yesterday. Well, *my* yesterday. For you, it never happened. That's how I knew what was on the test, how I knew what score you got, and how I was able to predict what those kids wrote down on my first day here."

I went on to explain how discard days and sticky days worked, as well as the events from yesterday's discard day.

"Wait. Didn't you ask me about this a while back?"

"I did."

"Dude, I am so confused."

"I know." I held up a finger. "But I knew you were going to say all this. Look, as I said, we've already had this conversation before. I'll prove it. A little while ago, I learned some things about you that you'd never told a soul, some things that only you could know, so that when we eventually had this conversation, I could repeat them back to you and prove that I could only have gotten the information from talking to you."

"During a discard day that never happened for me?" Zak repeated slowly.

"Precisely." I pointed to his notebook. "You ever remember telling me about your superhero drawings?"

"Uh . . . no," Zak said, pulling his book into his chest.

"But have you ever told *anyone* that halfway into that notebook, on the twenty-first page, you have a drawing of a guy in garbage-can armor that you plan to call Smasher Trasher? And that you used a picture of Mr. Wilding from the school's website as your model?"

Zak's face went slack. His notebook hit the floor. "That's impossible."

I held up a finger. "But completely explainable if I lived every day twice, wouldn't you agree?"

Zak wordlessly moved his mouth up and down. An alarm beeped on my phone. It was time for the nail in the coffin, for the reason why I had picked this particular sticky day to tell Zak.

"In fifty-two seconds, Mr. Rory will slam on the brakes to avoid hitting a dog. David Eggerton is going to fall out of his seat and roll into the aisle, and Nicole Campbell is going to fall on top of him. A bunch of students will pull out their phones, and it will be the first picture to ever be on both *Studs* and *Duds* at the same time. LeeAnna Sumsion's unzipped backpack will spill out, and her pink water bottle will roll all the way down to the front of the bus." I referred to my notes and started pointing around the bus. "He'll bonk his head on the window and start crying; she'll laugh hysterically; he's gonna say a cuss word."

I checked my phone timer and placed my hands on the seat in front of me to brace for the sudden stop. I stared at Zak and motioned with my head for him put his hands up as well. He hesitated.

I checked my phone again and then put it in my pocket. "Seven, six, five, four . . ."

Zak waited until *two* before putting his hands on the seatback. The bus lurched to a stop. Kids screamed as they were jolted forward into the next row of seats. David and Nicole tumbled into the aisle on top of each other; LeeAnna's backpack spilled out onto the floor. Some kids laughed; one started crying. A cuss word shot above the chaos, and a pink water bottle thudded to a stop near the bus driver.

Zak's eyes darted around the bus, taking it all in, processing my prediction with what he had just witnessed. He slowly turned to me. "Dude, you're like a psychic."

"No, my friend," I said, placing my hand on his shoulder. "I just live the double day."

CHAPTER 15

DOUBLE DAY DUO

(Sticky Monday—Sept. 20ᵗʰ)

I lay in bed, watching my phone buzz with a new text for about the tenth time in the last two minutes. It was 10:30 p.m., late for a sticky-day night, but I was expecting this. Before getting off the bus, I had given Zak a slip of paper with the final score and some key stats for tonight's New Orleans Saints versus Green Bay Packers game. The game had just ended.

Dude, call me.

Danny . . . The Saints just threw for EXACTLY 343 yards. The Packers had 274. The score was 34–21. Okay, man. I believe.

We NEED to talk.

Have you told anyone else about what you can do?

What do you use the double day to do? Have you ever tried staying up all night? Can you DIE on a discard day?

C'mon, man, you can't just swear me to secrecy, drop a bomb on me like that, and then go silent!

None of this makes sense. Danny, I'm freaking out over here, man!

CALL ME!

I let him sweat it out a bit more before calling him. Zak's face appeared on the phone before the first ring. "Danny, this is insane. Where have you been? You been doing a bunch of crazy stuff?"

"If you call assembling the patio swing with my dad and eating dinner with my family 'crazy stuff,' then yes. I've been doing *insane* stuff," I said. "It's my sticky day, Zak. My goal is to do the exact *opposite* of crazy stuff. I was actually going to bed." Even though I had already broken the ice with Zak about the double day, it was still a surreal experience to be talking so plainly with someone about it during a sticky day.

"Oh, right." I could see from the look on his face that this whole concept was a lot to take in. "So what's the plan for tomorrow? You going to solve some crimes or maybe even stop crimes before they happen or wait until the sticky day and then video crimes *as* they happen? You could capture some wild stuff to put on YouTube if you knew where to be ahead of time."

"What's with you and crimes?" I asked. "I usually spend my discard day faking sick and playing video games. *If* I go to school, it's to see what's on tests and pull pranks and stuff."

"So you *do* actually cheat on all your tests and quizzes?" Zak said, looking deflated.

"No," I replied calmly. "I do not cheat."

"Didn't you just say you go to school to see what's on the tests?"

I gave Zak a look like he should know better. "Since when is it cheating to look at a quiz or test *after* you've already taken it?"

Zak rolled his eyes. "But it's before you take it on the sticky day."

"I don't look at it on a sticky day, now, do I?"

Zak twisted his mouth to the side. "That's a technicality. So is that all the stuff you do? Video games, study tests 'after you've taken them,' and pull pranks?"

"I mean, that's not *all* I do. Sometimes I get bored and do some pretty crazy stuff. I ran my mom's minivan into a light pole in the grocery store parking lot once."

I thought Zak would think that was cool, but he just stared back blankly. "You are totally not using this power to its full potential."

"Hey, don't make me regret telling you about this, dude." I was giving Zak a hard time. Zak didn't know it, but it was precisely for his different way of looking at the double day that I had told him my secret in the first place.

Zak's eyes went wide, and he shook his head. "I *promise* you won't regret telling me. I'm assuming you told me because you wanted someone to bounce ideas off of and stuff, right? Well, I've got a ton of ideas, although first I need to ask you a bunch of questions."

"All right, hit me," I said, propping up my phone on a nearby moving box. "I've gotten very good at pretending like sticky-day conversations are the first time I've talked about something."

"Huh," Zak said, considering my comment as he glanced down at a sheet of paper. "That's weird. Anyway, for *my* benefit, I'll still go through my list. So, to start, how often do you use it to help people?"

"Uh, I don't know. Let me see. A couple weeks back I prevented my sisters from drawing all over the walls and ruining a basket of laundry with some shoe polish. Oh, there was this one time my mom set the oven on broil instead of bake and ended up burning a lasagna pretty bad. I made sure it was set right the next day." I was downplaying it just a bit to get a rise out of Zak, but the guy had made a pretty decent point on the discard day.

Zak pursed his lips and started an exaggerated slow clap. "You saved a lasagna. I mean, you're practically Batman."

"C'mon," I said defensively. "She burned it like *really* bad."

Zak wrote something down. "And I believe that already answers my question about stopping crimes. So, have you used your extra time to learn some skill like superhumanly fast? Because you realize you can practice twice as long as anyone, right? An instrument, a second language, up-close magic, et cetera."

"Up-close magic?"

"I don't know," Zak said. "Just some sort of skill."

"Uh, did I not mention how much gaming I do?"

"You're killing me, man." Zak shook his head.

"You know, I actually *have* killed someone before."

"Wait." Zak's face went slack. "You *have?*"

I rolled my eyes. "No, I'm just messing with you . . . or am I?"

I gave him a hard stare, then burst out laughing. I hadn't tried that one on him before. Even though Zak had a very different view of what I should be doing with the double day, talking to someone my age about it on a sticky day was like removing a backpack full of cement from my shoulders.

"Danny, let me be straight with you, man."

"Uh-oh," I said, "here it comes."

"Look, this is a crazy power, and it's wasted if you spend it cheating on tests—"

"I don't cheat."

Zak gave a small sigh. "Studying tests before taking them . . . again, driving into light poles, and playing video games. You could do some *incredible* things."

"Man, you sound like Dr. Donaldson," I said.

"That a bad thing?"

"Quite the opposite." My gut was right. Zak was the perfect choice. He was more than just someone to share the double day with. I didn't *enjoy* being challenged, but I knew I needed it. "Okay, Dr. Zak. What would you do, besides practicing the violin, because that's lame."

"Hey! Violin is cool."

I nodded. "I like seeing you so obviously wrong about something. It makes you relatable, you know?"

Zak waved a dismissive hand. "So are you *sure* you don't want to fight crime?"

"Dude." I held my hands up in disbelief. "I'm not even willing to look Jaxson or Braxlynn in the eye on a sticky day. I think I'm a few steps away from coordinating a drug raid or foiling armed robbery."

"Okay, okay," Zak conceded. "Just needed to confirm where we're starting from here. Let's start with that, then."

"Start with what?"

"With Braxlynn."

"Nope."

"Then with Jaxson."

"Uuuuuhhh, nope."

"C'mon, man." Zak laughed. "Work with me here."

"Zak, I may be new in Pocatello, but I've had plenty of discard days to push those kids' buttons and feel their wrath. I ain't ending up no dud."

"Well we gotta start somewhere." Zak paused and rubbed his chin. "If we're not going to save the victims of crime in our city, then we'll save the victims of bullies in our school. Gotham has Batman, Metropolis has Superman, and Snake River Middle School has Team Double Day!"

"Team Double Day?"

"Yeah, I know." Zak pursed his lips. "It doesn't have the right ring to it. Maybe the Double Day Squad, or the Double Day Defenders. Oh, wait. I got it. The Double Day Duo!"

"So we're superheroes now? Is that it?"

"I'll work on the official drawing," Zak replied, holding up his sketchbook. "For now let's work on some ground rules, like we can't *hurt* the bullies. We can't become the bullies ourselves. I've read enough comics to know that superheroes always have trouble with that. We can't become villains to take down the villains, you know? We need a code or something."

I placed my hand over my heart. "I promise to adhere to the Double Day Duo code, where I will not become a bully or kill anyone. I also promise to still spend some of my discard days playing video games, eating candy, and driving my mom's car very, very poorly."

"Needs some work." Zak cocked an eyebrow. "And I'm pretty sure we just agreed to scale back the video games."

"Oh, does that include you cutting out your nightly *Clash of Warbands* sessions?"

Zak's jaw went slack for a moment. "Who told you . . . Oh, I did, right?"

I nodded.

"This is so weird." Zak laughed. "So if we're not ready for Jaxson or Braxlynn, then where *do* we start?"

I knew the answer to that question just like I knew the answer to who I wanted to tell the double-day secret to. "We take down Noah."

"Hmmm." Zak weighed the name. "Noah *is* a sufficient punk. So what do we need to do first?"

"I don't know," I said, "but I feel like the answer has something to do with me playing a lot of video games."

Zak brought his palm to his face. "Of course you do."

CHAPTER 16

TEXCALIBUR

(Discard Tuesday—Sept. 21ˢᵗ)

The school bus doors thudded closed behind me, and I looked to see Zak saving me a spot in the last row, his eyes looking for all the world like it was his birthday and I was walking toward him with his cake, candles blazing. I shimmied down the aisle, dodging crumpled-up balls of paper and avoiding eye contact with Noah, who was busy gaming away on his phone. I might not like the kid, but you couldn't doubt his dedication to video games.

"Okay," Zak whispered as I took the seat next to him. "What day is it today?"

"It's Tuesday, Zak," I said blandly.

"You know what I mean," Zak hissed.

"It's a discard day."

Zak sucked at his teeth. "Yeah, but how do I actually *know* for sure that this day I'm having right now is just going to disappear? It just feels like a regular day to me."

I looked at Zak like he'd just insulted my mother. "What, you don't trust me?"

"C'mon, man, this is a pretty new concept for me. A little bit of assurance would go a long way."

I sat and thought a moment. I'd never had to convince anyone that they were actually living a discard day before. After a minute or so I got an idea. I stood up and cleared my throat. "Attention, all fellow bus riders. My name is Danny Day, and I have a very bad case of explosive diarrhea. That is all."

I sat back down with a smug look not befitting someone who had just announced to fifty kids that he had severe digestive problems. For a moment, Zak looked like he was going to switch seats, but he just shook his head and laughed. "Weeeellll, I will admit that that is slightly out of character for you."

"Slightly?" I said, knowing that no matter how many discard days I spent with Zak he would only ever have my sticky-day behavior as a reference.

"Okay, fine," Zak conceded. "I will admit that I did *not* see that one coming. So if it truly is the discard day, then what do you have planned so far?"

"Zak," I said blandly. "I don't know what's going to

happen any more than you do. Most of the time, discard days are for seeing what goes on, taking notes, and lots of knee-jerk reactions. Or I just play video games."

Zak rolled his eyes. "Yeah, you've mentioned that once or twice. So is that it? You take Noah down by just playing a bunch of video games and then coming out of the blue one sticky day and taking it to him?"

I eyed Noah as he pumped his fist in the air, stood up, and yelled something to the kid in front of him. Gloating, raging gamers like Noah annoyed me to no end. "No, it needs to be bigger than that. I've played with kids like this before. The moment things don't go their way, they start making excuses about how they were lagging, or they weren't used to the controller, or they're feeling sick, or the game glitched, or the sun was in their eyes, or whatever. If I just eventually beat Noah in a Brown Bag Game, I don't think it'll be enough. I'm not looking to dethrone this punk for a day. I'm looking to take him out for good."

"Geez," Zak said. "Remember the code, man. You can't actually strangle the guy with a controller cord."

"All my controllers are cordless, Zak. What do you take me for, a noob or something?"

Zak pressed his lips together. "Nice to see you taking issue with the controller cord after I accuse you of strangling Noah."

I shrugged. "Discard Danny is edgy like that. So look, I've got . . . well I *had* pretty good evidence that Noah is actually cheating during Brown Bag Games. I would have caught him red-handed on a sticky day if not for an unfortunate run-in with Jaxson."

"Okay, well, just use the double day to catch him again." Zak spoke as if I hadn't thought of that idea before.

"It might take a while for the stars to align," I explained. "I'll need to keep taking screenshots of the stats at the end of every game in hopes I can get something useful for our resident *Champions Royale* expert to interpret."

The bus lumbered past a speed bump as it pulled into the school zone and over the curb to the school parking lot.

"Expert?" Zak said, confused. "You mean there's someone that knows the game better than you?"

I glanced toward the front of the bus at a mop of black curls poking above the seat. "*Way* better than me. And if we're talking about taking down Noah, I don't think there's anyone on the planet that's thought through it more than she has."

"So I know I'm still pretty new here," I said, tilting my head as I read the spines of all the game cases proudly displayed on a small shelf in the Roost, "but what's the extent of what a shadow team is allowed to do in a Brown Bag Game?"

"Nothing crazy," Freddie replied, tracing a new chibi-style drawing of Lara Croft on her whiteboard. "They basically just avoid shooting their friends until the end and team up on shooting other people. Nothing that's like super obvious, I guess."

"Doing something like giving someone the wizard's cloak would be off-limits, then?"

"Uh, does Mario like mushrooms?" Freddie turned and folded her arms, suspicion written across her face. "Did someone actually try and give you the wizard's cloak today?"

"What? No, I don't even have a shadow team, Freddie." I looked around the tree house as if checking if the coast was clear. "I have it on good authority, though, that Noah is cheating."

Freddie's eyes narrowed. "How good is that authority?"

"Preeeetty darn good." *If she only knew.*

Freddie moved her lips around as if she was swishing her mouth with the new information to see how it tasted. She snapped her fingers. "I bog-squashing knew it!" Freddie stomped the wooden floor. "Noah is good, but no one is *that* good. Oh, I wish I could get him back, just *once*. Just one time, I'd like to see him get what was coming to him."

"You wanna?" I asked.

Freddie stopped and stared at me. "What? Get him back? Of course I spud-thumping *want* to. I want to make a million

160

dollars a year streaming on Twitch. I want to fly to Paris on a private jet. I *want* to do a lot of things, Danny, but that doesn't mean I'm able to actually do them."

"Just play along for a second," I said, plopping down on an old camping chair Freddie had hauled up to the Roost as a guest seat. "Let's just pretend like we managed to get solid evidence that he was cheating, a screen capture or something. How would you use it?"

"Weeeellll," Freddie mused, pacing the small tree-house floor. "The temptation would be to post it online or send it around on the Spud Gamers group chat, but that wouldn't be good enough."

"I don't know. Sounds pretty good to me," I replied. "He'd be disgraced at that point, wouldn't he? His title of Poky's greatest gamer would be destroyed. He'd lose everything."

"Sort of." Freddie's tone hinted that she'd thought this through before. "It's not like he'd cough up all the money he's taken from people over the years. Also, while there would be plenty of upset gamers, I just know he'd have some explanation, some way to spin the evidence so it doesn't look as bad. It's like a superpower you get when you're a salty-headed, arrogant worm like Noah."

"What do you suggest, then?" I asked, picking up an Xbox controller and turning on the TV.

"Noah likes a spectacle," Freddie said. "He doesn't just

like getting kills; he likes shouting about it from the top of his lungs. He doesn't just like winning; he wants everyone watching. You need to catch him at his grandest moment, when he thinks he's on top of the world, and have it all come crashing down." The edge in Freddie's voice could have been forged from rage or revenge, but it wasn't. It was a plea for justice, to finally be free of a plaguing, oppressive weight.

"So we use that info somehow to take him down during a Brown Bag Game?"

Freddie shook her head, her eyes distant as though she was already seeing the moment play out. "I don't want to just out Noah and be done with it. I want to tee him up for a downfall that will be talked about by Snake River gamers for the next *decade*. We take him down at the Shoebox Game."

"The what, now?"

"It's like the Brown Bag Game on steroids. It only happens twice a year, though. Once in the spring and once in the fall. All the gamers meet at a park. Twenty-dollar buy-in. Winner take all. It's in like a month."

I did the quick mental math. Although you had roughly twenty-five people playing in any given Brown Bag Game, that only represented about half the people who regularly played. If there were fifty people at twenty bucks a pop . . . "That's *a thousand dollars*, Freddie."

"I am well aware, Danny." Freddie sighed. "I was dumb

enough to save up for it a year back. I'd be happy just to see Noah fall, but I can't even begin to tell you how much a win would change my life."

She didn't openly fawn over the thousand bucks like most kids would do, but I hadn't forgotten our conversation during my first visit to the Roost. How Freddie needed a new bike, new clothes, even money just to help her grandmother. It was that moment that my whole plan shifted on its axis. It wasn't that I didn't want Noah to lose, it was just that I wanted Freddie to win even more. Luckily, if I pulled this off right, I could kill two birds with one stone.

CHAPTER 17
TOILET TALK

(Discard Tuesday—Sept. 21st)

I pulled my bike up to my garage and punched in the four-digit code. The large door opened with the sound of a castle gate rising. How humanity could invent the smartphone but couldn't figure out how to make a quiet garage door was beyond me. I squeezed through a hoarder's nest of moving boxes, tools, camping gear, and sports equipment. My mom had gotten the house unpacked and straightened away, but my dad hadn't had time to so much as take the packing tape off anything in the garage. It was unlike my dad.

I opened the door to the house and almost tripped over Sarah and Alice as I entered.

"Bike ride, Danny?"

"Bike wide?"

They must have heard the garage door. It was like their dinner bell for a bike ride.

"Not today, twinsies."

I tried to walk past, but they latched on to both my legs, repeating their pleas as I dragged them over the tile floor with heavy steps like I was trudging through waist-deep snow.

"So what did you two stinkers get up to today that I have to undo, huh?"

"We just played, Danny."

"Yeah, Danny, we just pwayed and wed stowees."

I stopped when I reached the carpet and glared down at my sisters' chubby innocent faces. "You know, it would make my life a whole lot easier if I could come home and you two would just confess to everything you did while I was gone. I know you did something. There's always something."

"Oh hey, Danny. You're home," my mom said, walking down the stairs and entering the living room. Fuzzy white specks dotted her hair.

"You get like a really aggressive case of dandruff or something?" I said, pointing.

"Did I what?" My mom looked at her hair and picked out several of the white fuzzies. "Ah, yes. I just finished restuffing the couch cushions."

"Why'd you have to . . ." I glanced down at my sisters

and knew from the looks on their angelic faces that this was their doing.

"We pwayed in da snow, Danny," Sarah said, nodding.

I took out my discard-day notebook and made a note. I wasn't sure how I was going to keep my sisters from unzipping the couch cushions, but I'd think of something. I turned to my mom. "Have you ever thought about keeping them in some kind of a kennel during the day? Uncle Paul used to have those big hog-hunting cages. They would work great. Put a few stuffed animals in there, a mini fridge with Go-Gurts, a bowl of Goldfish, you'd be set for hours."

My mom picked another fuzzy out of her hair and narrowed her eyes at me. "The girls would find a way out."

I laughed despite myself. I had been convinced my mom was going to reprimand me for suggesting we lock my sisters in cages. Her joke, plus the fact that no attempt at dinner had been made despite it being past six o'clock, let me know everything I needed to about what kind of day she was having.

"Did you have fun on your playdate?" my mom asked, going to the kitchen and removing several Tupperware containers from the fridge. It wasn't that I hated leftovers, I just didn't like having them for both the discard and the sticky day. And if we had *two* days of leftovers that made *four* days for me. There was only so much reheated shepherd's pie one kid could take. I made another note in my discard-day book. I couldn't always have an effect on whether my mom made a fresh meal, but if there was even a *chance*, I'd go for it.

"It's not a playdate. Mom . . ." I stopped when I saw a smile creep over her lips. She was getting a rise out of me. It was good every once in a while to remember where Discard Danny got his mischievous streak. It might explain the twins as well . . . maybe. "Is Dad working late again?"

My mom clicked her tongue. "Chiropractor again, actually. His neck is still giving him fits from when he fell asleep at the table the other night."

"Seriously?" I said, a pang of guilt lancing my gut. My dad was going through a rough patch. "He didn't exactly get hit by a car."

"Just wait until you're forty, Danny. Life gets less forgiving. I once knew a guy who was constantly popping his neck. Would torque it super hard. Over and over again. One day, *snap*, broke his own neck."

"Really?"

"No, but it could be true, and—"

"That's all that matters." I finished my mom's sentence. My mom had no idea how many times she'd gotten me with that on a discard day. How did I never see it coming? "Gonna chill upstairs for a bit, Mom."

"Okay, but stay off your phone. There's plenty of other things to do in life."

I tickled the twins until they released their holds, and I ran upstairs before they could reattach themselves. When I got to the safety of my room, I pulled out my phone and dialed Zak's number.

"Yo," Zak said, picking up yet again on the first ring. I couldn't tell where he was for a second and then noticed what looked like a shower curtain.

"Are you on the toilet?"

"Uh, yeah." Zak shifted his eyes side to side. "You called, so I thought it was urgent."

"Nothing is so urgent that I need to talk about it while you're on the toilet. Let's just agree to that."

"Fair enough, but you'll have to let me know again tomorrow, right? This whole day apparently disappears in like six hours."

"It'll disappear for *you*," I said, pointing to Zak through the camera. "I, however, will be forever scarred with the memory of FaceTiming you while you're taking a poop."

"Blessing and a curse, man." Zak shrugged. "I still can't wrap my mind around it. Today doesn't seem any different from any other day. I don't feel like I'm going to forget."

"Yeah, well, you will," I said, taking out my notebook and flipping through the day's entries. "How was violin practice? Lame as always, I assume."

"Violin is *not* lame. How was wasting your time playing video games with Freddie?"

"Actually . . ." I drew out the word. "I think I discovered how I want to take down Noah, or at least when."

"Really?"

"There's apparently a big tournament coming up called the Shoebox Game. More money, more players, more prestige. I'm sure Noah will be pulling out all the stops to win."

"And that's where we take him out." Zak finished my thought. "But how?"

"I'm not sure," I said. "We start with trying to get evidence of Noah cheating, but that won't be enough. Liars lie their way into things, and they'll lie their way out of them. Once we have the video evidence on a sticky day, I'll have to brainstorm with Freddie some more. Even though she's got the video game knowledge, it's tough when she doesn't know the resource she has with the double day."

"Why don't you tell her?" Zak asked.

"The tournament's in a little over three weeks. Even if I was completely confident that I wanted to tell her, we simply don't have the time."

"Let's see, here." Zak pretended to look at a watch on his wrist. "Hey, Freddie, I live every day twice—here let me prove it. You then say something amazing, and presto. That took all of eleven seconds."

I clicked my tongue in disappointment. "You do realize

that it took me like eight bus rides and two weekends of trial and error before I came up with an approach where you both believed me and didn't want to turn me in to the insane asylum, right?"

Zak looked at me like I'd just accused him of skipping violin practice to play video games. "You can't be serious."

"Serious as a Tater Tot competition at the Idaho State Fair."

"That's pretty serious," Zak admitted. "All right, then. First step to you dethroning Noah is catching him cheating."

"Oh, one other thing." I held up a finger. "I don't want to dethrone him."

"What? What are you talking about?"

"I want *Freddie* to dethrone him." I went on to explain about Freddie's need for a bike and her embarrassment about her hand-me-down clothes. "She's had a rough go, man. I feel like she needs to win as much as Noah needs to lose, and that's saying something, because he *really* needs to lose. I want Freddie to win the Shoebox Game."

Zak smiled and nodded. "Well, look at you. Discard Danny does have a heart. When did you say this Shoebox Game was?"

I switched over to my phone's calendar. "It's on the . . . crud."

"It's on the crud?"

"It's the same day as the football game my dad is taking me to," I said, trying to do the mental math on when the game started and when the Shoebox Game started.

"I'll be there, too," Zak said. "It's a morning game."

"Yeah," I said, still trying to see how I could pull it all off. "I think there's time. I'm sure other kids will be going as well. It'll be tight, but I can't skip the game. He's been super busy and this means a lot to him."

"I'm sure you have my dad to thank for that," Zak said. "I told you he's a pretty driven guy. He probably pushes his team hard."

"At least that explains why my dad has suddenly started practicing the violin thirty minutes a day."

"Makes total sense." Zak laughed. "So now what?"

"Well, in addition to playing in every Brown Bag Game, I'll need my skills on point. That means a lot of practicing."

"So, you're going to try to get evidence of Noah's cheating, somehow turn that against him during the biggest tournament of the year, all without him knowing, *and* set Freddie up to win." Zak stared at me with a look like he wasn't sure if he should say what was on his mind. "Isn't this, I don't know . . . unnecessarily elaborate?"

I channeled my best disappointed-father face. "Maybe if I wanted to be totally *lame* about it. You're tapped into the double day now. You gotta think big thoughts, man."

"Don't look at *me*," Zak said. "I was trying to get *you* to fight crime, remember?"

I rubbed my chin. "You gotta think big thoughts . . . that don't have me fighting crime against actual dangerous criminals. Think appropriately proportioned big thoughts."

"This is going to take some getting used to." Zak breathed a sigh. "I got your back, man."

"Thank you." I gave a single nod.

"Now I'm gonna hang up so I can flush the toilet and get out of the bathroom. My legs are asleep."

"Forever scarred by the memory, Zak. Over and out."

CHAPTER 18
RED-HANDED

(Sticky Monday—Sept. 27th)

My alarm clock blared the original Super Mario Bros. theme song as I blindly fumbled to turn it off. I rolled over, grabbed my sticky-day notebook, and scribbled down everything I had memorized from my discard-day notes. There was something to stay ahead of the twins, a few facts for classes, a handful of clever comebacks, and the big one: where and when I could finally catch Noah cheating.

It had been nearly a week since the toilet conversation. A week of taking endgame stats to Freddie on a discard day and then staking out a spot on the game map on the sticky day in hopes of catching Noah red-handed. Even with Freddie's wizardlike powers of interpreting endgame stats, Noah had frustratingly slipped through my fingers every single day.

One time I got stuck in a battle right when I dropped and missed my window. Another time I didn't have a good spot to hide. The other times my hiding spot wasn't good *enough*, and I got jumped by other players before SpudMasterFlex even showed up. We were one week closer to the Shoebox Game and had nothing to show for our efforts. Part of me worried that the cheating weasel simply *couldn't* be caught, that whatever cosmic force had me repeating days also kept Noah from losing at *Champions Royale*.

I ate breakfast, moved the laundry soap before the twins could dump it all over the floor this afternoon, and kissed my mom goodbye before heading for the bus.

Zak sat predictably in the last row, rubbing his hands together like I was a waiter bringing him his long-awaited entrée.

"Okay, what day is it today?" Zak whispered as I sat down.

"Sticky day."

"You know," Zak said, twisting his mouth to one side. "Although I totally believe you every time you tell me, it's still a struggle to like *really* believe. I mean, what if you tell me it's a discard day to get me to do something crazy, but then it's actually a sticky day and I'm stuck with it?"

"Hmmm." I looked to the bus ceiling. "I hadn't really thought about that, but that does give me a lot of great ideas."

"Danny," Zak said with a look that told me not to even

think about it. "We still need to come up with some way that can help reinforce my belief in this whole crazy thing."

Zak had actually brought this concern up several times, so I was prepared. "Okay, okay. How's this? Every sticky day, you write down a number. Show me that number on the next discard day. I will then be able to miraculously tell you what the number is on the following sticky day. It doesn't help convince you that it's a discard day and your actions won't matter, but it should help you keep faith that there was a discard day you don't remember."

"So for me, you'll just be able to magically guess a number I wrote down and kept secret from the day before." Zak paused. "I guess that could work."

"Of course it could," I replied. "You came up with it last night."

"This is still so weird," Zak mumbled as he took out his notebook and wrote down a number. "So did you and Freddie figure out on the discard day where Noah might be cheating in *Champions Royale* today?"

I craned my neck to see Noah sitting toward the front of the bus, his bright red, flat-billed hat sticking out like an angry zit on the end of a seventh grader's nose. "I'm actually feeling pretty good about today. Freddie's almost positive Noah got the wizard's cloak handed to him in a cave on the south side of Joyless Jungle."

"What do *you* think?" Zak asked.

"I think the Shoebox Game is in less than three weeks, and we're running out of time."

"You running out of money, too?" Zak asked, pulling out his wallet. "I can spot you a few bucks if you need it."

I waved him off. "Nah, I'm good, man." I paused, listening to Noah's grating laughter shoot above the school bus chatter. "For now."

Later that morning, I sat in Mrs. Marlow's first-period class and stared across the room at Elise, the pale anime girl in the panda-eared hoodie I had noticed my first day in class. Three hours from now, a photoshopped picture of her and Po from *Kung Fu Panda* would be at the top of *Dud Spuds* with the question "Ship or Dip?" By the end of the day, the post would have 113 likes and forty-seven comments. Even though I was focused on taking down Noah, it was getting harder for me to ignore the other things that I could fix, that I *should* fix. It was gonna be a rough day for Elise.

"Anybody?" Mrs. Marlow asked the class. I hadn't heard the actual question, but that's what Discard Danny was for.

I raised my hand. "Fort Hall was established in 1834 by an explorer named Nathaniel Jarvis Wyeth."

"Very good, Danny." Mrs. Marlow beamed. "The boy from Texas, teaching us a bit of Idaho history. Very nice."

At lunchtime I made my way to the gamer tables and

motioned for Freddie to save me a spot. First, I had some unfinished business to attend to.

"Cool shirt, man," I said, walking up to Noah. He was wearing the same *Double Dragon* T-shirt from back when I thought I was going to catch him the first time. I took it as a sign that balance was about to be restored to the double-day universe.

"Do you even know what game it's from?" Noah asked.

"It's hard to say," I said, inspecting his shirt.

"Shows how legit *you* are," Noah scoffed.

I looked up at Noah, both eyebrows rising. "Oh, I know it's from *Double Dragon*. I was just trying to see if it was for a specific version. I mean, the NES version is a classic, but I much prefer the one released with the Sega Master System. The level designs were a lot closer to the arcade version, but I'm sure I'm not telling you anything you don't already know. Oh, and did you see the movie they made?" I forced a chuckle. "I think it might be worse than the Mario Bros. movie. Actually . . . I take that back. Nothing's worse than the old Mario Bros. movie, but *Double Dragon* was *really* bad, am I right?"

"Uh . . . yeah," Noah said, hesitating just a moment before regaining his composure. "The Sega version is the best."

I smiled inwardly at the unsure look on Noah's face. Sticky Danny lived for these low-risk, high-satisfaction burns. They wouldn't do anything to invite trouble, but they kept people on their toes.

I took my seat next to Freddie and dropped my two dollars in the brown bag. She passed the bag down the row without putting any money in since she was sitting this one out.

"What was *that* all about?" Freddie hissed, casting a quick glance at Noah.

"A very small taste of some very large things to come."

Freddie scrunched her eyebrows. "You're weird."

"I will take that as a compliment," I said as I readied my phone and joined the game lobby. Thirty seconds later the game began. I chose to drop into some trees on the south side of Joyless Jungle, just outside where the wizard's cloak was supposedly going to be handed over to Noah. The last few times I tried this, I got jumped by other players passing through, and since I didn't have any weapons I either got killed or sent running for the hills. I crossed my fingers it wouldn't happen this time.

"Why are you just sitting there?" Freddie asked.

"Quit watching my screen," I said to Freddie a bit more sharply than I intended. My nerves were getting to me. If she caught Noah cheating red-handed, she might do something drastic. I couldn't afford that. Not on a sticky day. She looked sheepishly at the table, and I was quick to apologize. "Sorry, I'm not mad. It just makes me nervous when people are staring at me. It's like when I'm trying to take a pee."

"People stare at you when you pee?" Freddie asked, a disgusted grimace contorting her face.

I just shrugged.

"Boys are weird," Freddie said blandly as she got up to check out other players' screens.

After a little more than a minute, I watched Spud-MasterFlex move into position, crouching in the tall jungle undergrowth. He wound up and pelted an unsuspecting player in the head with a holy grenade, engulfing him in a flash of blue and gold sparks. It was actually an incredible shot. Despite being a complete turd, Noah was pretty darn good at the game. SpudMasterFlex grabbed the eliminated player's loot and hid inside a nearby shallow cave.

I held my breath as if Noah's character could hear my actual breathing and crawled through the undergrowth to get a better view. If he spotted me now, my cover would be blown and another day would be wasted. It wasn't just that I could feel my heart beating, I could *hear* my heart beating. The pulsing thump filled my ears, sweat beaded along my forehead. I made to wipe my palms on my pants and nearly dropped my phone to the floor.

"Focus," I mumbled to myself, starting my video capture.

After a few more seconds, a player with the gamertag FancyPrance approached. Noah held his fire. I held my breath. I quickly scanned the area to make sure I wouldn't get jumped. This was it, the key piece of evidence I would need to mark the beginning of the end for Noah.

FancyPrance walked straight for SpudMasterFlex and crouched into the small cave. I could still see both of them. FancyPrance dropped the wizard's cloak and left. Five seconds later, SpudMasterFlex was floating toward Fangthorn Peak, sparks of lightning crackling from his fingers.

"Yes," I grunted. I looked across the table to Freddie, who now stood peering over the shoulder of another player. She'd stand there and watch Noah torch the entire playing field, curse his name as he took the brown bag yet again, and wonder how he did it. Odd, considering she was the one who had gotten to the bottom of that question during the discard day. SpudMasterFlex was a great player, but I now had proof that he was an even better cheater.

CHAPTER 19
HOG HUNTING

(Sticky Monday—Sept. 27th)

"I bug-chuggin' knew it!" Freddie stomped so hard on the floor of the Roost I thought she was going to put her foot through the boards. She dragged her finger across the screen of my phone and rewatched the wizard's-cloak exchange between FancyPrance and SpudMasterFlex. "I can't believe you actually got this. How did you know where to be? That cheating, rat-bagging, worm-squirming, blister-licking ninny!"

I couldn't contain my laugh at her string of insults. It was a good thing I hadn't let her watch my screen as it happened in real time; she would have climbed the lunch table and throttled Noah. "Call it a hunch. So now that we have it, what do you want to do with it? Our end goal is to dethrone him during the Shoebox Game, so how do we use this to our advantage?"

Freddie tapped her lips with a dry-erase marker, her entire face tightly knit with concentration. She walked to her whiteboard, brought up her forearm, and with two broad swipes erased every single one of her chibi drawings.

"What are you doing?" I asked in shock.

"No time for cute little cartoons, Texcalibur. We're at war. We need to strategize." On one half of the board, Freddie drew two circles and labeled them *SpudMasterFlex* and *FancyPrance*. She connected them with a line before drawing a dozen more circles, labeling each of them with a question mark. On the other half of the board she wrote titles to multiple columns: *Gamertag, Real Name, Weakness, Strength, Role.* "FancyPrance's name is Adam Sipherd, known friend to Noah. Head-to-head he's garbage, but he can be a frustratingly effective third-partier."

Freddie wrote down the information as she spoke, the strong smell of dry-erase marker filling the small room. Under the *Role* section she wrote down the word *gifter.*

"So I take it from all this"—I motioned to the whiteboard—"that you want to track down Noah's entire shadow team."

Freddie tapped her lips with the butt of the marker. "You're gut-gobblin' right I do. If they're all in this thing together, then they're all coming down together."

I looked at the empty circles on the whiteboard. There was no telling who or how many goons Noah had helping him on his shadow team, but Freddie was right. If we couldn't root out everyone that was propping Noah up, then we ran the risk in the Shoebox Game of falling into the same trap that Noah set each and every Brown Bag Game.

"All right, then, Commander FreddieCougar." I stood up and held out my hand. "We're officially at war with Noah and his shadow team."

Freddie's eyes sharpened as she grabbed my hand and shook it formally. "Except they don't even know it."

"And trust me." I smirked. "They never will."

(Sticky Friday—Oct. 1ˢᵗ)

I repeated my strategy of taking the endgame stats to Freddie for evaluation and staking out the most likely spots during the sticky-day Brown Bag Games, but by the end of the week, I'd only managed to discover one more cheater: RigaTortoise, a stocky blond girl named Ophelia Higginson. It wasn't that I couldn't find people dropping weapons and gear for Noah, it was just that it was always the same two people: RigaTortoise and FancyPrance.

I *knew* there were more cheaters out there, but they must have been helping in different ways. Zak had even been secretly keeping tabs on Noah during and after lunch to see if he slipped anyone some money after the Brown Bag Game but had never seen anything suspicious.

Freddie was able to identify a few potential cheaters by seeing who scored kills in close proximity to Noah but never attacked him. While that helped focus our efforts, it didn't *prove* anything. There were a thousand different reasons why someone did or didn't do something in a game like *Champions Royale*. The more I played the game in the evenings and at the Roost, the more I learned the secrets of the map and the strengths and weaknesses of each item. Even the wizard's cloak had its downside. You could float around, do crazy up-close lightning damage, and command the dragon, but your defense was totally nerfed, you had no long-range attack, and you were a magnet for alchemical fire. Aside from the weapons, there were like a trillion magical objects ranging from the Vest of Invisibility (which did what you thought it would) to Akbain's Portal, which would instantly transport you one time to anywhere on the map.

I also found out that there were a bunch of other items similar to the wizard's cloak that Noah removed from the Brown Bag. Every area on the map had some sort of monster to summon: Haunted Pines had werewolves, Lost Labyrinth had Minotaurs, Dryout Dunes had giant scorpions, and so on. The item needed to summon and control those monsters always spawned somewhere away from that region. Since Noah was the reigning Brown Bag champion, he could choose the game, which included tweaking the variant. Limiting it to just the wizard's cloak and the dragon made things a lot easier to control. For the Shoebox Game, however, that custom variant would be pulled back, and the full chaotic glory of the *Champions Royale* map would be on display.

I boarded the bus on a sticky-day Friday morning and walked over to Zak.

"Discard or sticky?" Zak asked as I sat down.

"Forty-nine," I said, repeating the secret number. "Sticky."

"Darn it," Zak said, writing down another number to confirm the next sticky day. "I bet you do some pretty crazy stuff on discard days."

I feigned an apologetic expression. "Well, I'm *sorry* I'm such a boring friend when I know I can't get away with murder. I've tried to get *you* to do some 'pretty crazy stuff' on discard days, by the way. You're not exactly the rebellious type."

"I can be rebellious," Zak scoffed.

"Dude, last week you wouldn't skip violin practice because you said it would be like skipping out on putting on underwear . . . which can be super liberating, by the way."

"Look, discipline equals freed— Wait, what?" Zak's

eyebrows shot to the ceiling. "Are you talking about missing violin or not putting on . . . you know what? I don't want to know. So I'm *not* that rebellious. Fine. What did we figure out yesterday, at least?"

"I figured out there are three different underground entrances in Greedy Mines that take you straight to Ghastly Gravestones."

Zak shook his head. "You just stayed home and played video games?"

"Yes, Zak," I said plainly, as if calmly responding to my sisters' question of whether they had to put on clothes before going to church. "Have you ever gone to school for like *ten* days in a row? It's exhausting. We each have our role to play in this war on Noah. If I'm not in tip-top video-gaming shape, how can I help during the Shoebox Game? And don't worry, you were just as disappointed with my decision yesterday evening. You almost didn't tell me your daily secret number. You do realize I always have to hear these things from you twice, right?"

"Huh," Zak said, considering the comment. "Well, we all have our roles to play, as you said. I'm your annoying conscience. So what's the plan now? I can try to keep tracking Noah during class breaks and stuff, but I would bet he just sends the money through an app or something. I think this is a dead end."

I kicked the problem over in my mind. Whether it was exchanging items in the game or money in person, it didn't look like we were going to catch any more cheaters out in the open. So how did we rustle them out of hiding?

"Let me call Freddie for another opinion," I said, taking out my phone. "She's good with this kind of stuff."

"*Call* Freddie?" Zak straightened and looked toward the front of the bus. "Hey, where is she?"

"She's faking sick today," I said without looking up from my phone. "We played video games online together almost the entire discard day."

I looked over to see Zak giving me a flat stare.

"Hey, you should try it sometime," I said, tapping my phone to call Freddie. "Oh, and remember. No talk about the double day."

Zak mimed zipping his lips shut.

Freddie picked up after the second ring, her untamed black curls filling most of the screen, the unmistakable backdrop of the Roost behind her.

"Danny? Uh, hey . . . what's up?" Freddie flitted her eyes between her phone and the TV before giving two unconvincing coughs. "Not feeling well today."

"It's seven thirty a.m., Freddie," I said. "Shouldn't you be resting or drinking lots of fluids or something?"

"I can't rest until I rank up to platinum tier," she said,

quickly dropping all pretenses of being sick. "And I'll drink the plentiful blood of my fallen enemies. Now, how can I help you?"

"Looks like we got the right person," Zak said with a nod. He and Freddie still didn't know each other that well, but our joint quest to dethrone Noah would solve that pretty quick.

"Oh, hey, Zak," Freddie said, a hint of embarrassment hanging on her words. "Didn't know you were there."

Zak gave a little wave to the camera, but Freddie was too busy looking at the TV. Zak leaned in close to the phone and lowered his voice. "So Danny tells me you and he are going to take down the great SpudMasterFlex."

"Did Danny recruit you, too?" Freddie perked up. "Please tell me you've agreed to karate chop him in the pus-bubbling skull."

"Uh . . ." Zak hesitated. "Not exactly. More here for ideas and strategies than anything. Plus, I think I'm more the bodyguard type than the hitman or assassin."

"Ah," Freddie said, deflating a bit. "Okay, so what's up?"

I ducked below the seatback in front of me and lowered my voice as well. "So, we were just saying that we don't think we're finding the cheaters fast enough, and we're running out of time before the Shoebox Game. We were brainstorming ideas."

"Ratbag, cow poop!" Freddie shouted before putting down her controller. She'd apparently lost her game. She grabbed her phone and angled it toward her whiteboard, which now included Ophelia's name as well as a bunch more info on potential cheaters. "So, I just want to double-check here. You're saying all threats of physical violence are off the table? 'Cause I bet we could get them to spill the beans on the other cheaters if Zak put one of them in a headlock or something."

Zak cocked an eyebrow. "Yeah, that's off the table."

"Monkey dung." Freddie snapped her fingers and erased a line from her board. "Well, there goes that idea. So what does that leave us with?"

"We were hoping *you* would know," I said.

"We've gotten what we can from spying, threats of pain and death are off the table . . ." Freddie gave an over-exaggerated glance of disappointment. "I suppose asking nicely isn't an option. Hog bog, this Noah is squirrelly."

"Wait, that's it," I said, holding up a finger.

"What's it? Asking nicely?" Freddie asked. "I highly doubt that is going to work."

"Hogs." I nodded with a self-satisfied smirk.

"How is *hogs* the answer to your problems?" Zak asked.

"Hear me out," I said, still piecing my thoughts together. "So back in Texas, my dad used to take me hog hunting. There are millions of the things. They tear up farmers' land, breed like crazy, and stink to high heaven. They're like a statewide infestation of two-hundred-pound cockroaches. Anyway, with how many of them there are, you'd think they'd be easy to find, but there's no fooling a hog's nose. They'll smell you a mile off if the wind's in the wrong direction, and you'll never see a thing."

"So how do you hunt them?" Freddie asked.

"The *hard* way is to track them. Move slow, read the signs, but it takes forever. The smart way isn't to *avoid* their sense of smell. It's to use it *against* them."

Zak twisted his mouth. "And how do you do *that*?"

Zak was a smart kid, but he obviously wasn't much of a hunter. "By laying bait. You find something that they can smell for miles that they can't resist. They'll come in by the herds."

"So you're saying that we try to bait the cheaters?" Zak asked. "But what do we use for bait?"

"Money," Freddie said plainly.

"Bingo," I said, snapping and pointing to the camera.

A shrill call of Freddie's name sounded in the background. "Oh, sorry, guys, I gotta go," Freddie interjected. "That's my gammie. I'll have to catch ya later."

With a quick wave, she hung up.

"I told you she was good." I turned to Zak. "If these

cheaters like getting money from Noah, we'll just have to give them a *whole* lot more to turn on him."

"Okay," Zak said. "But where will we actually *get* a whole lot more money?"

"Doesn't really matter," I said, pocketing my phone. "I only pay people bribes on discard days."

CHAPTER 20

RIGATORTOISE

(Discard Monday—October 4th)

Zak pressed his lips together and looked nervously around the bus. "Are you *sure* this is a discard day?"

I glanced sideways at Zak. "Yesterday was Sunday, Zak. That would make today the first Monday of the week. I'm sure."

"Well," Zak said, fiddling with something in his jacket pocket, "yesterday is *always* the day before for me, and I only ever have *one* Monday in a week. It's not like I wake up on a sticky day and remember the crazy stuff that happened on a discard day. I'm flying blind here."

"Oh, stop your whining," I said. "You remember how I told you that you never do anything crazy on a discard day?"

"Yeah."

"Well, consider this your first big step."

Zak took a couple of deep breaths then pulled his hand out of his jacket and handed me a roll of dollar bills. "I can't believe I'm doing this. You *better* be right. You *are* acting way more rash than usual, and I can't ever really remember *seeing* you act rash, so that's probably a good sign."

I looked through the bills. Tens, twenties, and even two fifties. There had to be close to three hundred dollars here. "Yeah, well, my parents aren't big on cash, and this much is well beyond my personal savings. If we're gonna get these cheaters to come out of hiding, we need strong-smelling bait."

"My parents are going to *kill* me when they find out."

"If they kill you, you'll only be dead for like half a day," I said, playfully slugging Zak on the shoulder. "You've come so far. See, doesn't it feel good to be a little rebellious on a discard day?"

"No. It doesn't," Zak said, breathing out and putting his head down between his knees. "It feels like I'm going to throw up."

"It'll pass." I patted Zak on the back. It was weird to see him like this. He could stand up to the town's most ferocious bully, but borrowing a bit of money from his mom's purse had him nearly passed out on the floor. The sticky-day part of me understood every bit of his anxiety, however.

I stashed the cash in my jacket as the bus pulled up to the school. I may not have known who the cheaters were, but I had a pocket full of bait, video evidence, a discard day, and two places to start: Ophelia Higginson and Adam Sipherd.

Ophelia Higginson, aka RigaTortoise, was short and broad, and had razor-sharp blond bangs that looked like they'd been cut with the help of a straightedge. She was quiet and sat in the back row of my first period next to Elise, the anime girl. Since she typically spent most of her between-class time and lunch hour with Noah and the gamer group, the tricky part was going to be finding a time when I could get her alone to propose the bribe.

At lunchtime I picked a table apart from the gamers and sat with Zak and Freddie to reevaluate the situation. We watched the brown bag get passed around, the students discreetly slipping in their money before handing it down the line. Knowing what to look for, I was amazed we'd never been caught by a teacher. At one point Ophelia stood, and I got ready to make my move. When she picked a wedgie and sat back down, I knew we needed to work out a different strategy.

"I'm guessing you haven't had any luck yet?" Zak asked.

I dipped a golden, crispy Tater Tot into some fry sauce and popped it in my mouth. How did I ever live without these things? "Nothing. This girl attaches herself to Noah like a phone to Braxlynn's hand."

Freddie put her elbow on the table and rested her chin on her hand. She mumbled when she spoke. "The Shoebox Game is in less than two bum-busting weeks. What do we do if we never get a chance to bribe her?"

"We'll get the chance," I said, eyes fixed on Ophelia.

"How much you end up getting for the bribe?" Freddie asked.

I gave Zak a look and pulled out the roll of bribe money.

Freddie's eyes went so big I thought they'd overinflate and pop like a balloon. "Is that *real*?" Freddie hissed, frantically looking over both shoulders.

"The money is quite real," I said. "The bribe will not be."

"Where did you get it?" Freddie stammered. She was acting like I'd just pulled the Triforce out of my pocket. However strange Discard Danny was to Zak, he was going to be baffling to Freddie.

"Freddie," I said, making sure I had her eyes. "I'm gonna need you to trust me today."

Meeting Discard Danny was always a shock to the system for those who only remembered Sticky Danny. It was a moment (or series of moments) of such uncharacteristic behavior that people questioned whether they knew me at all. My parents had said almost those exact words dozens of times over the years. Freddie, however, gave a different response. One that stunned me as much as Zak's explanation of what he would do with the double day. She simply pursed her lips, squared herself, and nodded. "I trust you."

Her sincerity was so pure, it halted me for half a breath. I could probably still make the discard day work without Freddie, but knowing that she had my back, whether I was Sticky Danny or Discard Danny, with no explanation of what a double day even was, was a type of trust I didn't know I'd been desperately missing until I suddenly had it.

I nodded to Freddie and pulled out my phone. I searched online for RigaTortoise's profile and began drafting a direct message.

I know you've been helping Noah win during the BBG. I've seen you give him two wizard's cloaks, one giant healing potion, and walk over a bear trap so he could get a magical mace . . . and that's just in the last few days.

"Here we go." Zak took a deep breath.

"Wait for it," I mumbled, and reassuringly patted Zak on the leg. "No one look at her."

Our joint attempt to suddenly not look at Ophelia was probably as noticeable as just staring at her. I watched her freeze out of the corner of my eye. She slowly looked up from her phone and scanned the lunchroom. A few seconds later, three jumping dots appeared at the bottom of my screen. She was typing her reply.

Is this the new kid from Texas? I have no idea what you're even talking about.

"Time to play hardball," I said, teeing up and sending two of the videos I'd recorded of her helping Noah.

Let me refresh your memory. I mean, this was ALL THE WAY back to last week, so I see how you might forget. Shall I send a few more? Maybe to the whole BBG crew? I'm sure they'd love to know how helpful Noah's shadow team can be.

There was a long pause before Ophelia's reply.

What do you want?

Names. I know SpudMasterFlex is paying you to help him. But I guarantee he's not paying you THIS much. It's yours if you tell me who else is helping Noah.

I sent a picture of a fifty and two twenties. Zak wiped at a sheen of sweat forming on his forehead.

He doesn't pay me and no one else is helping him. I'm the only one.

I'll give you a hundred and fifty bucks if you tell me the others.

You think I'll ruin my friendship with Noah for a hundred and fifty bucks?? You AREN'T a mind reader after all. There AREN'T any others. I'm the only one.

"A bit squirrelly, this one. Looks like it's time to take it to the next level."

I want names or I start posting videos.

There IS NO ONE ELSE! I'm the only one Noah trusts and the only one good enough to help him.

"Wow," Zak said, looking up from my phone. "I'd definitely rat you out for a hundred and fifty bucks."

"I would have done it for the original ninety," Freddie added.

"Thanks, guys." I rolled my eyes.

"He must be paying her a huge amount of money," I said. "No way anyone could *actually* be friends with that turd. Well, Ms. RigaTortoise, if you don't think anyone else is helping Noah, then the truth shall set you free." I selected the two videos of FancyPrance helping SpudMasterFlex and sent them to Ophelia.

I waited for her reply, but she never typed one. I could see her watch the video, her jaw dropping and eyes bulging in surprise. She tapped her phone several times over the next few minutes, most likely replaying the videos to make sure she was seeing things correctly. She stood, tugged on her wedgie, and turned to loom over Noah.

"Dude, I honestly think she didn't know," Zak said, now openly staring at Ophelia.

"Oh, this should be good," I said.

Ophelia thrust her phone in front of Noah's face, who was busy playing a game.

"What the crud, Phee?" Noah yelled.

"You want to explain this to me?" Both Ophelia and Noah were talking plenty loud for us to hear them from a distance, even with the lunchroom chatter.

"Explain what?" Noah stopped and watched the two videos of FancyPrance, his face flushing a brighter shade of red with each second. "Phee, it's not what it looks like."

Ophelia's face contorted with rage, and I thought for sure she was about to punch Noah in the mouth. "I'm not stupid, Noah. I know how the game is played. Adam is obviously helping you. You said you trusted me to be the only one." Ophelia burst into tears as she spun and ran away.

"You're such an idiot," Noah said, turning to Adam and slapping him on the back of the head.

"Should we go after her?" I asked.

"Don't look at me," Freddie said. She was keeping it together, but she had just witnessed me completely blow our cover to Noah. I could only imagine the freak-out she was bottling up at the moment.

"I don't think she has much more to tell us," Zak said. "It looks like she honestly didn't know about anyone else."

I looked at Adam Sipherd, a mousy kid with scraggly brown hair, cower and rub the back of his head where Noah had slapped him. "I'm thinking we probably should have started with FancyPrance."

"We try again on the next discar—" Zak barely caught himself. "On the next day? That is to say, tomorrow. Should we try tomorrow?"

"Nah," I said. "Not when I'm on a roll."

I looked up FancyPrance online and sent him the videos of him cheating with Noah.

Your turn . . . I've got videos of three more
people. If you tell me the rest of the people
helping Noah then I'll give you eighty bucks.
I'll get the answers from someone else if you
don't help. Either way I will find out and only
one way has YOU getting eighty bucks. Your
move, FancyPrance. I'm only asking once.

I waited ten seconds and sighed when I read the answer.

Texcalibur, I seriously don't know anyone's
name. I thought it was just me. I swear it.
Please don't send the videos. Noah will
seriously not be my friend anymore.

You're friends with a turd and you've been
helping that turd cheat at the BBG and steal
kids' money for a long time. How much money
does he give you and how does he give it
to you?

He buys me different Champions Royale skins.
I get really good stuff if I give him good items.
He gives me cheaper items if I help him just a
little, but it's always worth it.

**How did he first contact you about helping
him cheat?**

**It was a long time ago. I almost beat him once
and then he contacted me about how I could
get a lot of cool skins. He doesn't care about
the money. He cares about being a legend. I've
told you everything I know. Don't send out the
videos. Please, man.**

"*Skins?*" Freddie growled. "He's selling himself for *skins?*
I should walk over there right now and—"

"You'll get your chance, Freddie." I reached over and
patted her on the forearm. "At the Shoebox Game."

I paused for a good while before I sent my final text.

The truth shall set you free!!!

I went to the Brown Bag Game forum, clicked SEND
MESSAGE TO ALL and posted the videos with the message,
*There's a new king in town. Riga and Prance didn't cooperate, so
now you know they're cheaters, along with Noah. I've got A LOT
more videos with a lot more people. If you don't want to be exposed
as a cheater, private message me immediately. If I don't hear from
you in five minutes, your video is going up next.*

"Savage," Zak said, shaking his head and glancing over at the gamers as they all read the message. Freddie pulled out her phone and checked the message as well with a look like she was trying to hold her pee after chugging a gallon of water. "But what are you going to do after five minutes if no one gets back to you and you have no videos to send out?"

I leaned over and whispered to Zak while Freddie read and reread the message. "Nothing. It's a discard day, big guy. You gotta think by different rules. Usually it doesn't make sense to shoot yourself through the leg to hit your target." My phone dinged as two private messages popped into my inbox. "But it does on a discard day."

CHAPTER 21

BE A BUDDY

(Discard Monday—Oct. 4th)

By the end of the school day, I'd been able to grow the list of confirmed cheaters from two to five. Only two had private messaged me, Regan Russell and Scott Brinton, but they had each given up another name once I dangled fifty bucks in front of their faces. I then contacted those two names, Robin Bourke and Aaron Griffin. Robin denied the accusation and dared me to find *any* proof of her cheating. Zak told me she was a neighbor of his and was a pretty cool girl, so it was probably more likely that Regan didn't actually know another cheater and just threw Robin's name out there to get fifty bucks. Aaron, on the other hand, must have sent me thirty texts pleading for me to not tell anyone. With about thirty players in your average Brown Bag Game, five decent players was probably enough to help a player like Noah win almost every time, but I was convinced there were more out there.

The final bell rang, and I made my way straight to the bus, anxious to discuss what next steps we'd take with our new information. I passed Zak by the bike rack. He was talking to one of his judo buddies.

"Hey, Zak. Hurry up, man. Lots to discuss."

"Yeah, yeah," Zak said. "I'll be there in like two minutes."

I took out my notebook and scanned my daily notes as I made my way to the back of the bus. I felt a tug on my sleeve and stopped to see Freddie chewing her nails and staring at me.

"I still don't understand how you're able to get so many of those videos, Danny. You'd have to be in the exact right spot at the exact right time."

"Yeah, pretty amazing what you can come up with when you can read minds." I tapped my head knowingly.

Freddie looked around and hunched down, speaking in a low voice. "Look, I trust you, but you gotta help me understand the strategy here. I thought we wanted to do all this closer to the Shoebox Game. So what's the plan now? I'm not even sure Noah will show up now that he's been outed as a cheater. You gotta fill me in on the details, Danny."

"I will, I just need to—"

Someone slapped my notebook to the floor.

"What do you think you're doing, punk?"

I looked up to see none other than SpudMasterFlex himself, both fists clenched and nostrils flared. "I *was* talking to Freddie. But *now* I'm staring at Snake River's biggest cheater. What are you up to?"

The kids on the bus gave out a low *ooooh*.

"I bet you think you're so clever."

"No." I shook my head. "I've *proven* I'm clever. Just like I've *proven* that you're a rotten cheat who also happens to know squat about retro games. I'm onto you now, Noah. Your reign ends at the Shoebox Game."

I squared off with Noah. My whole body tensed and my heartbeat revved up like someone pressing a gas pedal to the floor of a car still in park. Noah was furious and I was on a discard day. Not exactly the recipe for a peaceful resolution.

Noah opened his mouth for what I thought was going to be some clever comeback. It wasn't. He cleared his throat and spit in my face. I winced and made to wipe away the loogie when Noah jumped me, clawing and biting like some kind of rabid badger. I yelled as Noah sank his teeth into my shoulder and knocked me to the floor. I scrambled backward and used the space to kick Noah off me. He lunged again but stopped short, dangling like a marionette. Zak had him by the back of the shirt.

"Break it up, break it up!" Mr. Rory, the school bus driver, yelled as he shuffled down the aisle.

I rubbed my shoulder and winced, trying to hold back tears. "That lunatic spit in my face and bit me on the shoulder." I pulled up my T-shirt sleeve to reveal a set of purpling bite marks.

Mr. Rory pursed his lips as he grabbed Noah from Zak. "You're not riding home on *my* bus, mister."

"I can't *walk* home!" Noah yelled, flailing as Mr. Rory escorted him off the bus.

"Never know till you try," Mr. Rory said, and turned back toward me. "You all right, kid?"

"Yeah, I'm fine . . . as long as he isn't infected with the zombie virus."

"Oh my gosh, Danny." Freddie bent down to help me to my feet.

I stood up and rolled my shoulder as Freddie and Zak walked me to my regular seat toward the back of the bus.

"What happened?" Zak asked. "I can't believe he *bit* you."

"I must say having you around to pull bullies off of me on discard days is coming in pretty handy." I flipped through my notebook and tried straightening out the now-bent pages.

"But could you try and show up just a *little* bit sooner? I'm taking a lot of damage here."

"Beggars can't be choosers," Zak said. "That's what my dad always says. Plus, I bet you won't even feel a thing tomorrow."

I rolled my eyes, wincing as I gingerly touched the bite mark. "Now you're making double-day jokes, huh?"

"You said I need to think differently."

"Discard day? Double day?" Freddie asked, looking from me to Zak. "What are you even talking about?"

Zak's eyes widened in panic. I waved a hand. "It's a discard day, Zak. Don't worry about it." I turned to Freddie. "I'll tell you some other time."

"So are your parents going to be mad?" Zak asked.

"What, that I got bit?" I said. "No, I won't tell them about this. It's not like I got my face pounded in. I can hide a bite mark."

"Not if you turn into a zombie," Zak countered.

"More likely he'd turn into a lying, whining cheater," Freddie said. Zak and I both laughed. "Maybe that's how Noah formed his little shadow team."

"Would make a lot of sense," Zak said. "So what do we do now with all those names? Get them to turn on Noah during the Shoebox Game?"

I shook my head. "If we can. I'll have to test who's loyal

to him and who can be persuaded to turn, but I want Noah walking into the SBG thinking everything's under control. I don't want to run the risk of anyone squealing and blowing the plan. I say we keep digging to find more cheaters. If we can get them to turn on him, then we've got a good shot."

"Look, I still feel like I'm in the dark here a bit, but I don't think we'll need to convince his shadow team of anything," Freddie said.

"What do you mean?" I asked.

"If you can get more evidence of them cheating, then maybe instead of turning Noah's team against him, we can get the honest gamers to band together and fight the cheaters. I can promise you I'm not the only one sick and tired of Noah's reign. There's more of us than there are of them."

"Like one big shadow team. I like it." I nodded at the idea as I looked out the window at a scowling Noah, who now stood in front of the school with Vice Principal Woodard.

"I wonder if Ophelia and Adam are still even going to have his back after all this," Freddie said. "I guess when you have to pay people to be your friends it's easy come, easy go."

"Easy come . . . ," I echoed softly. My mind lingered on the phrase, the seed of a deviously good idea taking root. "There's one last angle we haven't explored yet."

"And what would that be?" Zak asked.

"He'd never believe it right now, but between now and the Shoebox Game ol' SpudMasterFlex and I are going to become the best of friends," I said, leaning out the window and giving Noah an enthusiastic wave. "Be a buddy, not a bully!"

CHAPTER 22
STRATEGIES

(Discard Saturday—Oct. 9th)

That discard Saturday, Freddie stood at her whiteboard. The morning call of songbirds seemed to come from right outside the Roost. In addition to information about Noah's shadow team there was now a complete list of Shoebox Game participants, their gamertags, known strengths, weaknesses, shadow teams, and potential ties to Noah. At the top of the board was a countdown: *Days to SBG—6.*

"So that now makes seven confirmed cheaters," Freddie said, drawing a frowny face next to the name Master-Cheese116. "And you said you don't have video evidence of this one?"

I pulled a sucker from my mouth and shook my head as I read over the list of nearly fifty names. "Nope. This one was a . . . credible confession, let's call it." In truth, this last one had come after a few sources pointed me to the same player (MasterCheese116), and I kind of threatened him with a judo-style beating from Zak. Would Zak ever do something like that? Of course not. Would Zak have even consented to send me videos of him body slamming and nearly breaking a kid's arm in his latest judo tournament if he'd known I was going to use them to intimidate MasterCheese116 into fessing up? Not a chance. But if Zak couldn't remember what happened in the discard-day past, was it really my place to remind him?

Freddie took a couple of steps back and surveyed the board. "I seriously don't know how you manage to get all of this bog-squashing info. I'd hardly believe it if you didn't produce so much blasted video evidence."

"I've got a few tricks up my sleeve," I said, putting the sucker back into my mouth. "If Noah thinks he's the only one with secret helpers, he's sorely mistaken." The odd thing was that my number one secret helper didn't even know she was my secret helper. Freddie's ability to break down post-game stats and draw conclusions on how the game had played out was like some expert tracker looking at faint indentations in the earth, dew missing from grass, and half-broken twigs and divining which direction an animal had gone when most people would just see trees and flowers. Cheaters confessing names of other cheaters showed me who to look for; Freddie's post-game stat breakdown showed me where and when to look.

"So of the seven confirmed cheaters," Freddie said, reading down the list, "we have video evidence of six. Three are dedicated to dropping off useful items like potions, weapons, and armor. One spies on key players and has her earbuds patched into Noah's so she can whisper information like player locations and what weapons they have. The last three are essentially bodyguards. Very few of them are aware of any of the other cheaters. We've also got most everyone else assigned to a shadow team. Now the trick is seeing which of the seven cheaters can be turned, if any, and which of the shadow teams would want to combine into one big shadow team against the cheaters during the Shoebox Game. How we're going to figure that out without anyone squealing to Noah, I have no clue."

"I've got a few ideas," I said.

Freddie rolled her eyes. "Let me guess. Mind reading."

"Bingo." I was tempted to tell Freddie about the double day. Her knowing would actually make things a lot simpler, but her freaking out about me magically living every day twice would make things a lot more difficult. We were zeroing in on a solid Shoebox Game plan, and, with only one week left, we needed Freddie focused and on her A game.

Freddie looked at the list of cheaters and clicked her tongue. "With this many cheaters I'm not even sure he makes any money during the Brown Bag Games."

"Probably not anymore," I said, "but do you honestly think he's doing this for the money? I doubt he started with seven people on the payroll. He probably got close to losing and then added one, then another, then another, until it was just all about maintaining the image of a champion, no matter the cost. He's cracking, Freddie, and we're gonna be the ones to break him."

"I hope you're right. You think we have time for a few quick games before Zak gets here?" Freddie asked, pulling out her phone and checking the time.

I did the same. "Yeah, we've got enough time for one for sure. Two if you get killed as quickly as you did last time. Heck, maybe even *three* if you die that fast."

Freddie grabbed the whiteboard eraser and tossed it at my head. I threw my arms up and blocked it at the last moment. "Very funny, Mr. Sit Back and Wait for Me to Do All the Dirty Work. Is there anything else I can help you with this round to make you more comfortable while you hang out and snipe? Maybe there's some secret magical cushioned chair I could find and bring back for you."

I laughed, wiping dry-erase residue from my forearm. As it turned out, Freddie and I actually had very complementary play styles. I liked to sit back and work the long-range game, picking people off, while Freddie was much more the "kick down the door, guns blazing" kind of gal. We worked so well together as a little shadow team of two that Freddie finished second at the Brown Bag Game two sticky days ago. She had quickly become a thorn in Noah's side, and I felt more confident than ever about going into the next phase of our strategy.

"You still good about the plan on Monday?" I asked as Freddie brought up *Champions Royale* on the TV.

Freddie shrugged. "Look, it's gonna stink to lose my only wingman, but if you going all undercover on Noah is gonna set us up for a glorious victory at the Shoebox Game, then yeah, I'm good."

"The one way we can guarantee someone from Noah's shadow team will turn on him, is to become part of his shadow team," I said. "Keep your friends close—"

"But your enemies closer." Freddie finished the thought. "I'll use the week to keep running those sniping drills you showed me, although I seriously don't feel like I'm getting any better. It just isn't my thing."

"Freddie, you get more kills than I do," I said, mumbling my next words. "You also die quicker, but you'll get it."

"No guts, no glory." Freddie shrugged, not the least bit bothered by the tease.

Halfway through our second game I got a text from Zak, letting us know that he was out front. We ran our players into a huge firefight and managed to take down a few people before being crushed by an ogre.

"You ready to go see what Noah gets up to on a Saturday?" I asked.

Freddie paused as she turned off the TV and lifted up the tree-house trapdoor. "Texcalibur, this was *my* idea. Well, you inviting Zak along for backup was *your* idea, but I'm not about to let my fear of Noah stand in the way of taking him down."

"Doesn't that kinda mean that you're not afraid of him?" I arched an eyebrow.

"No." Freddie spoke with a matter-of-fact tone. "It means that maybe I've just decided to be epically courageous and that I know we need to make sure we've flushed out all the cheaters that we can, and I'm willing to do my part."

"Fair enough." I chuckled, holding up my hands in surrender. Freddie may have not known all the things that Zak and I were doing with the double day to make this plan work, but she was no less committed to seeing it succeed. Once she knew that she had a couple of friends at her back, it was awesome to see how her confidence had blossomed.

Freddie took a deep breath and nodded, gesturing for

me to descend the ladder. "Now that that's settled, lead the way . . . for once."

I hesitated, placing a hand on my chest as if deeply offended. "Was that yet *another* jab at my playing style?"

"You're the mind reader." Freddie smiled. "You tell me."

CHAPTER 23
ROCK, PAPER, SCISSORS

(Discard Saturday—Oct. 9th)

We scrambled down out of the tree house and ran to the front yard to see Zak waving at us from the passenger side of a shiny blue Ford truck. He climbed out and helped me load my bike into the back before we all piled in.

"So you must be Danny and Freddie," Zak's dad said with only a hint of his native Ghanaian accent. He turned around and shook our hands with what was basically a human bear paw. I'd seen baseball gloves smaller than Zak's dad's hand. I buckled my seat belt and ran my hand over the smooth, black leather interior. I glanced over to Freddie, who couldn't have looked more awestruck if Zak had picked us up in a helicopter. I doubted she was used to traveling in a car this nice. Heck, *I* wasn't used to traveling in a car this nice.

After a few minutes, we pulled up to the Pocatello mall, in all its small-town Idaho glory. I'm pretty sure there were grocery stores in Texas that were bigger than the entire Pocatello mall, but, size notwithstanding, it thankfully had the essentials: a GameStop, a pretzel place, a Cinnabon, a Hot Topic, a comic book shop, and a movie theater. Any other stores were pretty much just fluff. Even more important than that, we were hoping to find one more thing at the mall today: Noah.

Earlier in the week, Freddie had caught wind that Noah planned to be at the mall on Saturday morning as part of a promotion for his dad's business. We'd kept tabs on Noah during school hours, but thought we might be able to learn something by seeing what he got up to on the weekend. With that bit of information, I had developed the perfect plan of attack.

☐ Step 1: Buy and relish cinnamon roll from Cinnabon.

☐ Step 2: Go by Noah's family business to see if he is hanging out with any other potential cheaters that would need to be investigated.

☐ Step 3: Browse video games at GameStop.

☐ Step 4: Browse cool T-shirts at Hot Topic.

☐ Step 5: Buy a pretzel.

☐ Step 6: Check on Noah again.

☐ Step 7: Look at comics.

☐ Step 8: Maybe buy another cinnamon roll (it is a discard day after all).

☐ Step 9: Go home.

I read over the steps written in my notebook and had to say that I had rarely put together a better plan for a Saturday morning. We got out of the truck and made our way to the food court. We walked past the Arby's, Sbarro, and Wok This Way, the smell of warm, sweet, cinnamon goodness guiding us to the counter of Cinnabon. I got an order of cinnamon roll centers, while Zak got twisted churros. When it came time for Freddie to order, she froze.

"I'm fine, uh, I don't want anything—"

"Special?" Zak finished her sentence and then turned to the cashier. "She'll have a normal cinnamon roll. I got this one." Zak pulled out a twenty-dollar bill and handed it to the cashier.

Freddie stood wide-eyed, staring at Zak like a kid would Santa Claus. "Are you serious?" Freddie said, reverently taking her cinnamon roll from the worker.

"Yeah, it's no big deal." Zak brushed it off. But it was a

big deal, to Freddie at least. Not that I'd ever really doubted my decision to tell Zak about the double day, but he did have an uncanny ability to continually reassure me I'd made the right choice. Zak was a good dude to the core, and he had just cemented his friendship with Freddie on the unbreakable foundation that is a fresh, gooey, cinnamon-flavored roll. Whatever else happened on this discard day, I'd need to make *sure* I repeated this moment on the sticky day.

After scarfing the cinnamon rolls, we made our way to Noah's dad's business, which was coincidentally directly across from GameStop. A flashing LED sign hung over a shop with blacked-out windows.

"The Pocatello Escape Room," I read.

"Well, he doesn't win any bonus points for originality, but it does look pretty awesome," Zak said.

I'm not sure why it irked me that Noah's family business was something legitimately cool like an escape room, but it did.

"Let's do this," Freddie said, taking a big breath and leading the way into the store.

The lobby had a pair of leather sofas and smelled faintly of fresh paint. Four movie-style posters were hung on a brick wall, depicting the various rooms you could try: Lost in Space, Back to Reality, and the Magic School Bus. The fourth one, Brain Teaser, had a creepy picture of a zombie with the words

Coming in October at the bottom. Underneath each poster was a leaderboard with times and names.

"Hey there, kids," a man said from behind the counter on the opposite side of the room. "Welcome to the Pocatello Escape Room. We've got a weekend promotion going on. All the games are half off, although I would suggest the Magic School Bus for a group your size and age. I've got another group that's about to hit the time limit in there, so the room should be free in about five minutes. You're what, sixth and seventh graders?"

"Sixth grade," I said. "We're actually in your son Noah's class. We play video games together at lunch."

"Ah," Noah's dad said, his jovial customer-service-oriented demeanor dropping a touch. "That's probably the only way you'd ever get his attention. I wouldn't be surprised to hear that his teacher has to send him a text to ask him a question in class."

I actually laughed at the comment. Noah's dad seemed about as frustrated with Noah as anyone . . . almost.

"Is Noah here?" Freddie asked.

His dad pressed his lips together and raised his eyebrows in the exact same expression my dad gave me when I knew he was about to tell me something less than the truth, but he didn't care to hide it. "He hasn't quite made it in yet. He's at his mother's for the weekend, but should be here anytime now."

I noticed Freddie give a thinly veiled sigh of relief. She

was brave enough to face Noah, but it didn't mean she'd be disappointed to not have to go through with it. Just then three kids came out of a door on the far side of the room. Had it been a sticky day, I would have nearly fainted. Jaxson, Braxlynn, and an older boy, who, judging by his similar look and build, could only be Jaxson's brother, came walking toward the counter.

"Welcome back," Noah's dad said, his salesman smile returning. "Did you unlock the secrets of the mysterious magical school bus?"

"We would have solved it forever ago, but my *genius* little brother here kept reading his codes backward." Jaxson's older brother whacked him upside the head as they went to a bank of lockers to retrieve their jackets and phones.

Noah's dad gave an uneasy laugh. "Well, don't be too hard on him, the rooms aren't supposed to be easy. Do you want to take a picture? We'll put it up on our Facebook and Instagram pages." Noah's dad motioned to a corner of the room with a stack of signs that said things like TOTAL GENIUS!, ALMOST!, and NAILED IT!

"As long as you have a sign that says 'I'm with a complete moron.' We easily had that top spot on the leaderboard until we put Bozo the Brainless here in charge of using the cipher wheel." Jaxson's brother shoved Jaxson, who almost tripped over a small end table.

An awkwardness settled on the room like a stifling fog. Jaxson noticed Zak and gave him a slight nod but didn't say a word. Braxlynn briefly looked up from her phone and inadvertently made eye contact with Freddie.

"Oh hey, Braxlynn," Freddie squeaked.

Braxlynn rolled her eyes and went back to her phone, her face oozing with disdain. Something inside me snapped. I took a step forward to say something, but Freddie beat me to it.

"Hey, Braxlynn," Freddie said more forcefully, clearing her throat as she leaned down to get Braxlynn's attention. "I said hey."

Braxlynn slowly tore her gaze from her phone and looked at Freddie like she was something stuck on the bottom of her designer shoe. "Uh, hey."

"Yeah, hey, as in 'Hey, how's it going?'" Freddie took a step forward, growing more confident with every word. "Or 'Hey, remember when we used to be neighbors and would do stuff and you didn't have your face glued to your phone?' It's okay if you actually talk to me, you know? My hand-me-down clothes aren't contagious."

For a moment it was like all the oxygen in the room had been sucked out through an air lock. Braxlynn's disgusted look gave way to true surprise as Freddie amazingly held her gaze. I knew Freddie had talked about being brave, but I wouldn't have been more surprised had she suddenly sprouted a second head.

I took a half step toward Freddie. It was a small movement that I'd hardly meant to even do, but with everyone else standing still it was especially noticeable.

"Well, at least someone's got his girl's back," Jaxson's older brother said.

Braxlynn folded her arms and glared at Jaxson, her eyes echoing the comment. We all waited, the tension growing like someone slowly tuning a violin string tighter and tighter. I braced myself for some biting comment from Jaxson, but he said nothing, not with his voice at least. His message was in his look. I'd been pounded by Jaxson before on a discard day, but being hit by this murderous stare was somehow worse than being clobbered by his fists. It wasn't just the threat of one beating, but the promise of a *hundred* beatings. Despite my discard-day self, I swallowed hard.

When Jaxson finally moved, it was only to grab Braxlynn's arm and march out of the store. He bumped into a sign advertising the weekend promotion and knocked it to the floor but didn't bother stopping.

I stood there, looking back and forth from Freddie to Zak, trying to process exactly what had just happened. In life's game of Rock, Paper, Scissors, people like Jaxson and Braxlynn were rocks to my spineless sticky-day scissors. They used their position and status to smash others, but never did it occur to me what kind of person would be the paper . . . until now. Freddie could never crush them; she would never beat them at their own game. She could stand up to them, however, and use her courage to stifle them.

People like Braxlynn had looks, money, and popularity, and they used them to elevate themselves and put others down. People like Zak had those same things and used them to buy people cinnamon rolls. Jaxson was athletic, and he used it to bully people, while Zak used his physical gifts to *stop* the bullies. He was like a rock that smashed the bully rocks. Noah was good at games and gloated, while Freddie was good at games and wanted nothing more than to share with others. I stared at Jaxson's older brother, who still stood at the counter. Apparently Jaxson got picked on as much as he picked on others, but it wasn't like Freddie didn't have older brothers who made her life miserable. She even had to wear their blasted hand-me-down clothes just to add insult to injury. Some people seemed to act a certain way *because* of their environment, and others acted a different way in *spite* of it. What made the difference was beyond me.

"Friggin' wuss," Jaxson's brother scoffed and followed Jaxson and Braxlynn out the door. "Wait up, Bozo."

There was an extended pause before I turned to Freddie. "Epically courageous, huh?"

Freddie shrugged, trying to play it off like it wasn't the most significant social moment of her life. She might have convinced me had she been able to restrain the purest, most genuine smile I had ever seen in my life.

Noah's dad shook his head. "Kid kept blaming his little brother. We got cameras in there, you know? That older kid couldn't figure his way out of a paper bag. So now that *that's* all over with, you want to give it a go?"

"You guys in?" Zak asked, righting the knocked-over sign before removing his wallet.

Freddie clapped and rubbed her hands together. "I feel like I could wrestle an alligator right now."

Noah's dad barked a laugh. "No gators in here, but this Magic School Bus room has only a thirty percent completion rate, so your work will be cut out for you."

"You give Danny one crack at anything like this, and he'll have it figured faster than anybody," Zak said, turning to me and flashing a meaningful look. "Guaranteed."

"Is that right?" Noah's dad said, the uncomfortable feeling left by Jaxson and his group lifting. "We'll have to see about that."

Our discard-day time was 53:21. Respectable, but not enough to earn us a spot on the leaderboard.

"We'll see you next time." Noah's dad waved as we left the escape room and walked out into the mall.

"What do you want to do next?" Freddie asked, her eyes glittering.

"We could see if they have an exotic-pet store," I offered. "Maybe they have some alligators we can wrestle."

Freddie playfully punched me in the arm. "Sounds like a plan," she said, skipping away.

"Have you ever seen her like this?" Zak asked as we watched her almost collide with a sunglasses kiosk.

I shook my head. "I cannot say that I have."

Freddie's glee lasted the entire afternoon. She was a different person. Well, maybe not a *different* person. More like a purer, happier version of herself. It was an image that stayed with me the rest of the discard day and into the sticky day as we returned to the mall and sat again at the food court, cinnamon rolls and churros on small paper plates in front of us. Freddie was nervous now. Nervous at the prospect of meeting Noah. She had no idea that he wouldn't be there. That we'd instead find Braxlynn and Jaxson.

I repeatedly checked the clock and absently prodded my cinnamon roll centers with a plastic fork.

"You all right, Danny?" Zak asked.

"Yeah, yeah, I'm good, man." I had thought before that it was impossible not to enjoy a cinnamon roll, but I had been wrong. I watched the minutes tick by and slowly chewed my food. If we left within the next two minutes, we'd be at the escape room when Jaxson, Braxlynn, and Jaxson's brother came out, but the thought of Jaxson's glare kept me glued to my seat.

I forced myself to look at Freddie, to confront the fact that if I backed down now, then there was no telling how long, if ever, it would be until she had a moment like she'd had on the discard day.

"Let's go." I sprang to my feet, not trusting my courage to last.

"But you're not done with your cinnamon bites," Freddie said.

"C'mon," I said, walking briskly to the escape room. Zak and Freddie hurried to their feet and followed me as we made our way through the mall. I stopped in front of the escape room and checked the time. They'd be out in the next minute.

"We going in?" Zak asked.

I took a deep breath. "Yeah, let's . . ." I trailed off as I saw the weekend promotion sign that Jaxson had already knocked over.

"Let's what?" Zak asked.

"Let's go to GameStop first, though," I said, breaking my stare and turning around. "I want to check something out real quick."

By the time we came out of GameStop, Jaxson, his

brother, and Braxlynn were long gone. Despite setting a blistering time of 33:46, dumbfounding Noah's dad and earning the top spot by more than ten minutes, it all seemed a bit hollow.

I'd always thought selfishness was a Discard Danny thing, but I wasn't so sure anymore. I guess it was only fitting for life's game of Rock, Paper, Scissors. If rock smashes scissors, and paper covers rock, then scissors was destined to cut paper.

I looked at Zak and Freddie as we bought our ridiculously large pretzels toward the end of our mall trip. Freddie dipped her pretzel into a cup of yellow cheese sauce and took a bite, laughing as it ran down her chin. She couldn't have been happier with how the day had gone, or at least *she* thought she couldn't. *I* knew, however, that she could have, and I'd robbed it from her. I had felt like I was making progress with reconciling my sticky-day and discard-day halves, but maybe I was only kidding myself. I was no better than Braxlynn. I criticized her for her false image of perfection that she peddled around online with her filters and curated poses, but wasn't that the *exact* same thing I was doing with my sticky day?

Choking down guilt with every bite of my pretzel, I vowed to never disappoint my friends again, but even as I had the thought, part of me was afraid that I could never keep that promise.

CHAPTER 24

FRENEMIES

(Sticky Monday—Oct. 11ᵗʰ)

It was sticky-day Monday. I set my lunch tray down on the table and took a seat a few spots away from Noah. I glanced over at Freddie and gave a nearly imperceptible nod. This part of the plan had a few moving parts, so yesterday's discard-day performance during the Brown Bag Game had to have been just right. Luckily, our practicing had paid off. I cued up my game and wiped the sweat from my palms on my pants. I could do this. I knew exactly where SpudMasterFlex and his bodyguards would be dropping in and had shared my strategy with Freddie during the bus ride to school.

I put my two dollars in the brown bag and readied my character, a cloaked elf with a wooden mask. Now that I knew who Noah's minions were, I couldn't believe that I hadn't seen it before. That was the thing about these battle royale games, though. You were so focused on the mad dash for resources and weapons that any evidence of foul play just got lost in the chaos.

Freddie and I dropped into the middle of a rocky outcrop just north of Bandit's Bog, and I quickly snatched up a bow, slingshot, and belt of throwing knives. To the south, SpudMasterFlex and his three bodyguards landed on opposite ends of the bog. We had good cover and the high ground, but Bandit's Bog was famous for its good weapon and item drops. If you could get in and come out alive, you were usually pretty well set up to do some damage.

I pushed up the hill and flanked one of the bodyguards with the gamertag BooterScooter. Peppering her surroundings with arrows, I drove her back to take cover behind a ridge . . . directly below Freddie, who hid behind a set of three large boulders. As planned, Freddie pushed against one of the huge stones and sent it tumbling down the hill.

FreddieCougar splattered BooterScooter

"You gotta be kidding me!" Carolyn, aka BooterScooter, cried from the far end of the lunch table.

I smiled. Getting a boulder kill didn't happen all that often and was one of the more embarrassing ways to die. I sprinted into the bog and found my next target, MasterCheese116, who was busy harvesting attack-boost flowers near the base of a huge tree. I stuck him with two arrows, one in each leg, before he even knew he was being watched. His character dropped to the ground, unable to walk. FreddieCougar came sprinting over a nearby hill, and I gestured toward the crippled MasterCheese116 before taking off to find the third and last bodyguard, CatHissEverdeen. Ten seconds later, another kill notification flashed across my screen.

FreddieCougar pelted MasterCheese116

By now, Noah would be getting nervous. Two of his most trusted bodyguards were down within the first minute of the game and both by Freddie.

I spotted CatHissEverdeen by an open treasure chest at the base of a gnarled swamp bush. I fired a pair of arrows while she donned a suit of heavy plate armor. My shots went wide, and she spun to see my unarmored elf retreat to the trees. Sensing an easy kill, she immediately came barreling after me. I ran in a zigzag pattern and watched throwing-axes thud into the trees around me. I turned the corner behind a row of wild hedges, sprinting past FreddieCougar as she tossed out a bear trap. Within seconds, CatHissEverdeen, fully armored, turned the blind corner and lumbered straight into the trap. Regan Russell, a few seats to my right, yelled as Freddie finished the kill.

FreddieCougar put CatHissEverdeen out of her misery

Three down. One more to go. Freddie would have collected the gear from three different kills. Everyone watching the kill notifications knew that she'd be stacked with loot. This couldn't have worked better. By the time I ran back up the hill to get a better view of the area, FreddieCougar and SpudMasterFlex were already exchanging shots. I rushed downhill and looped back behind SpudMasterFlex. He didn't even know I was there. He had gotten too cocky, too used to winning. I pulled my bow, sighted in my target, and fired as many arrows as I could . . . at FreddieCougar.

I pressed forward and sprinted straight for Freddie, forcing her to shift her attention from Noah to me. I dodged her incoming shots and returned fire, shooting the last of my arrows. I ran past her, forcing her to turn her back to SpudMasterFlex, who predictably took the opening to press his advantage.

SpudMasterFlex assassinated FreddieCougar

"Moldy monkey butts!" Freddie yelled as she slapped the table, causing everyone around her to jump. Her performance was so convincing I'd have to tell Freddie later that she had a future as a drama nerd if this Shoebox Game didn't work out.

I turned my character around to face SpudMasterFlex, made sure that he saw me, and bowed. He paused for a second and returned my bow . . . just before he threw an ax at my head.

SpudMasterFlex chopped Texcalibur

"Gal darn it," I hollered. Before the match was even over, I pulled up my messenger and shot a note to SpudMasterFlex.

The competition is getting better. Your bodyguards aren't. I could have put a knife in your back, but I protected it instead. I'll do it permanently for $5/game, plus $1 for every kill assist I get. I'll be at the Shoebox, but so will Freddie. I heard she came up with the money. My price for that event is $30 plus $5 for every kill assist. Freddie has gotten really good. You need me.

I waited for the game to finish and Noah to collect the brown bag. I watched as he walked out of the lunchroom and paused to check his phone. Ten seconds later a message popped up on my screen.

You're hired.

CHAPTER 25

COOKIES AND TOTS

(Discard Friday—Oct. 15th)

I finished another online round of *Champions Royale* and put my phone down, rubbing my face with both hands. It was late. Just thirty more minutes left in the last discard day before the Shoebox Game. I had spent the entire week playing the game every moment I could spare. Most of my afternoons had been at the Roost, while my lunches were spent serving Noah the Brown Bag Game on a silver platter. It was a weird balance to maintain.

With the help of his shadow team and being able to play the field on a discard day, I could have set up my *mother* to walk away with the brown bag. The Shoebox Game wouldn't be so easy, however. The Shoebox Game forum showed fifty-four confirmed players, the most I'd ever seen for a game.

That meant over a thousand dollars was going to be on the line. The shadow teams would be tighter than normal, and everyone would be bringing their A game. The rules were also different. All the monsters, weapons, and items would be available, and every player would have three lives instead of just one. It was going to be chaos, and the best place from which to strike at Noah would be his inner circle.

In addition to my gaining Noah's trust over the last week, Freddie, Zak, and I had also put considerable effort into testing which shadow teams would squeal back to Noah when shown evidence of his cheating ways. It wasn't hard to tell which ones would. Noah wasn't exactly the non-confrontational type once he found out someone was conspiring against him. We were left with around thirty players who I could reasonably trust to band together to seek and destroy Noah and his team of cheaters. Once the playing field was leveled, it would simply be up to the best man or woman to win.

The cheaters that could be flushed out had been flushed out. Whatever practicing I could do had been done. Noah trusted me completely, and Freddie was chomping at the bit for her chance to put SpudMasterFlex in his place. The only thing left would be to send out the message to the non-cheaters with evidence of Noah's foul play to get as many shadow teams to band together as possible. I'd do that the morning of the Shoebox Game. I didn't exactly want to spring it on them at the last minute, but the longer people knew, the more of a chance that the info would make its way back to Noah.

My stomach grumbled. It was as trustworthy an alarm as my phone for a late-night, discard-day snack. I got up to make my way downstairs when I heard the garage open. Was my dad seriously just coming home? I stood at the top of the stairs and waited. A minute later he came quietly into the house, walking by the light of his phone to the kitchen. I debated whether or not to go downstairs. If he was coming home this late on a Friday night, I doubted he'd be all that happy. But I had been meaning to catch up with him some more about the football game tomorrow. I couldn't afford to be late to the Shoebox Game.

I walked downstairs, sure to make a bit of noise so I didn't scare the crud out of my dad when I wandered into the kitchen in the middle of the night.

"Danny?" my dad said, flashing his phone light in my direction. He stood at the kitchen counter, his tie loosened and skewed to one side. He reached over and turned on the single light above the sink. "What are you doing up?"

"I was coming down to get a glass of water. Are you just getting home?"

"That I am, Danny boy." My dad breathed out. "Look, son. I got some bad news. I don't think I'm going to be able to go to the football game tomorrow."

"Oh," I said. My initial reaction was relief. Getting back from the game in time to go to the Shoebox Game had been a big worry for me. When I saw the look on my dad's face, however, that relief soured to guilt. This meant a lot to my dad and should have meant more to me.

My dad slowly shook his head from side to side. He reached up into the cupboard and removed two glasses, clinking them down onto the counter. He turned and got the milk from the fridge and a packet of Oreos from the pantry.

"Don't tell your mother," he said, stripping back the top of the Oreo package and filling the glasses with milk.

"How many can I have?" I asked, plucking my first one from the package. I snapped one of the sides before dipping into the milk. You got the best milk penetration that way.

"I find with Oreos that you should never start with a number." My dad grabbed two and dunked them at the same time.

We sat in silence for a while, our entire focus devoted to the enjoyment of cookies in the dark.

"I'm sorry I've been so busy, Danny."

"It's okay, Dad," I said.

My dad grabbed a paper towel and wiped black crumbs from his lips. "No, it's not. I'm starting to think this whole thing was a mistake."

I scrunched my eyebrows. "What whole thing?"

"Taking this job. Coming up here." My dad stared off to the side as he spoke. "If it ain't broke, Danny, don't fix it." This wasn't like my dad, or at least it wasn't like the dad I knew.

"I don't know, Dad," I said, reaching for another Oreo. "Sometimes you got to break something perfectly good so you have the pieces to build something even better."

"Oh yeah?" My dad turned down his mouth in surprise. "And where'd you hear that?"

"Saw it on a Lego box."

My dad gave a quiet chuckle. "I am glad to see you doing well. Your mother was worried that the change might, well . . . that it might be hard on you."

My dad didn't like to discuss the "early days" before Dr. Donaldson, but I could read between the lines well enough.

"I'm doing fine, Dad," I reassured him. "So what happened at work today?"

My dad looked to the ceiling and grunted, massaging the back of his neck with one hand. "You ever forget to back up a presentation that you'd spent weeks preparing, only to accidentally save over the top of it?"

While my dad was generally a pretty happy guy, he did come home from work a bit grumpy on occasion. I'd only ever used the double day in those instances to steer clear of him or ensure he didn't make things worse by forgetting something around the house. It had never occurred to me that I might actually be able to help solve the root of the problem at work.

"What time did it happen?"

"Twelve nineteen p.m.," my dad recited. I got the feeling he'd had to talk to more than one person about it today. "I tried the whole afternoon to find some sort of backup or temporary saved file. I'll have to spend all weekend re-creating it since the presentation is on Monday. Sorry, buddy."

"Don't worry, Dad," I said, plunging my ninth Oreo into my milk. It'd been a while since I'd had a moment like this with my dad. A shame we weren't having it on a sticky day. "It's gonna turn out all right."

(Sticky Friday—Oct. 15ᵗʰ)

"You okay, Danny?" my dad asked at the breakfast table. The twins sat in their chairs, smashing their muffins into crumbs and mush.

"Yeah," I said, making a show of rooting through my backpack. "Hopefully I forgot this assignment in my locker. It's due today."

My dad took a swig of orange juice and brought the cup to the sink. "If I had a dollar for every time I'd forgotten something over the years, we could retire to the Hawaiian Islands."

"Wouldn't that be something?" my mom added from the kitchen, stirring a pan of scrambled eggs with a spatula.

"Maybe us absentminded folks should stick together," I said. "Send each other daily reminders or something. If we're both half-brained, maybe we'll round each other out."

"Ha," my dad responded, patting the twins on the head and giving my mom a kiss on the cheek before briskly walking to the door. "Maybe so."

"Badge, Dad," I said, pointing to his work ID badge.

"Well," he said, and jogged back over, plucking his badge off the counter and shaking it in the air. "Maybe you're onto something."

My dad rushed out the door, and my mom gave me a look that said she knew I was up to something but was committed to not prying. She'd seen enough of these last-minute morning reminders to my dad or moving random objects out of reach of the twins to know that Dr. Donaldson hadn't exactly "cured" me of my premonitions.

I finished my breakfast, put my backpack on, and headed for the door to catch the bus.

"Hopefully you find that lost assignment, Danny," my mom called from the kitchen, her lack of real concern revealing exactly how much she didn't believe my story. Not a lot got past my mom.

"I think there's a pretty good chance."

The rest of the morning went smooth, up to and including the last Brown Bag Game that I would ever have to help Noah win. I felt dirty taking payment from Noah, but that money would pay for both Freddie and me to play in the Shoebox Game, so that had some good irony to it.

After Noah walked away with the brown bag, I made brief eye contact with Freddie across the lunchroom. I gave her a quick smile, and she replied with a funny scrunch of the nose. I'd kept my distance from Freddie during bus rides and lunches ever since I started working for Noah. It was probably a ridiculous over-precaution, but the closer I got to the big day, the more nervous I was that something would pop up to derail our plans.

I walked aimlessly around the schoolyard, staring at my shoes and thinking about all the work we had done to prepare for Saturday. I had never put so much time and effort into having one day go a certain way in my entire life. Not even when I snuck out of the house and into the movie theater in the middle of the day to see the last *Venom* movie. I had a lot riding on this. I didn't get anxious about many discard days, but getting a good first crack at the Shoebox Game tomorrow would be absolutely vital for making sure everything went off without a hitch and allow me to adjust my plans if needed.

My phone buzzed, and I pulled it out. It was an alarm to send my dad a reminder. Four minutes from now he would save over his presentation. I stopped walking and worked on my text.

Yo, old man. I just found my assignment. This is your daily friendly reminder to back up all important documents, and to remember to

"Hey!" someone yelled.

I jumped, and my phone tumbled from my fingers, falling to the grass. I looked up, and the blood drained from my body. Jaxson stood not four feet in front of me.

"You taking pictures of Braxlynn?"

"I'm what?" I managed, looking over his shoulder to see Braxlynn and the Clique sitting on their bench. I must have unknowingly wandered over to their bench and stopped behind it when I'd gotten my alarm.

"You were standing behind Braxlynn and her friends with your phone up, doofus. What else would you be doing?"

I blinked hard as if trying to start my brain like it was an old truck engine struggling to turn over on a bad battery. If I didn't send that message to my dad in the next minute or two, then his presentation would be lost. I'd fail him just like I had when he fell asleep and screwed up his neck. *Way* worse than that, actually. But this was a sticky day. This was Jaxson. This looked bad. I needed evasive maneuvers. Abandon ship. Hit the ejector seat. Emergency evacuation. But I just froze.

"I . . . uh," I stammered.

"Yeah, that's what I thought, Texas turd," Jaxson said. "Let's see what's on your phone."

Jaxson made a move to grab my phone off the grass. "Don't touch my phone," I blurted. I wasn't thinking, or maybe it was just some other part of me that was thinking. Just as Jaxson bent down, I reached forward and pushed him as hard as I could. He toppled backward, rolling into Braxlynn and her friends and knocking them down like a human bowling ball scoring a strike. I snatched my phone and ran faster than I had ever run in my life.

"You're a dead man!" I heard Jaxson yell as I zipped between students, sprinting back inside the school, not daring to look behind. I had no plan, no refuge in mind. My shoes squeaked as I flew around a hallway corner. I couldn't find anyone. It was like I was running for my life in a zombie apocalypse wasteland. I had to find a teacher. Where did they friggin' eat lunch?

I heard a door slam open down the hall behind me followed by the heavy slap of sprinting steps. Jaxson would catch me. He'd pound me to a pulp. I barreled around a corner and slammed into an unsuspecting student, his small basket of Tater Tots launching into the air.

"Sorry!" I said, desperately swimming past the kid.

"My tots!" he yelled after me.

Tots . . . wait. Mr. Wilding! Jaxson's thundering steps grew louder. I looked around. Racing forward, I took the next right and dashed up the stairs three at a time. Out of breath, legs ready to collapse, I burst into Mr. Wilding's office.

Mr. Wilding, sitting at his desk, popped out of his seat, his glasses bouncing off his nose. "My goodness!"

"Mr. Wilding." I quickly shut the door behind me and pressed my body against it, shoulders heaving. I took my phone out and sent my text message to my dad. Two minutes to spare. Hopefully he'd see it in time. "Let's hear all about your grandpa and the history of Tater Tots."

CHAPTER 26

DISCARD SBG

(Discard Saturday—Oct. 16ᵗʰ)

"It's gonna be a great day," my dad said from behind the kitchen stove. He flipped half a dozen golden pancakes on the griddle with one hand and prodded at a pan of sizzling bacon with the other. My sisters giggled as they launched handfuls of fluffy scrambled eggs across the table and onto the floor. "It should be a fantastic game. The Idaho State Bengals haven't won their first five games since 1995. They've got a great team this year. Their quarterback's actually from Katy, Texas, would you believe it?"

My mom stumbled out of the bedroom, her hair like a bird's nest and dark circles under her eyes. My mom almost never left the bedroom without being done up, so I knew it could only mean one thing: She was sick.

"Good morning, sunshine!" my dad said, briefly glancing up from draining the bacon grease into an empty tin can.

"Good morning," my mom croaked.

"Sleepy mommy. Go to sleepy, mommy," the twins yelled.

My dad made up a plate of food and set it down at my mom's spot at the table before he even noticed my mom's condition. "Are you okay, honey?"

"I'm wonderful," my mom said, grabbing her plate of food and taking it to the couch, where she slumped down. "Enjoy the game. Don't worry about me. The twins will keep me company."

My dad loved and took care of my mom, but she'd have to be in worse shape than slightly groggy for him to miss a game when he had tickets. Common cold, headache, even the flu wouldn't have been enough. Pneumonia was a maybe.

"You're a trooper, my love," my dad said, walking over to my mom and giving her a kiss on the forehead. "I'll make it up to you. Danny, you almost ready? We need to be heading out."

My text message had come just in time. I'd gotten a reply from my dad when Mr. Wilding was discussing the method his grandfather Merle Wilding had used to congeal the potato scraps into a patty and then eventually a Tater Tot. I'd managed to avoid Jaxson the rest of the afternoon, mainly because I had his and Braxlynn's schedules memorized for just this reason. I wasn't looking forward to that one eventually catching up to me, but I had a Shoebox Game to worry about first.

While seeing the ISU Bengals was a far cry from going to an NFL game in Texas, it took less time to drive, park, and walk to the stadium than it took to just get onto the freeway in Houston. The stadium was small enough that I was able to easily spot Zak and his family up in one of the box seats.

Before settling in, I pulled up my pre-drafted message entitled Grand Shadow Team: Cheaters Among Us. I scanned the list of thirty recipients we'd handpicked as Shoebox Game participants who'd proven they wouldn't squeal back to Noah. With a tap of the screen the message was sent. The wheels were in motion.

The game was a good one, but it was hard to focus with the Shoebox Game on my mind. The score was tied during the last few minutes of the fourth quarter, and I couldn't help but repeatedly glance at my phone and cross my fingers that it wouldn't head to overtime. The opposing team drove the length of the field and set up for a game-winning field goal. With the crowd cheering wildly, I'm pretty sure I was the only ISU fan that was actually rooting for them to lose, and lose they did. The ball sailed through the uprights and gave the Weber State Wildcats a three-point victory.

My dad cursed under his breath but was happy when I told him how much I had enjoyed the game. Zak texted me to wish me luck and let me know that he'd be pretty late to the Shoebox Game since his dad was taking him to meet some of the players. That was fine. Zak's part in this plan was over. It was up to me and Freddie now. The roads were pretty busy getting home, but it was only the difference of five or ten minutes. Not exactly Houston traffic.

We walked back into the house to a war zone of toys, stuffed animals, and couch cushions. Bags of cereal were dumped all over the carpet. My mom was passed out on the couch, and my sisters' mischievous laughter echoed from upstairs.

"Oh dear," my dad said. "Danny, can you start cleaning this up? I'll get your mother to bed."

I checked my phone. I had twenty minutes before the Shoebox Game started. It would take me five minutes to bike to the park if I hustled. "Sure, Dad." I launched into a cleaning frenzy that would put Mary Poppins to shame, and on a *discard* day to boot. By the time I had things somewhat back to normal, I had eight minutes to get to the park.

"Wow, nice job, son," my dad said, inspecting my handiwork.

"Thanks, Dad. Hey, I know it might be a bad time, but a bunch of kids from school are meeting at the park right now for a big game, and I was wondering if I could go."

"The park? That's great. Better than you being cooped

up playing video games or something. I'd give you a ride, but I need to keep one eye on the twins and another on your mother. Actually, probably both eyes on the twins."

"Thanks, Dad. No problem. I'll ride my bike."

I rushed out to the garage, hopped on my bike, and raced down the street. It was a gorgeous fall day. I zipped through the streets and made my way out to the river, the autumn wind whooshing past my ears. Even though it was a discard day, I was still nervous, and the bike ride felt good to burn off some of my anxious energy. I glanced back and saw a couple more kids on bikes behind me, no doubt hurrying to get to the Shoebox Game as well. I made good time getting to the park and turned the final corner, only to slam on my brakes. I bucked off my seat and almost flew over my handlebars as my bike skidded to a stop in the gravel. Jaxson stood in the center of the path.

"Care to read my mind, Texas turd?" Jaxson said, as two of his henchmen came up behind me, blocking my retreat. I was surrounded.

I swallowed hard. I knew I'd have to confront Jaxson sooner or later, but this was sooner than sooner. I didn't have much time left to get to the Shoebox Game, and once the game started, you couldn't join late.

"I don't know what's on your mind, but can I please get past? I've got to get to a game."

Jaxson made a buzzer sound effect. "Wrong answer. Give me your phone, turd."

"Look, man, I can't give you my phone, but I didn't take a picture of Braxlynn. I swear to you."

"Then why won't you show me your phone?" Jaxson took a step toward me. I didn't have *time* for this. If I gave him my phone, there was no telling what he would do with it. If I didn't give him my phone, he might just take it by force. If I could get to the clearing with the other gamers, there'd be enough kids to step in and stop this. I ran away from him once, I could do it again.

"Fine." I put my hands up. "I'll show you my phone, but when you find nothing, you have to give it right back." I dismounted from my bike and very slowly set it down. I'd have to do this quick. As I put the bike on the ground, I grabbed a handful of gravel and flung it in Jaxson's face. He flinched backward, and I dashed in the direction of the clearing where the other gamers were gathered. I could do this—

I slammed into the dirt, flattened by what felt like a pickup truck. I wheezed, my lungs paralyzed from the impact. I gulped for air, Jaxson's voice filling my ears. "You think you're clever? Read my mind and tell me what happens next."

He flipped me over and put his knee on my chest, making it even harder to jump-start my breathing. My lungs would collapse. I'd never breathe again. Jaxson's rage and carelessness would kill me right here and now.

I finally, somehow, took a rasping, shuddering breath.

"C'mon, Texas turd stain. Read my mind."

I should have said something like, *I've learned my lesson. I won't talk to you or Braxlynn ever again, oh great Jaxson, king of Snake River Middle School.* But it didn't really matter with kids like Jaxson. I had thrown gravel in his face, run from him twice, and denied him looking at my phone two days in row. He wasn't going to just let me off the hook. In situations like this, Discard Danny went down in a blaze of glory.

"It's hard to do when there's nothing there . . . Bozo the *Brainless*."

Jaxson paused, his face twisted in a mix of surprise and rage, most likely wondering how I knew what his brother had called him at the escape room in front of Braxlynn . . . then he went *nuclear.* He bellowed like a madman and pummeled me with heavy, hard fists. He stood up, and I curled in like an armadillo as kicks pelted my body. There was no one to pull him off me this time. Sometime during the beating I must have blacked out, because by the time I opened my eyes, Jaxson and his goons were gone . . . with the front wheel of my bike, apparently.

I grunted and gingerly sat up. My head swam and throbbed

like my heart was now lodged in my skull. I sighed but stopped short, a shooting pain lancing through my ribs like the ghost of Jaxson was still getting in shots.

"What the deuce?" I said, looking down at the crotch of my pants, which was wet. "Don't tell me I . . ." I trailed off as I saw my discarded water bottle. How very classy of Jaxson and his buddies. I looked around for my phone and finally saw it discarded in the dirt some twenty feet away.

I looked at the time. "No, no, no." I gritted my teeth and struggled to my feet. I left my bike and hobbled down the trail to the Shoebox Game as fast as my busted-up body would take me. Noah's taunting voice echoed from the trees as I approached the designated spot. A huge crowd filled the hidden clearing, a perfect place for a secret gathering. About twenty kids were still in the game with huddles of people around each of them looking over their shoulders. Freddie was still in it, but so were six of Noah's cheaters.

I limped over to Freddie, who saw me out of the corner of her eye but didn't look over. "Where have you been? It's a disaster." Freddie's fingers blitzed over her phone, and she sounded on the verge of tears until she glanced in my direction and did a double take. "Holy fish farts and rat boogers, what happened to you? Are you okay?"

I wiped some blood from my nose, which I just now noticed was bleeding. "Who, me? I'm great. Just thought I'd go play with Jaxson and his buddies on the way over. I'm not late, am I?"

"Danny, take a seat or something." Freddie put her phone down to help me get settled against a tree. "Just chill for a second and let me focus."

I stole a glance at Freddie's screen. She was doing well with six kills and two lives left and looked to have a little squad of her own as they pushed their way to Fangthorn Peak. Her improvised shadow team, however, turned on Freddie before she even had a chance to threaten SpudMasterFlex and his cheater punks. It was hard to blame them too much. It was supposed to be an every-man-for-himself game after all. Eventually they'd have to turn on each other, and without someone to watch her back, Freddie had to fight off both SpudMasterFlex's crew and part of her own. Her last death came at the business end of a two-hundred-yard snipe from SpudMasterFlex. She ended up placing eighth overall.

Noah stood on top of a picnic table, grabbed the shoebox, and roared in victory. Half the crowd started to boo and a few frustrated kids yelled for their money back, but no one had the guts to make a move. The reaction from the gamers only seemed to make Noah's smile grow wider.

"We need to get you to a hospital or something," Freddie said, putting her phone down and inspecting my battered face.

I knew how much winning this Shoebox Game had meant to Freddie. I knew she was dying on the inside, but for her to bottle it all up and look after me just showed how good of a friend she really was.

"I'm fine, Freddie. It looks worse than it is."

"Have you *seen* what it looks like?" she said, eyebrows rising.

"Uh, no, actually."

"Pleasure doing business with ya, puke stain," Noah said to Freddie as he walked by, shoebox under one arm and a trail of his cronies in his wake. "I would tell you to stick to solving escape rooms, but I enjoy taking your money too much. I truly hope to see you again next year . . . if you can scrounge together enough money."

Freddie stood up and took two steps toward Noah, her nostrils flaring like an enraged bull ready to charge. "You're a cheating, snot-gargling dork face. And half this group knows it! Come play me online, and I will wash the floor with your blood and use your skull for a mop bucket."

Noah actually took a step back at this last comment. "Whatever, psycho," Noah said, warily eyeing Freddie as he retreated to the trees.

"Wow," I managed. She wasn't kidding about this epically courageous thing. "Savage."

Freddie turned to me, shaking and with tears welling in

her eyes. "I can't *believe* that mold-sniffing turd nugget got the last laugh. He won *again*, Danny. We . . . lost."

I nodded slowly. She was right. I had never been beaten so thoroughly and completely in my entire life. Not only did I fail to get the information I would need to pull off a sticky-day victory, but I had no idea how I was going to get past Jaxson to even *play* in the Shoebox Game. Heck, my football team had even lost.

Maybe if I hadn't run my mouth to Jaxson, I could have made it to the Shoebox Game on time, but I hadn't even tried. Discard Danny just did his thing yet again. After robbing Freddie of her moment at the escape room, I had vowed to never let her down again, and yet here I was.

I turned and spat a loogie of blood onto the grass, thankful I had the double day to fix my mistakes and terrified because I had no friggin' clue how I was actually going to do it.

CHAPTER 27
YIN AND YANG

(Discard Saturday—Oct. 16ᵗʰ)

I peered over the steering wheel of my parents' minivan, headlights illuminating a dark gravel road on the edge of town. I saw a sign for the rock quarry and kept driving, trying my best to keep the car straight. I had waited until just after eleven o'clock for my little joyride for several reasons. One, I wouldn't be able to "borrow" my parents' car until they were asleep. Two, fewer people on the road meant that I might actually reach my destination without someone noticing me and calling the cops. And three, in less than an hour, at midnight, no matter what I was doing (asleep or wide awake) the double day would work its magic, and I would find myself waking up on sticky Saturday. That way I didn't have to worry about making my way back home or the fallout from my parents freaking out if they happened to find me and the car missing.

I parked the van next to the quarry's perimeter chain-link fence and opened the trunk. I removed a large backpack and a big pair of bolt cutters, which I used to snip an opening in the fence. The backpack (its contents clinking and clanking) probably weighed half as much as I did and would have been difficult to carry even without my bruises from earlier in the day. My parents hadn't really accepted the excuse that I had crashed my bike into a tree, but I didn't want to spend the evening in a battle between my parents and Jaxson's, so I stuck to my story.

I walked around the quarry for a while until I found the biggest pit and gingerly lowered my backpack to the ground. I unzipped it and took out a cup of my mom's fine china. I tossed it over the edge of the pit and watched it fall until it shattered against a boulder with a satisfying *crash*. I threw another cup and Frisbeed out a plate before calling Zak.

"Hello," Zak said groggily.

"Hey, man." *Crash.*

"Dude, it's like the middle of the night."

"No," I said, launching a bowl end over end into the night air. "It's eleven forty-seven."

"Are you *outside?*" Zak asked, turning on a lamp and sitting up. "What the heck are you doing . . . wait. It's still discard Saturday, isn't it?"

"Yep." *Smash.* "I took my parents' car down to the quarry to blow off a little steam and smash some stuff. I would have invited you, but something tells me you would have said no."

"What makes you say that?" Zak said, yawning.

"Uh, *you*, actually. I've asked you before. You said no. We've been over this, Zak. You're always along for the ride, but you're much more comfortable with Sticky Danny's speed."

Zak rubbed his face with both hands. "Well, considering that's the only Danny I actually know, I'd say that isn't a bad thing. And for the record, I think I've gotten into a sensible amount of mischief in my time, thank you very much. I apologize if stealing a car, breaking into a quarry, and destroying valuables is just slightly over the line for me. Every time I meet Discard Danny it's like it's the first time for me, by the way. So what's going on?"

I pulled out a Snickers bar, unwrapped it, and took a bite. "I don't know how I'm going to pull it off tomorrow. I need to go to the game with my dad, and there's no way to stop the twins from destroying the house. At the very most I will have about ten minutes to make it to the Shoebox Game, I have no one to give me a ride to the park because my mom is sick, and I have no way of knowing where Jaxson's buddies started following me."

"Can you go a different way or something?" Zak asked.

"Not with the time crunch. I was looking it up on Google Maps and couldn't really see a different route out there that I could take in time. You sure you can't get home any earlier?"

Zak clicked his tongue. "No, man. I didn't get home until like an hour after the game. I could try shooting Jaxson a text in the morning, but I'm not sure what good it would do. We know each other, but we're not friends."

I grabbed a stack of plates and spun them out into the air one after another. "So do I even *try* to go? Did you *see* my pic on *Duds* today? It has more comments than the last ten posts put together."

"You saw that, huh?" Zak said, scratching the back of his neck.

"Uh, yeah, Zak. I saw that." After I'd dragged myself home from the Shoebox Game, I checked *Dud Spuds* and was greeted with a pic of me unconscious in the dirt next to my bike with the caption *Probably should have kept his training wheels on a little bit longer. Got scared, peed his pants, fell down, got a boo-boo.*

"I've got an idea," Zak said tentatively. "You won't have to face Jaxson and Noah won't win, but you aren't going to like it."

"Sounds pretty good so far. I'm listening."

"You familiar with something called a scorched-earth strategy?"

I *was* familiar with the term. It had come up a few times in social studies when talking about conflicts like the Civil War and World War II. When an army withdrew from or advanced through a location it would sometimes burn everything useful to the ground so the pursuing enemy would be left with nothing. *Scorched Earth* was also the name of one of my favorite old-school computer games, which was probably why I actually remembered the term.

"You're saying if I can't win the Shoebox Game that I *destroy* it?"

Zak shrugged. "It's an option. One anonymous phone call to someone like Noah's dad with the details of the Shoebox Game and the whole thing would go up in smoke. You'd probably get a lot of kids in trouble, but if you made the phone call early enough then no one would question why you didn't show. You could probably even make up an excuse for Freddie to stay home. Live to fight another day."

However much I didn't want to be the guy to bring down the Shoebox Game, Zak's plan was probably the best one I had right now. But there was no way I could know what the ripple effect would be of nuking the Shoebox Game. With that many kids getting in trouble, there would be a few that would confess about the Brown Bag Game. Destroying this one chance could destroy all future chances as well.

It was a last resort. One I didn't want to take. I *had* to

figure out a way to ditch Jaxson and make this work. My stomach tied itself in a knot. Even if I *did* manage to make it to the Shoebox Game, I never got the chance for a dry run. I would be flying blind on the sticky day. I had no idea how and if the shadow teams would band together, whether I would make a critical error, whether I had discovered all the cheaters, or whether Noah had some other trick up his sleeve. Getting to see how the Shoebox Game played out on the discard day had been crucial to my plan. "I don't want to give up, but I can't see that look on Freddie's face again. Not on a sticky day." I pulled out some more china and tossed it on the rocks.

"Can I tell you something else, Danny?" Zak said, yawning.

"I didn't wake you up to stare at you."

Zak twisted his mouth and gave a little sigh. "I think you should forget the scorched-earth strategy."

I was about to fling out another plate but stopped. "You just suggested it like two seconds ago."

"I know," Zak said. "I pointed it out as an option, but I don't think it's the solution. Consider fully, act decisively. It's a judo thing."

"Okay, Sensei Zak. How do I not fail Freddie, then?"

"This might sound a little weird, but I don't think this is really about Freddie."

"What are you talking about?" I said, tossing the plate. "Of course it is."

Zak slowly shook his head. "Look, this whole Shoebox thing started as a way for you to bring some balance to your double day, remember? Pull your yin and yang together. I think that describes Discard and Sticky Danny pretty well. Freddie became part of it, and she's awesome and I want her to win as much as anybody, but you haven't been doing this just for her. It's okay to admit you're doing this for you, because honestly . . . you need it. Here, look at this."

Zak turned his phone around and pointed it at a wooden-framed quote. Japanese symbols were at the top with the English translation below.

" 'Vision without action is a daydream, and action without vision is a nightmare,' " I said, reading the words.

"Remind you of anyone?"

"Maybe." It was pretty clear. Discard Danny acted without much thought, and Sticky Danny thought without much action. "Okay, so what *do* I do?"

"You gotta pull together your yin and yang."

I knew what he meant; I just couldn't see how it was possible. I also knew that it needed to happen. Nuking the Shoebox Game would be like avoiding Jaxson at the escape room all over again, not just because it would let Freddie down, but because it would let *me* down.

"Pull together my yin and my yang, huh?" I said, fishing around in my bag for the last few pieces of tableware. "I knew there was a reason I chose the only half-Japanese kid in town to be part of the Double Day Duo."

Zak rolled his eyes. "Yin and yang are *Chinese*, Danny. You chose me because I'm awesome and I'll answer your phone calls at midnight."

"Or on the toilet."

"I would never."

"You *would*." I nodded knowingly. I checked the time: 11:59 p.m. I wasn't ready, but it didn't matter. Sticky Danny and Discard Danny had to come together on this. Somehow I had to have both vision and action and find the guts to do everything without a practice run. Before I threw out the last piece of fine china, all went black.

CHAPTER 28
YAY, BIKE RIDE

(Sticky Saturday—Oct. 16ᵗʰ)

Two days in a row of my Dad's Saturday breakfasts were usually a double-day treat I would never pass up, but I hardly touched my pancakes, bacon, and eggs. After breakfast, I made sure to hide all the cereal at the top of the pantry and joined my dad in the car. I was used to having to do a bit of acting on a sticky day, but it took all my best moves to keep my dad from noticing the dread that gnawed at me like a hundred zombie rats. I'd normally use a sticky-day football game to make some amazing prediction of the score or a certain play. I'd only guess it directly on the nose every once in a while. Sometimes I'd even say the right score but guess the wrong team. I didn't want to come off as a psychic or anything, but I did have fun with it. Not today, though. Today I was too distracted.

I sent Zak a text letting him know the situation, but that I knew he couldn't do anything to help me. The football game ended the same way it did on the discard day, and we rushed home to the same chaotic situation minus the cereal, which actually saved me about five minutes of vacuuming.

"Wow, nice work, son," my dad said, looking over the clean room.

This was it. The moment had arrived so fast, and I still didn't know what to do. "Thanks, Dad. Hey, would it be possible for you to give me a ride to Riverside Park? There are some friends from school meeting up there, and I don't want to miss out. I can get a ride home."

"How about you take your bike? It'd do you good to get some exercise, yeah? Plus I need to keep one eye on the twins and one eye on your mother."

"Or both eyes on the twins," I added.

"Took the words right out of my mouth."

Crud. I was a dead man. My time was up, and I didn't have a plan. Defeated, I took out a business card I'd grabbed from the Pocatello Escape Room and looked at the contact number. I knew I needed to stand up to Jaxson, to meld my yin and yang, but there was no way to do that without getting my face beat in, missing the Shoebox Game, and becoming the Dud Spud of the decade. My only out was scorched earth, and I figured calling Noah's dad would probably do the trick.

I took a deep breath and dialed *67 for a caller ID block before punching in the rest of the numbers. I glanced over my shoulder and walked out to the garage, where my dad wouldn't hear me.

"If it wasn't for my friggin' little sisters," I mumbled while dialing. "The whole world revolves around them. They could get away with murder, all just because they're sooooo cute."

"Pocatello Escape Room, this is Gary."

I froze. This was it. There'd be no turning back once I made this move. Sticky Danny was in the driver's seat, and his foot was on the gas. I sighed, glancing around the garage at the clutter of unorganized tools, camping equipment, and empty moving boxes.

"Hello? Is anyone there?"

I turned and stared at the twins' bike trailer, which currently sat on top of the lawn mower. The bike trailer. That was it! I hung up the phone and sprinted inside to find my dad.

"Dad," I said, trying not to sound more excited than I should. "You know what? You've been working hard, and mom is sick. How about I pop the twins in the trailer and take them on a bike ride?"

My dad couldn't have looked more shocked if I had asked him if I could drive the minivan to the park . . . but it was a good kind of shocked. "Well, I don't know, son. That's awfully kind of you. They do love bike rides. Do you think you can pull them?"

"Dad, no problem." I stared expectantly at my dad. There was no way my mom would let me take the twins by myself, but my dad was way laid-back with this kind of thing. He always talked about how when he was a kid, he'd leave the doors unlocked and stuff.

"Okay, but don't be gone too long, yeah?"

I thanked my dad and rushed upstairs. "Hey, girls, you want to go on a bike ride?"

"Bike ride?" they said in unison, popping up from under a mountain of stuffed animals.

"Yay, bike ride!" I said enthusiastically, and clapped my hands.

I ran to the kitchen and filled up two sippy cups with apple juice, checked the twins' diapers, and shuffled them out to the garage. They tottered over to the trailer, which was essentially a small tent on wheels at the end of a pole, and climbed in. I fastened the trailer to the back of my bike and buckled the twins in their seats before zipping the tent portion shut.

"Let's go, you little stinkers," I said, pushing off and heading down the driveway. "Let's hope your adorable powers overrule Jaxson's jerk strength."

"Dorble powers!" the twins yelled as I pedaled furiously down the street.

My legs burned as I tried to keep good time. I'd saved a few minutes by not having to clean up cereal but had spent those minutes getting the twins in the trailer. I needed to hustle. At the corner of Tyhee Road and Rio Vista, I spotted Jaxson's two friends about twenty yards back. I brought my bike to a stop and made a show of going around to check on the twins, unzipping the door and talking very loudly.

"Hello, Alice. Hello, Sarah. Are you being good girls?"

"Yes, Danny," Sarah said. "We be da best girls. Bike wide!"

I leaned down and gave them each a hug before zipping them back up and continuing down the road to the park. I glanced over my shoulder a few times but saw no trace of the two goons. A few minutes later and I came up on the spot where Jaxson had beaten me to a pulp. I slowed down as I turned the corner and braced myself for Jaxson. I hit my brakes and came to a stop. There he was in the middle of the trail, just like on the discard day.

"Hey, Jaxson, what's up?" I said, trying and failing to steady my voice. As if my heart wasn't beating hard enough from the ride, it now it felt like it was about to erupt from my chest and flop onto the gravel.

He hesitated as he noticed my sisters in the trailer. "What are *you* doing?" I could tell he wanted to add on an insult like *turd* or *doofus*, but the way he said the phrase was enough of a threat.

"Oh—you know—out for a ride," I stammered as I glanced back at my sisters before forcing myself to meet his eyes. It was the same look of restrained anger I'd seen at the escape room. I got an idea. "Trying to be a good *older brother* and all. You know how it is."

"Danny's da best!" one of my sisters yelled from the trailer. "Bike wide!"

"You know how demanding siblings can be," I said, forcing a laugh.

Jaxson narrowed his eyes, then slowly pedaled his bike next to mine. He spoke low so my sisters couldn't hear. "You're a dead man. Turd stain."

I must have been holding my breath, because by the time he turned the corner, I felt like I was going to faint. I'd done it. Sticky Danny had gotten past Jaxson.

"Let's go to the park!"

"The park," I said, turning the word over in my head. I checked my phone. "The Shoebox Game. I can still make it."

I pushed off and pedaled like I was in the last leg of the Tour de France. The girls squealed with excitement every time I went over a bump. I pulled through the trees and saw a group of what had to be a hundred kids scattered around the small clearing, either idly chatting or with their faces buried in their phones for some last-minute practice. No doubt some were talking about the message I had sent earlier in the day. With only fifty-four confirmed players, the remainder of the crowd must have been there for support. Freddie's face lit up like a Christmas tree when she saw me.

"I was getting nervous," she said, glancing down at the time on her phone.

"What—that I wouldn't show?" I laughed, removing my helmet and wiping the sweat from my forehead. "Nothing in the world could have stopped me from making this."

"Glad to hear it," she said. From the look on her face I could tell that she was focused. "You ready to roll?"

"Yeah, I just gotta go pay first."

I walked over to the central picnic table, where about a dozen kids gathered around Noah. The shoebox, spray-painted gold, sat in the middle of the table.

"Hey, no little kids allowed!" Noah said, looking over my shoulder at my sisters, who pressed their faces against the mesh siding of the trailer.

"Stuff it," I said, pulling out my money and jamming it in the shoebox. "It's on like *Donkey Kong*!"

"We want to play!" one of my sisters screamed.

"One moment," I said, holding up a finger and running back to my bike.

"Okay, girls, you need to sit here and be quiet for a few minutes while I play my game." I bent down and looked at my sisters through the mesh siding. I might as well have asked a fish to stay dry, but it was worth a shot.

"We want to play a game," Alice said, pointing to my phone.

"Yeah, we want to pway a game," Sarah echoed. "We want the game."

I glanced back and saw a scrawny kid with long black hair stand on top of the picnic table and cup his hands around his mouth. "The Shoebox Game starts in five minutes!"

I had to think of something to keep these girls busy.

"Do you girls want ice cream?"

"Ice cream!" they yelled, throwing their little arms up.

"Okay, we can get ice cream, but you have to be good while I play."

"We don't want ice kweam," Sarah said, her chubby features scrunching.

I grunted a sigh. "If you girls weren't so darned cute . . ." I trailed off, getting an idea. I looked around at the crowd. I needed someone I knew who looked like they were bored.

"Hey, Amy!" I called out, walking up to one of the girls I'd done the mind-reading trick to the very first day at school. She was standing by herself with no phone, the most desperate of all positions to be in. "Sorry to bother you, but I had to watch my sisters and really wanted to play in the game today. Do you think you could play with them for a little while?"

"Did you read my mind again, or could you just tell from my face that I was already bored?"

"Uh, both?"

She followed me over to my sisters, who were just beginning to finagle the zipper open on their trailer.

"Hey, twinsies, I brought a friend." I unzipped the door the rest of the way and then turned back to Amy. "I owe you big-time."

"I require an IOU of one free mind-reading trick of my choosing."

I held out my hand, and we shook on it. I would have agreed to just about anything at that moment. "Deal."

I got my phone out, fired up the game, and joined the private Shoebox Game lobby. All the training, all the planning, all the strategizing, it was all behind me now. I had made it. I felt like just getting here was challenging enough, but now we had to take down Noah. This was a sticky day weeks in the making. It would be a sticky day to remember. "*Now*, it's on like *Donkey Kong*!"

CHAPTER 29

STICKY SBG

(Sticky Saturday—Oct. 16th)

The same scrawny kid with the long black hair got back up on the picnic table with a small clipboard in one hand. "Registration is now closed. There are fifty-four participants for this year's fall event. The Shoebox Game is *Champions Royale*, solo variant with three lives each. All items, monsters, and weapons are unlocked and available on the map. Best of luck and may the best player win!"

I sat against the trunk of a thick oak tree and jostled my earbuds into place. Butterflies spun around my gut like rocks in a clothes dryer. This was supposed to be my second time going through this. There were too many unknowns. Would the shadow teams band against Noah and his cheaters, and for how long? In the end, there could be only one winner, and even the non-cheaters would eventually have to turn on each other. Luckily, I had three lives to figure it all out, so that at least gave me a fighting chance.

You ready for this, Texcalibur?

A text from Freddie flashed across my screen. She sat about twenty feet away from me to avoid suspicion that we were working together. I looked in her direction, and we locked eyes. She was ready. I tried my best to reflect that same confidence, but I didn't feel it. I gave a shallow nod and wiped my sweaty hands on my pants, cracked my knuckles, and watched the countdown timer on my screen tick away: 5, 4, 3, 2, 1.

"And so it begins!" the in-game *Champions Royale* announcer bellowed.

My character dropped from the sky. I floated over to the far south of the map near a formation of rocks called Ogre's Boulders. Noah had sent me a message the day before saying that he planned to drop on Lonely Island, which was directly west of Ogre's Boulders. We were supposed to meet near the bridge by the edge of Wishing Well Woods as soon as we geared up.

Two other players floated in to my right and landed about a hundred yards to the northeast at Buried Boneyard, a giant overturned skeleton of an ancient dragon. I checked all the usual spots under loose rocks, in hidden crevices, and on top of the tall boulders and came away with a ten-pack of throwing stars, some light armor, a blue-strength short sword, and the Staff of Vipers, which would allow me to command an army of snakes at Bandit's Bog. Not a bad start. I scrambled to the top of the boulders and peered at the other two players grabbing loot at the Boneyard. They definitely weren't in any hurry to attack each other, which was good, because one of them was FreddieCougar and the other one was BuckinBlueBronco, a non-cheater from my second-period class. They were also both wearing white sashes on their belts. The item was part of the default skin, so every player had one, but no one ever wore it. Today, unbeknownst to Noah and his crew, it was the marker of someone who had accepted my invitation to the Grand Shadow Team.

I selected the emote to have my character wave and then point to the west. They waved back in reply, and I hopped down and ran to my meeting point with Noah. There were plenty of ways I could play this, yet another reason to want a discard-day practice run. I could sabotage Noah right off the bat, kill a couple of people for him to gain his trust before stabbing him in the back, or wait until the very end. They all had their pros and cons, but *Champions Royale*, like many other battle royale games, was all about momentum. You wanted to take an early lead, gather the good gear, build a bigger lead, and ride it to the end. A slow start was usually a quick end.

I waited just inside the tree line of Wishing Well Woods near the Lonely Island bridge. A notification flashed up on my screen.

SpudMasterFlex clubbed StanTheM@n

Ten seconds later, I saw SpudMasterFlex cross over the bridge, hefty club in hand. I leaned out from behind the trees and waved him over to the cover of the dense woods. He glanced around and sprinted toward me. I scouted the way to the middle of the woods, where a stone well stood in the middle of a small clearing. Players could drop an item down the well and crank the handle for ten seconds to pull up a higher-class item. You could do it as many times as you wanted, but the ten-second requirement left you exposed each time. With me on guard, however, SpudMasterFlex would technically be able to upgrade all of his gear.

I crept into the clearing and scanned around before turning and waving Noah forward. He ran up to the well, tossed in his wooden club, and cranked away on the handle, pulling up a woodsman's ax. I motioned for him to go again, so he dropped the ax into the well and pulled up a frosted broadsword, which could shoot ice shards as long as the player had full health. He turned to go, but I selected the "strut my stuff" emote, which made my character strut around like a supermodel on a fashion runway. It made my elf character look ridiculous, but it was the universal sign for showing off your armor. Noah got the message, removed his armor, and tossed it in the well . . . just as FreddieCougar hit him with a bottle of alchemist's fire. SpudMasterFlex spun around to see where it had come from, but it was too late.

FreddieCougar melted SpudMasterFlex

"Are you kidding me?" Noah screamed as he shot up from his seat at the picnic table. A murmur washed over the other gamers as they saw the kill notification.

I was sure Noah was boring holes into the side of my head with his eyes, but I didn't look up. My cover was blown. There was no turning back now . . . or was there? I sprinted over to Freddie and Bronco as they sifted through SpudMasterFlex's loot. I got their attention and dropped all my weapons at their feet. FreddieCougar stared at me and shrugged, not sure what I was up to. I selected an emote to make my character kneel and bow his head. She nodded before swiping at me with her newly acquired frosted broadsword. My player iced over, and she swiped at me again, shattering my body into a hundred frozen pieces.

FreddieCougar shattered Texcalibur

"What?" I yelled, doing my best to imitate an angry Noah. The move was risky. I willfully gave up one of my three precious lives early in the game in the hopes that Noah would still trust me. I could have used that life to get rid of other players or even go toe-to-toe with Noah, but eliminating SpudMasterFlex was not an easy task . . . unless I could walk him into another trap. After I did it a second time, he'd know something was going on and the gig would be up, but then he'd only have one life left, I'd hopefully have two, and Freddie might still have all three at that point. It was worth the risk.

I respawned and dropped through the sky. I didn't know exactly where SpudMasterFlex would drop, but I knew that he'd be trying to meet up with more of his cheaters, get geared up, and make his way to Fangthorn Peak as soon as he could. There were now other monsters to control, but the dragon would still reign supreme.

The map was huge, and the chances of stumbling on Noah without a designated meeting spot were very slim, unless I went straight to Fangthorn. Dropping in on Fangthorn wasn't

281

something I typically did since I didn't ever seem to get very good loot there, and without the wizard's cloak, the dragon was useless. I needed to find Noah, however.

I steered my glider to the east side of Fangthorn Peak about halfway up, where a small thatched-roof village sat perched on a ledge. Luckily, the houses hadn't been looted yet, and I managed to scrounge together a steel breastplate, a magical throwing spear, and the Ring of Meteors, a pretty powerful magical object that could rain down chunks of flaming rock. It wasn't very accurate, but if you needed to cause a lot of damage over a given area, there wasn't anything better in the game.

Two kill notifications popped up for Freddie, followed by a third. I smiled. She was on point today. I walked to the edge of the village to a large telescope mounted precariously next to the ledge. The village was high enough that I could get a decent view of a good portion of the map. I scanned from Joyless Jungle to Floating Castle, past Bandit's Bog, Towering Trees, and Haunted Pines. Multiple skirmishes appeared in the distance, but I saw no sign of SpudMasterFlex. It killed me to play this slow and cautious. I wasn't exactly as aggressive as Freddie, but I definitely wasn't the type of player to just hide in a bush and wait the game out. I needed more gear.

SpudMasterFlex darted FreudianSlippers

I read the kill notification. It was from eighty-three yards out. An impressive shot with the blowgun. Nothing got me itching to duke it out with SpudMasterFlex in a long-range showdown like seeing him bag a snipe. If I was going to hang around Fangthorn waiting for Noah, I was at least going to loot the place, especially with the magical items no longer restricted. There were things like the Helm of Infinite Sight, which would let me find anyone on the map; Darkon's Blackness, which would turn the whole map pitch-dark for five seconds for everyone but me; the Enchanted Timekeeper, which would rewind the last five seconds of gameplay if I ever got killed; and so on.

I left the village and made my way around to one of the numerous caves that ran through the mountain. After checking out a few of the best spots, I unearthed a bow with a quiver of lightning arrows and a pair of ventriloquist boots, which made my footsteps sound like they were coming from a different direction. A neat little item, but nothing incredibly useful for what I would have to do. Two kill notifications appeared on my screen that made my stomach drop.

MasterCheese116 splattered BuckinBlueBronco

SpudMasterFlex mauled FreddieCougar

"Revenge is sweet, baby!" Noah yelled, pumping his fist.

"Crud," I said under my breath. I glanced over at Freddie, who mumbled to herself. Noah had found Freddie, and by the looks of it, he'd also found his reinforcements. The game didn't tell me where the deaths had happened, but *how* they happened gave me a clue. For a player to get splattered, they had to get crushed by a boulder. For a player to get mauled, they had to get attacked by a wild animal. Either of those could happen all over the map, but there were only a few places where both were *likely* to happen. I'd seen people get both crushed by falling rocks and mauled by sand panthers just outside of Spasm Chasm. Lonely Island also had some spots that had both steep cliffs and hidden beasts, but that's where SpudMasterFlex had started this round. I didn't think he'd go back there so soon. The other place was actually just northwest of Fangthorn Peak. Aside from a huge anti-dragon ballista mounted at the top of the tallest tower, Floating Castle had boulder-tossing catapults stationed all over its walls. The neighboring area, Joyless Jungle, was full of giant apes. Spasm Chasm was closest to where I had last seen Freddie at the wishing well, but there was a portal from the well to Joyless Jungle, so it was impossible to be exactly sure where they were. At least now I had a few spots to look.

I sprinted back out to the telescope but stopped when I

saw another player, ThePinkEraser, searching the thatch-roofed village. She wore full plate armor and rocked a flaming battle ax and an infinity bow. This chick was ready to do some serious damage. Luckily, she also had on a white sash. She turned her head to glance down the mountain as she drew her bow. She pulled the string back, and an arrow magically materialized, nocked and ready to fire. The infinity bow never ran out of ammo. It was one of my favorite weapons in the game. She paused, aiming for a second, then let the arrow fly, followed by another and another. Her arm cycled back and forth as fast as the game would allow, ripping a flurry of arrows into the sky. She either had really bad aim or a lot of people to shoot.

I crept around a few large rocks and peered down the mountainside. Three familiar cheaters stormed up the base of Fangthorn Peak. BooterScooter commanded a small army of dog-sized scorpions, while CatHissEverdeen and RigaTortoise lobbed up vials of alchemist's fire that fell short of ThePinkEraser's position but started the nearby trees on fire, almost certainly blocking ThePinkEraser's view. If they were storming up the peak, then they'd be clearing a path for SpudMasterFlex. Noah usually didn't have his goons work together like this, but he wouldn't be taking any chances on losing the Shoebox Game. Not with that much money and rep on the line. The gloves were off.

A trio of kill notifications informed me that Freddie had just cleaned house with a lightning bomb. "Keep it up, Freddie," I whispered to myself.

I turned my attention back to ThePinkEraser. I could always drop a shower of meteors down on the three cheaters' heads or run down the mountain and flank them, but SpudMasterFlex's goons weren't my goal. My goal wasn't to cut off the arms of this beast; it was to go for its head. I retreated farther up the hill and watched the scene play out. ThePinkEraser knew her stuff and managed to kill off Booter, her scorpions, and Riga, but in the chaos of the attack, CatHiss looped around to her back and finished her off with a hunting spear.

I waited and watched, my heart pounding like I was the one who had just battled to the death in hand-to-hand combat. Where was SpudMasterFlex? Would he still trust me? As if in answer to my worries, a kill notification popped up on my screen.

SpudMasterFlex zapped ZanzibarLaser

"Zapped?" I whispered to myself. "That means he has the . . ."

A figure broke from the distant tree line of Joyless Jungle, floating in the air and draped in the wizard's cloak. It was

SpudMasterFlex. To his left, MasterCheese116 rode on the back of a giant ape, escorting SpudMasterFlex across the open ground to the base of Fangthorn Peak. They scaled the mountain toward my position near the top and were joined by CatHiss. This was the moment of truth. I selected the "hands up" emote and came out from my cover. I saw the group raise their weapons but stop short. They looked to SpudMasterFlex, who gave a thumbs-up before continuing to the top of Fangthorn Peak and the base of the dragon's nest.

I blew out a sigh of relief and followed SpudMasterFlex as he approached the dragon and shocked it with wizard's lightning, causing the most powerful monster in the game to wake up, stretch its wings, and roar. The only question now was when and how to turn on Noah. SpudMasterFlex's body would be defenseless while his dragon roamed the skies raining down destruction on the entire map. That's what the two cheaters and I were supposedly for: to protect SpudMasterFlex while he had his fun. I could wait to kill him and make a grab for the wizard's cloak, but CatHiss and MasterCheese would be on me like stink on a monkey before I so much as equipped the cloak. I could try to kill the cheaters first, then kill SpudMasterFlex, but I was the least equipped person on this blasted mountain. The best option was to level the playing field. Take away Noah's biggest advantage before he even got a chance to use it.

A string of notifications scrolled in the corner of my screen like *Star Wars* credits on fast-forward. Something gnarly was going down somewhere on the map. Freddie's name kept popping up. One, two, three, four kills. She was playing out of her mind . . . until I heard her yell a pair of nonsensical cuss words. I looked over to see her face-palm, and I didn't even have to check the notifications to know what had happened. She'd seen an opportunity to do maximum damage and hadn't shied away. I looked around at the characters next to me. Maybe it was time to follow Freddie's lead.

"Things are about to get interesting," I whispered to myself as I equipped the Ring of Meteors, aimed it at my feet, and called down the fiery heavens.

"What's happening?" I heard Noah say from across the way as large circular shadows dotted the ground of Fangthorn Peak. "What is happening?"

Three seconds later, a shower of flaming rocks thundered down around us in a glorious explosion. A wave of kill notifications lit up everyone's screens.

Texcalibur obliterated MasterCheese116

Texcalibur obliterated CatHissEverdeen

Texcalibur obliterated SpudMasterFlex

Texcalibur obliterated the Mighty Dragon of
Fangthorn Peak

Texcalibur—Quad Kill!!

Texcalibur obliterated himself

CHAPTER 30
OUT OF THE SHADOWS

(Sticky Saturday—Oct. 16ᵗʰ)

The whole crowd gasped as they saw the notifications come across their screens. They either gasped from that or from the string of cuss words Noah shouted in my direction.

"You friggin' traitor!" Noah looked up and pointed at me from his spot on the park bench. "You stinkin' Texas jerk face. You *did* let me die at Wishing Well Woods. I knew it."

The cat was officially out of the bag.

"*Let* you die?" I shouted back. "Is everyone hearing this? You mean when you threw your *armor* down the wishing well and got jumped like a noob? This is a battle royale game, Noah. I would hope no one is *letting* anyone die, because that would mean that they had an obligation to *protect* them, and that, my dear friend, would be cheating."

I glanced up at Noah, whose face turned as red as a tomato. It was the kind of red only possible with the right mixture of nuclear rage and bone-crushing embarrassment. "Noah, if you're upset at me taking an opportunity to trade one of my lives for yours, two other well-equipped players, and your favorite pet dragon, I would like to think that that was a pretty sound decision. What do you say, everyone?" I yelled to the group, who continued to murmur.

"You're gonna friggin' pay," Noah blurted, seething.

"Don't know about that, but I'll tell you who's *not* gonna get friggin' paid today, 'cause there ain't no way you're getting that shoebox with one measly life left. Hey, everybody!" I announced. "Tons of loot at the top of Fangthorn. Spud's on his last legs. It's anyone's game now!"

The previously quiet clearing of fifty-four gamers burst into conversation. Players got up and ran to their best friends, disposing of all pretenses and huddling up in their shadow teams. Before I could think to move, Freddie plopped down at my side, black curls bouncing.

"Hello, you booger-flickin' bozo."

"Nice to see you, too, Freddie. Seen your name pop up a few times."

"Seventeen kills and counting." Freddie gave a huge smile.

"Where can I find you? I'm dropping in."

"Land right in the center of Lost Labyrinth," she told me, "and then tell me I'm not your best friend ever."

I did as instructed, floating to the far northeast of the map. When I touched down, I saw FreddieCougar wave me over to a hidden side corridor. She wore a full set of angel's armor, complete with large feathery wings, and had a bladed boomerang the size of a long sword. On the ground was a pile of gear.

"Good heavens, Freddie," I said, looking over the loot. "You've been busy." I picked up some armor, elven sprinting boots, and a diamond trident.

"Oh, and I've been saving these for you." Freddie's character dropped two more items.

I couldn't contain my smile. A sniper bow and the Helm of Infinite Sight lay at my feet. "Aw, you shouldn't have."

"I had an extra sniper bow, although it's not like I was going to use it anyway. Let's get going, cowboy," Freddie said, glancing at the corner of her screen. "There are thirty-seven people left, and they won't kill themselves off. Well . . . I mean, they probably will, but it'll be a lot more fun if we do it. Let's go find Noah and finish this. Call them out."

"Yee-haw."

FreddieCougar took to the sky as I dashed out of the maze. My magical helm let me zero in with Superman-esque X-ray vision on whomever I wanted. I scanned the map for the closest sign of other players and found a group perched at the top of Floating Castle.

"We got four on the castle," I said. "One's on the ballista up top, while three more are on the catapults. They're firing at a group of three to the south on the hills above Bandit's."

"I'll go north and squeeze the group on the castle. You do your thing."

Freddie flew up and tossed her giant bladed boomerang at the catapults. She eliminated the first two before they even knew what hit them. The ballista flipped around and began firing huge spearlike arrows through the air, but Freddie was too quick. She twisted and twirled out of the way as I sighted her attacker. Having a sniper in games when someone was stuck on a turret gun or catapult was just about my favorite thing in life. With two shots the castle was wiped clean, and we turned our attention to the three north of Bandit's Bog. They had control of a horde of bog vipers, but snakes weren't much of a threat to a flying, boomerang-wielding death angel and her sniper partner extraordinaire, not that Freddie even needed me this time. She was through with the group before I even had a chance to scope them. She was going to win this thing, and she deserved it.

I scanned the map, looking for SpudMasterFlex. He and three of his cronies were all the way over at Seaedge Fort, which sat at the end of a long peninsula on the far east side of the map. The game didn't let you fly over the sea, so the only way off that peninsula was through Spasm Chasm. They had their backs against the wall but were heavily fortified. They had boxed themselves in for one final stand.

We ran past Towering Trees and double-teamed a lone warrior riding on the shoulders of a huge ogre just outside of Peasantville. The kill notifications were coming fast and furious until a few caught my attention.

BuckinBlueBronco skewered MasterCheese116

TheReadyYeti poisoned CatHissEverdeen

SpudMasterFlex sniped BuckinBlueBronco

SpudMasterFlex sniped TheReadyYeti

"That's two from Noah's squad," I told Freddie. "But it looks like he's got a sniper bow." A swell of anticipation rose in my chest. It looked like I was finally going to get the showdown I'd been waiting for.

We mopped up a few last stragglers on our way through Spasm Chasm and the remaining player count in the top corner of my screen dropped down to four. With my helm,

I could already spot them. The only players left on the entire map were me, FreddieCougar, RigaTortoise, and SpudMasterFlex.

"Spud is hiding in the fort. Riga is . . . tucked behind some rocks to the west. She's looking to flank us, but I don't think she knows I have the helm and can see where she's at. Let me snipe it out with Noah while you flank Riga."

Freddie nodded and took off toward the stony outcrops to the west.

I zoomed in with my helm and fired a pair of shots right near where Noah was crouching, clicking them off the stone. "Knock knock."

Noah popped out from behind cover and returned fire, but the shots went wide. There were at least 250 yards between us, so any shot landed would have to be a good one. Noah could hole himself away in that fort for a while, but I knew one area I could attack to pry him out: his pride.

I stepped out from behind my cover. "May the record show," I announced to the assembled gamers, "that we both have sniper bows, but only one of us is in the open. The other one is hiding."

"Oooooh." The crowd reacted just like I wanted them to.

Noah had moved, but I purposefully sent a few more arrows zipping toward his old location to throw him off. Noah fired a volley of arrows in my direction and hopped down from the wall. I rolled out of the way and returned fire. He'd taken the bait. We were in it now.

We fired shots across the clearing, some in high arcs and others in straight shots, trying to force each other to dodge one and get hit by another. This wasn't just a cowboy quick draw.

Flashes of fire consumed the rocks to the west, and a kill notification popped up on my screen.

FreddieCougar scorched RigaTortoise

"Nice work, Freddie," I growled. "Only one thing left to do."

I felt myself zeroing in. My volleys were inching closer, my straight shots pushing Noah more and more to make a fatal error. I lured him into a pattern. Two straight, two up high, two straight, two up high. When I saw him fall into a rhythm, I fired a fan of four straight shots. The third one went straight through his helmet. Confirmed kill at 235 yards.

"Yes!" I bellowed, throwing my phone down. "There's a new sheriff in town—"

"Danny!" Freddie yelled.

"Huh?" I looked around confused as the crowd gasped. I snatched my phone off the ground as I watched my arrow pop back out of SpudMasterFlex's helmet and return to my bow. "The Enchanted Timekeeper! No!"

Before I could ready myself. My screen flashed red.

You have been sniped by SpudMasterFlex

"You were saying?" Noah's grating voice sounded from across the park.

I brought a palm up to my face. *That* was why a discard-day attempt would have been useful. How could I have been so stupid? It was like Noah had used a five-second double day to get the best of me. He'd beat me at my own game.

I switched to spectator mode and watched a volley of arrows thud into the ground around FreddieCougar. She dove for cover back toward the rocks but not before one of the arrows tagged her in the leg.

"Slug-sliming turkey butt," Freddie cursed.

"What's the matter, Freddie?" Noah called out, peppering the rocks around her with more arrows. "One of those didn't hit you, did it? Would be a shame, seeing as though I have the Basilisk's Curse. These arrows are just *dripping* with poison."

"I'm pinned down," Freddie hissed. "I've got sixty seconds till the poison does me in. What do I do?"

"Let's count it down, folks!" Noah taunted, turning to the assembled crowd. "Sixty, fifty-nine, fifty-eight . . ."

Only a handful of the other gamers joined in on the countdown, and I could see Freddie's breathing quicken.

"Well, help me out," Freddie hissed.

"Do you have anything in your inventory that might be useful at this range?" I asked, my brain stumbling for anything she could try. "Any magical item like Darkon's Blackness or something that would give you some cover or cure the poison?"

Freddie shook her head. "My boomerang won't even go that far. The only thing I have is a sniper bow, but if I try to snipe with Noah I might as well just bounce an arrow off the ground, shoot myself in the head, and save us the last fifty seconds."

However much I didn't want to admit it, Freddie was right. She was in a bad spot. I would have given up the double day for a month just to be able to trade places with her and snipe it out with Noah again, but, injured as she was, I wasn't sure even I could have done much.

I watched her poisoned health meter tick down like sands through an hourglass to Noah's victory. There had to be something I could do.

"Bounce an arrow off my head . . . ," Freddie mused, chewing on her bottom lip and flitting her eyes to my phone screen. "Wait! I've got an idea."

"Really? What?"

"Yeah," Freddie said, equipping her sniper bow. "Go to Noah's POV."

I hopped my spectating camera to Noah's point of view, not seeing how this could be helpful. He was zoomed in on the rocks surrounding Freddie. "Okay, what now?"

"Fifteen, fourteen, thirteen . . ." More of the crowd chanted now, their tone desperate for Freddie to try something. Noah stood on top of the table, bobbing side to side on beat with the countdown.

"Just hold steady," Freddie backed away from her cover slightly and sighted in on the same rocks. "And pray that all my practice has pleased the gods of the ricochet trick shot."

I shook my head. In every sense of the word this was a long shot, but it could still work. Freddie glanced between my screen and hers, trying to line up the shot. She stuck her tongue out and held her breath.

"You're not even going to *try*?" Noah scoffed. "Saves you the embarrassment, I guess."

"Seven, six, five . . ."

Freddie zipped off three arrows. All three clacked off the hard rock wall and zoomed toward SpudMasterFlex. The first two went high, but the third found its target right between the eyes.

FreddieCougar sniped SpudMasterFlex

The crowd's chanting died away at three seconds as a final notification flashed across everyone's screen.

FreddieCougar is victorious!

"I got him!" Freddie squealed as the crowd erupted into joyous disbelief. She dropped her phone and crushed me in a hug around my neck. "We did it!"

"It was all you, Freddie," I croaked.

"This is bogus!" Noah yelled from across the park. He frantically looked around for someone to agree with him. "That was a lucky shot, and you two were cheating the entire time! Is everybody seriously going to let a stinkin' cheater walk away with this thing?"

"You should talk!" someone yelled from the crowd. "How many Brown Bag Games did you cheat us out of?"

"I never cheated!" Noah squawked, sparking a chorus of boos. "You honestly think I need to cheat to win? What are you even talking about?"

"We want our money back, cheater! We've got proof!" The crowd shouted as it slowly closed in around the table.

"Yeah, Noah," I yelled from the back. "How about you give them their money back. I think you owe the crowd a few thousand bucks."

Noah looked around in desperation, like a mouse

hopelessly cornered by a hungry cat. "You want your money back?" He glanced down and paused on the shoebox. "Fine. Have it back." Noah bent down, grabbed the golden shoebox, and launched it into the air.

"No!" Freddie called out as dollar bills rained down onto the crowd, who instantly devolved into a frenzied mob, snatching up the loose cash.

"Stop!" I waved my hands above my head in a hopeless attempt to restore order. Freddie's prize money dissolved away into the crowd right before my eyes. Everything we worked for, yet again thwarted by Noah.

"Look out!" Freddie pointed over my shoulder and I turned just in time to see a charging Noah lower his shoulder and slam into my chest. I tumbled to the dirt as Noah fell on top of me, snarling and twice as rabid as the day he bit me on the shoulder. I batted away his flailing, scratching attacks as best I could. If getting pounded by Jaxson was like getting hit by a truck, this was more like getting mauled by a ravenous badger.

And then it stopped.

Noah was yanked off me and subdued with such efficiency that my savior could be only one person.

"Zak!" I exclaimed, brushing myself off and getting to my feet. My best friend currently had Noah folded like a pretzel and pinned to the ground. "You made it. It's almost like you knew I'd get jumped by someone in the end."

"I don't know what you're talking about," Zak said calmly as Noah weakly squirmed beneath him. "I came to support Freddie. I actually didn't think you'd make it past Jaxson."

"Thanks." I chuckled. "I hate to tell you, though, Noah threw the shoebox in the air and everyone took off with the . . ." I trailed off as I turned back around to Freddie, who stood still, glittering shoebox in hand. One by one the crowd of gamers came up and re-deposited their money, congratulating her as they went.

"Good game."

"Crazy last shot."

"Nice work, FreddieCougar."

With every dollar and compliment Freddie's smile got wider.

"We found money, Danny!" I looked down to see both my little sisters at my feet holding up handfuls of wadded cash. "Can we get ice kweam now?"

I bent down and picked up Sarah and Alice, one in each arm, and walked them to Freddie. "How about we give Freddie her money back and then I'll get you your ice cream."

"Yay! Ice cream!" the twins shouted, throwing the money into the air.

Freddie giggled as the money fell down around her. "Don't worry, Danny. Looks like I'm buying."

When the final gamer deposited their money in the

shoebox, I set my sisters down and cleared my throat. "The king of *Champions Royale* has been dethroned," I announced in a loud voice, pointing down at Noah. I grabbed Freddie's wrist and held it skyward. "Long live the queen!"

"You're such a bug-gushing goober," Freddie said, but I could hardly hear her over the roar of the crowd.

CHAPTER 31

ANOTHER DOLLAR

(Discard Monday—Oct. 18ᵗʰ)

"So, what do you say there, champ? You gonna still hold the Brown Bag Game?" I asked Freddie as we sat on a bench with Zak during lunch.

"I think so," Freddie said, smoothing her new, stylized *Champions Royale* T-shirt. She also sported a pair of brand-new jeans and black-and-white Converse shoes. Her untamable black curls had been trimmed but still kept their characteristic wildness. "I'm thinking of sticking with *Champions Royale* but doing teams of four with spectating on. Not sure how big of a crowd we'll draw, but we'll see."

"Something tells me you'll get quite a few people, Freddie." I nodded.

"What makes you think that?" she asked.

"I just sent you a link to something."

Curious, Freddie took out her phone. The screen was fixed, and it had a brand-new *Champions Royale* case. "Snake River Gaming All-Stars?"

A picture of Freddie's exuberant, victorious face was the top post of a new Instagram account along with the caption *Congrats to FreddieCougar, the new undisputed queen of the Shoebox Game!* She swiped to the side, revealing more pictures of the crowd, a screenshot of the final stats, and the kill map of where she'd scored her final shot.

Freddie looked up at me and Zak, eyes wide. "Did you do this?"

I shook my head. "No, actually. I have no clue who did it. Pretty cool, though."

Freddie smiled as if she'd won the Shoebox Game for a second time.

"Times are a-changing," I said, overlooking the scores of Snake River Middle School students.

The usual groups were on display: kids playing four square, basketball, football, or just chilling. There were the geeks and nerds of all variety: band, drama, art, D&D, and everything in between. Just beyond the blacktop, a shiny, mint-green cruiser bike was securely fastened to the bike rack . . . with *two* locks. I stared at

Braxlynn and the Clique up by the tree where Jaxson had slugged me in the stomach on my first day at school. He told me twice last week that I was a dead man, and I knew he wasn't one to forget a grudge. I was safe now with Zak at my side, but Zak couldn't always be there. Whether I liked it or not, Jaxson needed to be dealt with, and soon. For now, however, I was still savoring the Shoebox Game victory.

Noah sat against the school with Ophelia and one other person, all three hunched over their phones. Thirty-seven of the gamers had banded together to permanently expel Noah from any of their lunchtime games or tournaments. The only brown bag that punk would ever hold would be his home lunch. I smiled at the thought.

I turned to Zak. "I still can't believe you lied to your dad so you could leave the stadium and make it to the end of the Shoebox Game."

Zak held up a finger. "I did not lie," he corrected. "After you sent me that text Saturday morning telling me what happened at the Shoebox Game, I figured you might need some help, so I purposefully stuffed myself with nachos and chili dogs at the game. It was only a slight exaggeration when I told my dad that my stomach hurt and I had to go home. My integrity remains intact."

I gave Zak a slow clap. "Well done, maestro. This is progress, Zak. Doesn't it feel liberating?"

Zak shook his head. "There is a feeling that comes with eating three plates of nachos and two large chili dogs, and I'm pretty sure it isn't liberating."

"We all have our part to play, Zak," I said, patting him on the knee. "It *was* good that you finally got to rescue me from a beating during a sticky day for once."

"Wait," Freddie said, looking at Zak. "Did you say Danny sent you a text in the *morning* telling you what happened at the Shoebox Game?"

"Uh, yeah," Zak said slowly, realizing his mistake.

"But the Shoebox Game wasn't until *after* the football game," Freddie pressed. "And what in the toe fungus is a sticky day?"

Zak looked to me with eyes that pleaded for me to handle the situation.

I held out a reassuring hand. "Don't worry, Zak. I think the time has come."

Freddie turned to me and Zak, black curls bobbing. "Time has come for what?"

"Freddie." I cleared my throat and scooted forward. "I'm gonna need you to tell me something that I could never figure out unless you told me yourself."

"What are you talking about?"

I smiled, flitting my eyes to Zak. "I've got a secret to tell you."

"You gonna finally tell me how you 'read minds'?" Freddie said, fingers held up in air quotes.

"Yes," I said, nodding. "Yes, I am."

ACKNOWLEDGMENTS

My first thanks goes to my incredible agent, Lauren Galit. She loved Danny from the start, liberated my manuscript from the throes of querying, and took a chance on me and my story. She's always been honest, fair, and insightful. Thanks as well to Caitlen Rubino-Bradway, who worked side by side with Lauren to help me add to, sculpt, and polish my story for the big leagues.

I will be eternally grateful for Holly West, my editor, who was Danny's second champion, swooping in during submission like Gandalf on the back of a dadgum eagle to rescue my manuscript from certain doom. Her love and dedication to this story (along with Lauren's and Caitlen's) changed the course of my life.

To my small but mighty writers group, the Principal's Office (i.e. Allison Hymas and Ben Hewett), for always being on point, insightful, and giving me what I needed to make this story shine brighter. In a mad reading blitz, they came through with seconds left on the editing clock to make the ending truly pop. You guys are the best.

To my Friday night *Apex Legends* clan, Steve and Reg. It's nice to know that after all these years of gaming we can still hold our own and show the rising generation how it's done . . . some of the time. Hopefully out of Noah, Freddie, and Danny, I'm not the Noah of the group, but I'm pretty sure I know what Steve would say.

To my children, Abby, Owen, and Sienna. For always believing in Dad, supporting me, making fun of me, and being my inspiration. I will always remember Abby bringing a pillow and blanket into my office to delay bedtime night after night as I read another chapter to her. Her obsession with the double-day concept was a confidence booster, and her knowledge of the intricacies of middle school life were essential.

To my wife, Jill, who has been through it all. She has always supported this impossible dream, sustained me through my many failures, and loved me. In between edits on *Techno Wizard 2*, she asked me if I had another story idea. When I told her about *The Double Life of Danny Day*, she pushed me to write it. The first draft (one-third its current length) was knocked out three weeks later. So many dominoes needed to fall for this all to work, and Jill pushed over the very first one.

To my parents, who kept me safe and gave me space. Who inspired me to write and believed that I could do it. Dad, what I wouldn't give for just one more Saturday night with a small white bowl full of Oreos.

Thank you for reading this Feiwel & Friends book.
The friends who made

THE DOUBLE LIFE OF DANNY DAY

possible are:

Jean Feiwel, Publisher

Liz Szabla, Associate Publisher

Rich Deas, Senior Creative Director

Holly West, Senior Editor

Anna Roberto, Senior Editor

Kat Brzozowski, Senior Editor

Dawn Ryan, Executive Managing Editor

Kim Waymer, Senior Production Manager

Erin Siu, Associate Editor

Emily Settle, Associate Editor

Rachel Diebel, Assistant Editor

Foyinsi Adegbonmire, Editorial Assistant

Michael Burroughs, Senior Designer

Mandy Veloso, Senior Production Editor

Follow us on Facebook or visit us online at mackids.com.
Our books are friends for life.